They Tell Me You Are Cunning

A Novel by

DAVID HAGERTY

THEY TELL ME YOU ARE CUNNING
Duncan Cochrane - Book 4

FIRST EDITION SOFTCOVER
ISBN: 1622536150
ISBN-13: 978-1-62253-615-3

Editor: Darren Todd
Cover Artist: Kabir Shah
Interior Designer: Lane Diamond

www.EvolvedPub.com
Evolved Publishing LLC
Butler, Wisconsin, USA

Printed in Book Antiqua font.

BOOKS BY DAVID HAGERTY

DUNCAN COCHRANE
Book 1: *They Tell Me You Are Wicked*
Book 2: *They Tell Me You Are Crooked*
Book 3: *They Tell Me You Are Brutal*
Book 4: *They Tell Me You Are Cunning*

DEDICATION

For Diane, without whom....

CHAPTER 1

THE COLD FORECAST EVERYTHING THAT WAS to come.

When Mark and Eleanor Mulvaney returned to their condo from an excursion downtown, they felt Chicago's chill unchecked, the draft penetrating even their winter coats. The entry hall of their unit offered no more relief than the anteroom to the building downstairs, with its single-paned window and loosely framed door.

"Wait here," Mark said. "I'll stoke the super."

The boiler in their building had worked erratically of late, faltering as soon as the snow began. They'd complained to the manager several times already, but the maintenance man said it was just the pilot light blowing out. He kept odd hours, up all night and asleep during the day when they needed him, as reliable as the weather.

"It's late. Let's not disturb anyone," said Eleanor.

"We're customers. We deserve good service." Mark turned to descend the two staircases they'd just climbed. As he reached for the door handle, a gust of cold air surprised him. "Did you leave a window open?"

She gave him a look implying that he was being snotty, then raised the collar of her thin coat. "Why would I do that?"

That night, she had insisted on wearing something frilly and fashionable that she'd just bought at Marshall Field's instead of her warm but lumpy down jacket, like they were destined for the red carpet. To his mind, retirement meant never having to dress up again, and he didn't plan to spend the evening bundled in his camel hair coat, the one vestige of his professional wardrobe, nor to sleep through his wife's shivering.

Perhaps one of their children had come home to visit and left a window unlatched. Their son held keys in case his parents ever took sick. As a teen he'd been flaky and distracted, incapable of even taking out the trash prior to collection day, but since fathering children of his own he'd learned to attend to details. Their daughter, the chatterbox, could talk anyone into letting her in, except the coat rack sat empty, the boot tray still dry.

He opened the door to the powder room but saw all the casements shut and bolted.

Outside, the El screeched past, so loud it could have stopped on their back porch. Living a block from the tracks, he'd become deaf to the noise, but this overpowered all other sounds.

Only a few hours before, they had locked up the apartment and taken the train downtown to see *Glengarry Glen Ross*, David Mamet's new play, which was getting such rabid reviews. Truth was, Eleanor had dragged Mark to it. She said as a former audio salesman he could relate. "Why pay to see what I lived for forty years?" he said. To his surprise, he loved the conniving, posturing, and back stabbing. She complained: it was too profane, too cynical, his coworkers didn't speak like that. "You never heard how they talk to each other," he said.

The thought spurred him to check the front room and his own sound system, which took up an entire wall. Thirty years out of date, with vacuum tubes and turntables, hardly high-end compared to the CD players and subwoofers his customers wanted. Still, he felt a sentimental attachment to his old unit, even if it rarely rattled the walls any longer. It reminded him of his early years at Pacific Stereo—before the arrival of the big box stores—when he spent hours talking to other audiophiles.

The equipment appeared as always, with the thousands of records that surrounded it still in order, the out-of-print jazz albums segregated from the mono symphonic LPs. The furniture also looked as usual, the old couch dating from their wedding and the recliner he'd received on his retirement. Hardly proof of their security now, since it would take a team to carry them down the switchbacks of the stairwell. Beyond the front window, a dog barked and a snow-plow beeped, but inside the apartment he heard nothing. It felt warmer up front, too, less drafty.

Until recently, Wrigleyville offered streets safe enough that Eleanor could walk through Graceland Cemetery unescorted. Even returning from the El after dark, he didn't worry. Yuppies had infiltrated the neighborhood, fixing up the greystones and driving up the prices. Except in the past six months, some other tenants in his building had reported items missing from the basement—bikes and clothes they'd left in storage.

Some blamed the Bleached Bums, those Cubs faithful who'd spent forty years awaiting a pennant. Now and again one who'd adhered to the three-beer minimum would stumble onto their block having misplaced his parked car. With Wrigley Field only a short walk away, many locals suffered throughout the seasonal appearance of garbage and urine on their doorstoops.

Rather than complain to Chicago's finest, who patrolled the streets only when called, and then belatedly, Mark had joined the crowd. After so many years of catching only a game or two, he'd splurged on season tickets. For a change, the fans felt some optimism with Larry Bowa, Bill Buckner, and Leon Durham anchoring the middle of the order, plus newcomer Ryne Sandberg at second. Only, Spring Training wouldn't begin for two months.

He turned on the hall light and started a slow walk to the rear of the apartment, the wood floors creaking with each step. As he advanced, the temperature seemed to drop, like he was playing that game with his grandchildren, "you're getting warmer," except with the poles reversed. Odd. With all the electronics in the home, he made it a point to bolt all the windows before they'd left, even though it would take Spider-Man to access them along the third story. Lately, though, his memory had failed him, with objects going missing or turning up misplaced.

He checked his office where a saxophone leaned in the corner. After forty years of silence, he planned to take up jazz again in his retirement. Thus far, he'd only picked it up a few times, unable to recall more than the major scales, and reluctant to share his faltering first notes with the neighbors.

Another sight stopped him: an original Edison gramophone, which he'd been restoring, the wood case stripped and stained, the brass horn polished. All it lacked to make it sing again were a new belt and stylus. Surely a burglar would have taken that first. Again he checked the windows behind the blinds but found everything sealed tight.

On the opposite side of the hall lay the kitchen, which sat dark and empty. A tray of cupcakes rested on the counter, redolent of poppy seeds and orange zest, awaiting distribution at the local library, where Eleanor volunteered. Certainly cooled by now.

However, the rear door leading to the fire escape sat ajar, with a spray of dead leaves across the floor. That explained the draft. He paused to study the room. Nothing else appeared out of place—the pots and pans resting on the stove, the macramé plant hangers above the sink, so he examined the door. Up close, the lock looked undamaged. Perhaps they *had* neglected to close it.

"You left the back door open," he shouted to his wife.

"I don't think so," she said.

He walked toward the master bedroom to remove his shoes but paused on hearing a conversation, faint and crackly, in some language he didn't know. It sounded more like a recording than live people. Possibly sounds from outside.

Then a slim light distracted him, reflecting off something on his dresser as the sun would off water. He thought he saw a silver-plated comb and brush set that his parents have given them on the birth of their first child. Only, Mark had retired it to their bottom drawer years ago, a forgotten memento. A second later, the ray shone directly into his eyes, blinding him, although in his memory, he pictured the outline of a tall, slim man standing by the bed frame.

"Stop," said a thin voice. Something about the tone, a scratchy resonance, rang familiar.

"What are you doing here?" Mark said.

The man hesitated, then the light extinguished. In the near dark, Mark heard steps advance toward him, then saw the moonlight glint off something in the man's hand as he raised it overhead.

CHAPTER 2

BY THE SECOND YEAR OF HIS early retirement from public life, Duncan Cochrane had established a protocol that insulated him from the body politic.

He awoke to sunlight streaming through his condo, the plate glass windows of the high-rise unobscured by blinds or curtains. Compared to the formality of the executive mansion, with its antiques and sitting rooms, his apartment felt comfortably spare. He'd furnished it with only a double bed, a dresser, and a nightstand—no artwork, little furniture, mainly clothes and books. The building's round skeleton encouraged such minimalism, the whole looking much like a corn cob with rooms shaped like kernels, which required large blank spaces at the curves and corners.

When he'd rented the place two years before, he wanted to strip back his life to essentials, so he'd conceded most of his old furnishings to his estranged wife. As he left office, Duncan packed and stored the plaques, awards, and pictures from his tenure, displaying only a photo of his three children in their youth, gathered along the beach by their old home. Lindsay, his eldest, looked bronzed and glamorous in a linen top and Ray-Bans, while her sister, Glynis, covered up in a broad hat and long-sleeved dress. Their brother, Aden, barely into his teens, smiled slyly as though forecasting the misadventure that would fracture the family.

After standing through coffee and breakfast alone in his kitchen, Duncan descended to a gym on the lower level, where he walked on the treadmill for fifty minutes, ramping up the conveyor belt until it bounced beneath him. At that hour, most office workers had already departed while the underemployed had yet to arise, leaving Duncan to his own thoughts. This constituted a return to the purity of his undergraduate days, when baseball practice consumed every afternoon and games most weekends. However, after college he'd slipped out of shape, too focused on work and family. Only recently had he made time again for exercise, contracting his waist by two sizes and, if not equaling his former fitness, at least preserving it.

Following the workout, he returned to his apartment and began the business of the day, which mostly consisted of study. He favored history and economics, which taught lessons that he wished he'd known while in public service. His work had allowed no time for reading—other than legislation and government reports, neither very edifying—so he'd made a list of important texts and started at the top. Milton Friedman. Thorstein Veblen. Edward Gibbon. After four years focused on others, he craved self-improvement.

In truth, he preferred isolation to the hubbub of government. He'd purposely constricted his world to the community of his dwelling. Fortunately, the Marina Towers housed everything a man needed: groceries, restaurants, movies. A city within a city.

He considered himself one of its happiest inmates.

When he wanted escape, Duncan stepped onto his oval balcony and listened to the traffic below. From there he saw the Chicago River snaking around the erector set of downtown. The El rattled over the La Salle Street Bridge while autos inched across a dozen other spans connecting the Loop to its workforce.

The founders of Chicago got that right, leaving the waterfront open. Public parks and beaches stretched nearly the length of the city, without buildings or private property to obscure the coast. Unlike other big cities—New York or London—one had only to look east to escape the congestion and concrete of downtown.

Already the breeze off the lake felt warm and hazy, a sign of the humidity to come. Thankfully, he no longer dressed in suits and ties regardless of the weather, like some British gentleman governing colonial India. Instead, he embraced the casual comfort of anonymity.

For the first few months of his retreat, he'd tried to engage with the public. He'd dine at trendy restaurants, see old associates, talk of what came next, and people would treat him with the reverence of his old station, inviting him to their events, saving him a good table. Still, it felt put on, more nostalgic than genuine. Perhaps all men of importance eventually become obsolete.

His few excursions involved family: visiting his son downstate, talking to his daughter in Wisconsin, and seeing his ex-wife, all of which he anticipated that week.

By lunchtime he craved some diversion from his sanctuary, so he rolled the newspaper and descended to the coffee shop at street level. There the regular patrons ignored him, accustomed to a celebrity in their midst. Still, he sat at the counter, with his back to the tables, so he could watch people enter in the mirrored bar. He spoke only to the waitress, Florence, a cute brunette with dimples and a ponytail. She was almost too young to recall his term in office, though no doubt she'd heard about it. Showing a restraint uncommon for her age, she never mentioned it, and he obliged with few demands and generous tips.

He ignored the sizzle of hamburgers in the kitchen and ordered a BLT—a compromise for his new diet, the lettuce and tomato making up for the bacon.

While he waited, he studied the news. Mondale was leading in the primaries, with Jesse Jackson and others heckling from far behind, all vying to challenge Reagan. L.A. was building up for an Olympics without the Soviets. Famine struck Ethiopia. All felt equally distant to him.

The business pages noted that the S&P had doubled in three years, financing Duncan's idleness and his lawyers, but skeptics claimed it couldn't last, fretting about a trend toward hostile takeovers. After stripping TWA of all its assets, corporate raider Carl Icahn was targeting US Steel. Hard to see how that could threaten a bull market, but the precaution resonated with Duncan.

In frustration, he turned to the Metro section, which mentioned two prisons approved during his administration. Construction had nearly finished, with opening projected by fall. His legacy. He'd promised voters a state safer than the one he'd inherited. No parent should lose a child as he had.

A partisan battle had erupted within the legislature about which aging public figure to honor with their name. Perhaps they'd memorialize him, the Cochrane Penal Institute, the house that Governor Rambo built. Not likely.

At least weekly, he read coverage of himself. Invariably wrong. Reporters would write that he'd resigned from office. In fact, he'd chosen not to run for reelection. They'd claim that he'd lied about his son. In truth, he'd never spoken about him publicly. They'd allege that he'd misled voters about his crime bills. Ironically, those measures represented the truest words he'd spoken.

For a time he'd tried to respond, to clarify misstatements, but he found the interaction fruitless. Instead of transcribing what he said, the scriveners would counter it with accusations from people who barely knew him, attorneys both public and private who claimed to be investigating him but really fed off the state. Politics infected everything. Some days read like an autopsy, a search for the contagion after the parasites had dispatched him.

Once the food arrived, he set aside the scandal sheet to focus on his sandwich, the bacon crunchy, the lettuce crisp, the toast firm but not too dry. If only he found such pleasure in his other public dealings. As he enjoyed the last bites and eyed the potato chips on the side of his plate, a word startled him.

"Governor."

An address he'd not heard in some time, yet reflexively he turned to see a woman standing uncomfortably close. Instead of replying, he studied her and tried to guess her agenda. She wore a conservative gray blouse and her hair in a bob, more matronly than threatening, but her expression worried him: an anxious expectancy. Somehow he'd missed her arrival in the looking glass, no doubt distracted by the savory meal.

"I'm Catherine Fontanelle from the Innocence Inquiry."

He nodded, though the names meant nothing to him, and plotted an escape route via a back exit.

"Could I have moment of your time?"

Before he could respond, she sat on the empty stool beside him and laid a freckled hand on the countertop close to his own. Her features included a sharp chin and nose along with pale blue eyes and blonde hair streaked with gray. In her youth, she must have possessed great beauty, with a classic Nordic cool.

"I'm representing a man named Harry Flores." She paused to gauge his reaction, but he maintained a neutral face, the name unfamiliar. "He's incarcerated for killing a retired couple in Chicago."

The way she spoke, as though expecting all this to be familiar, perplexed Duncan. Why would he know such a person, or care?

"We believe he was wrongly convicted."

Duncan reached for the pickle but stopped himself when he realized that she anticipated a reply. From the kitchen he heard the rattle of a milkshake machine over a boom box playing some pop song about the sound of crying doves, a reminder that others might be listening. "And what is it you want from me?" he said.

"Support. To win his release."

Duncan signaled to the waitress for his check and lay his napkin funereally atop his plate, forgetting the pickle and chips. "I don't see how I could help," he said.

"He was tried during your administration and sentenced under your laws. If you were to publicly declare his innocence, it would—"

Duncan stood to extract his wallet. "I doubt that my word would sway anyone."

"As a former head of state? How could it not?"

"Miss, since my retirement, my influence has diminished greatly."

"You created the architecture of his incarceration. Don't you want to ensure that it's sound?"

Florence was preoccupied with other customers, so Duncan lay a $5 bill on the counter next to his plate. "I'm afraid the public perception about me," he nodded toward the newspaper, "is tainted."

"Which is precisely why we need your involvement. You're both a victim of violent crime and a prosecutor of it. Who better to campaign against the excesses of a penal state than someone who understands it from both perspectives?"

"I'm sorry, but I cannot help you," he said and strode to the elevator that would carry him back up to the security of his apartment.

CHAPTER 3

THAT DAY, THOUGH, DUNCAN HAD AN appointment he could not hold in house.

The one time he routinely departed from his cell was to visit his son, Aden, who lived ninety minutes southwest of the city. Each week, Duncan drove from the downtown skyscrapers to the fields of corn and wheat that populated downstate.

After retiring, he'd traded in his family sedan for an ice blue BMW 318i, a sporty two-seater more befitting a single man. Its trim efficiency pleased him: just enough power, with a hint of luxury in its leather seats and top-flight sound system, but nothing too showy or ostentatious.

However, in the parking lot of the Stateville Correctional Center, it stood out. There, people still honored Duncan's position. Instead of subjecting him to the visitors' area, with its screaming children and irritable guards, the warden let him use the staff entrance. He bypassed the metal detectors and walked unescorted down a long corridor to the medical offices, where he could speak to his son in private. The halls gleamed bright and clean—the floors freshly polished, the walls newly painted—smelling of chemical pine and disinfectant. On his first visit, the place had surprised Duncan with its sanitation, more like a hospital than the dungeon he'd imagined.

The exam room looked little different from a typical doctor's office, with a bed, a desk, and a chair. Except for the emptiness. The desk held no cotton balls, no tongue depressors. The cabinets, despite locks, held no bottles or drops or potions behind their tempered glass. Duncan understood the focus on safety and security, but what kind of weapon could be fashioned from a Q-tip?

Despite the scarcity, the room felt closed and stuffy, as though no fresh air could penetrate it. On contact, Duncan felt an irritation in his throat and a teariness in his eyes. He glanced to the vent to see it clotted with dust, the one place no one bothered to sanitize.

As usual, the boy was sitting at the ready when Duncan arrived, occupying a stool intended for the doctor. In the year of his incarceration, he'd come to look less like a college student and more like a man. Superficially, he appeared healthy, his hair cut short, his chest swollen with muscle, and his scrubs wrinkle-free. He'd pressed a seam into his pants—a tradition he'd never followed as a free man—by laying them under his mattress at night. The only signs of rebellion were tube socks covering both arms—like a mockery of the fashion for leg warmers, but they could have been purely practical—and his slumped posture, legs akimbo.

He greeted his father with a casual "hey" but did not move or face him. Many years had passed since he willingly submitted to hugs or kisses, and incarceration had only increased that distance, so much so that he rarely used the word dad. He treated their visits as an obligation, like Easter dinner with distant relatives.

Duncan sat perpendicular on the table intended for patients—close enough to touch, but not bold enough to try. "How have you been?" he said.

Aden shrugged his stiff shoulders and looked away at an angle. "The same."

"Staying out of trouble?"

Again the young man shrugged and said, "I keep busy." He'd never lost the sullen demeanor of adolescence, answering most questions in monosyllables unless drawn out.

"With what?"

Aden exhaled in frustration, but replied, "A GED program. For guys who need it. Sometimes I tutor them to earn extra scratch."

"Extra what?"

"Currency."

"They have money here?"

"Not money, currency: ramen, toothpaste, cigarettes, whatever you can barter."

"Very industrious." Duncan felt both pride and shame at his child's resourcefulness, so he sought another subject. "Are you making any friends?"

"People here don't have friends. They have cellies, partners, associates...."

"Well, are you making any of those?"

"Nobody here's worth the effort."

Duncan cast about the office for some inspiration but saw only a broken clock. "What about improving yourself, your education? When I was overseeing the system, they talked about starting college courses."

"Not here."

"Not even correspondence?"

"Guys here can't read. Why send them philosophy?"

"I know they have AA."

Aden twisted on his stool but kept his face half hidden. "I've done rehab. Remember?"

For three months prior to the revelation of his sins, Duncan had forced Aden to attend the Betty Ford Clinic, where he'd complied but never converted.

"What about therapy?" Duncan said.

"This place isn't about making you better."

"There must be something... productive you could do with your time."

The boy sighed heavily. "I get it, Dad, you want me to program, but there's nothing in this place for me but punishment. It's not like U of I. There's no clubs or sports to keep me out of trouble."

"What about work?"

Once more, Aden shrugged. "Nothing's open."

Involuntarily, Duncan glanced at the clock again to be reminded that prisons did not measure time in minutes. Intuitively, he knew that no more than a few had passed, and already he'd run out of conversation. He wished that for once he could connect with his son as something other than an authority figure to resent and resist, so he leaned forward and placed a hand over Aden's. The boy flinched on contact.

"There must be something positive in your life right now."

He squeezed Aden's hand, which felt rough and uneven, with scabs dotting both knuckles. "You've been fighting," Duncan said.

"I slipped."

"Slipped how?"

The boy did not reply, so Duncan shifted toward the wall where his son's glare was fixed. Again Aden turned away until his father said, "Look at me." When he did, Duncan saw a large bruise marking his forehead and a scratch cutting the length of his cheek. Both looked swollen and discolored, a sunset of browns and reds.

"As I said, you've been fighting."

"In here, you've got to." Aden shrugged as though it were a platitude.

"I thought you were in protective custody."

"That just means you bunk by yourself. There's still other guys in the pod."

"But why fight them? What's to fight about?"

The boy shook his head with frustration. "It's like at school. You've got to prove yourself."

"Won't that hurt your chances at parole?"

"Nobody here cares. As long as no one calls for the doc, the guards ignore it."

"Still, I don't want you getting hurt."

"I could kill any of these guys if I wanted to."

Even before his incarceration, Aden boasted about the skills he'd learned in military school: how to subdue and asphyxiate a man with his bare hands. Unfortunately, he'd applied those techniques to his sister, albeit inadvertently, he claimed.

"But you won't," Duncan said as forcefully as he could. "Remember, that's what landed you here."

The boy stared into his lap, pensive and distant.

"I know you blame me for your confinement."

Aden shrugged his indifference. "Not really."

"If it's any consolation, this was never what I intended. I sent you to school and rehab to reform you, so you wouldn't need... this." He swirled his arms to take in not just the room but the entire complex. "I did all I could to protect you, but some things even the governor can't fix."

Aden nodded vaguely and kept his face turned from his father.

"And remember why you're here."

Aden withdrew his hand before saying, "I don't need you to remind me all the time."

The scolding shifted Duncan's mood. Despite his son's guilt, he'd developed sympathy for his wretchedness. Maybe no parent could maintain a lasting anger with his children, regardless of the cause.

"This... " again he nodded to their surroundings, "is only for a short while. Soon you'll start over, become a man we can both be proud of. Only you can't let this place ruin you first. You'll put it behind you and grow into... who knows what. But it'll be something good."

Aden nodded and snuffled, though he made no move to wipe his eyes or nose.

"Your life won't be defined by this, or by what put you here."

Aden snorted and shook his head. "Everybody knows."

"Knows what, that you're locked up?"

The boy shrugged his overbuilt shoulders.

"What does everyone know?" Duncan said.

"What I did."

"How? Have you told them?"

"It's in the paper, Dad. Every week."

Duncan searched for something reassuring to say. "I thought they couldn't read."

The boy gave a half laugh but otherwise remained silent.

At once, Duncan felt a pang of guilt unlike any he'd experienced in months of critical news stories and discouraging legal briefings. He'd assumed that Aden too would outlive the infamy of his misdeed, but the taint lasted longer than he could have feared. "If we have to, we can move someplace new once you're released, start over."

"Not while I'm on parole."

"Then after that. Sometimes you have to reset your life. Just as I've done. Scandal is fleeting. It skips from person to person, place to place. So can you."

It sounded impassioned, but deep down, Duncan wondered if it would prove true.

CHAPTER 4

THE NEXT MORNING, DUNCAN AROSE EARLY for another unavoidable excursion.

The law offices of Barnham & Dreifort strained to impress, with leather couches in the lobby, Persian rugs in the offices, and antique furniture in the conference room. The mahogany table sat a dozen people, and all the chairs filled whenever Duncan entered. The firm's entire legal team contributed to the defense of their most prominent client, with some assigned to his son's appeal, others to a civil case from the man originally accused of killing his eldest daughter, Lindsay, and a third group to the grand jury investigation of Duncan himself.

Their chief partner, Dick Dreifort, always occupied the head of the table and presided over the reports. Though nearing retirement, he still possessed a quick mind and an imperious demeanor reinforced by bespoke suits and gold cufflinks. His lump of a body belied the power he held, which all rested above his slumped shoulders. One at a time, he called on his associates to detail the minutia of discoveries, depositions, and motions that made up each case. Typically, the summary took at least an hour, with more legal jargon than Duncan could absorb. He'd yet to learn the names of even half these advisers, thinking of them instead by distinguishing characteristics: the one with the gaudy watch, the one with the feathered hair, the one who wore Drakkar Noir. He presumed the intended message of this melodrama was how hard the firm was working on his behalf. Instead, he heard a meter running. So many people defending the ex-governor, yet all they'd accomplished thus far was hundreds of thousands in billable hours.

By the time each attorney had spoken, Duncan wished only to escape the room, but the team needed more information from him, more details of his administration to prepare his defense. Already they'd scrutinized all of his calendars, his memos, his speeches, even his notes to himself (*buy wife's b-day gift*), yet they proved insatiable, seeking the one fragment of paper that would betray an intent to mislead voters about his son's guilt. Two years before, when he'd announced his withdrawal from politics, Duncan assumed his morality play had reached its conclusion. Instead, it marked merely an intermission in his troubles.

For an interminable time, the attorneys discussed the limits of "parental evidentiary privilege" as it applied in these cases, where Duncan protected Aden for four years by withholding evidence against him. Their defense—that recent state court rulings shielded him from testifying against immediate family, even before a grand jury—was unsupported by federal precedent. Prosecutors called it obstructing justice.

As the advocates debated, Duncan turned to the wide window that gave an expansive view of Grant Park below. There people strolled through the tulip gardens, sat in the courtyard of the Art Institute, admired the rococo wedding cake that was Buckingham Fountain. Each year, the Petrillo Music Shell hosted jazz and blues festivals. Each summer, a quarter million people gorged themselves on hot dogs, pizza, and ribs at Taste of Chicago. The park represented the best that government could offer: an escape from the stresses of urban living.

"Governor?"

Duncan turned to face the jury of his advisers, who stared at him expectantly.

"Do you have anything to add?" said the lead attorney.

Their many expectant faces irritated their employer, who tired of people trying to capitalize on his vanity. "How much longer is this going to take?"

Dreifort sat back in his plush leather chair, which conformed to his round mass. "With your cooperation, we should wrap up before lunchtime."

"No. I mean these cases. How much longer are we going to be fighting these allegations? They are... paralyzing my family."

"Under our guidance, you've not been convicted of anything. Our strategy of—"

"My son has."

Dreifort stared at him as though preparing for a cross-examination. "We are representing Aden to the best of our—or anyone's—capacity. We remain optimistic about our chances on appeal."

"Even so, my family is wearing the mark of Cain as our insignia."

Dreifort reclined farther back. "What is it you're expecting?"

"To become relevant again. I can't hide forever, hoping people forget who I am, what I'm accused of. Even my son can't be hidden away. He'll be released someday, and he deserves a chance to remake himself. At some point, we have to create a new legacy for him... for me... for all my family."

"Which, through our efforts, you will achieve. However, escaping the predicament in which you find yourself now will require all of our tactical skill. Yours is an extraordinarily complex defense, one challenging even to a firm of our capabilities." Dreifort looked to his associates, who nodded sychophantically.

"Up till now," Duncan said, "your primary strategy has been to neuter me. How can I live as a public citizen when I'm not allowed out in public anymore?"

Dreifort nodded imperiously. "In private, you are free to do as you wish. Take a new job, make new friends, promote any causes you like, but do not seek redemption in public."

Duncan shook his head. "I have no private life. Everything I do winds up in the papers. How can I start a new career with my résumé posted in every gossip column?"

"Are you applying for work?" said the attorney.

Duncan ignored the hint of sarcasm and returned his gaze to the window, where clouds floated past effortlessly on winds off the lake. "I'm thinking about volunteering."

"Great idea, provided it's inconspicuous."

"Last week, someone contacted me." In the silence that followed, the air conditioner breathed so gently that it did not ruffle the papers on the tabletop. "An advocate for the wrongfully convicted." The attorneys busied themselves taking notes, all but Dreifort, who sat motionless, a king on his throne. "She wants me to lobby on their behalf."

"I don't see that as benefitting your causes."

Duncan returned his gaze to the outdoors, where people enjoyed the warmth of morning, heedless of his affairs. "It's a way to redeem my image."

"That won't hold any sway in a courtroom," Dreifort said. "Quite the contrary. If you start defending guilty people, it will make you look hypocritical: the father of a convicted man suddenly talking up injustice. You could provoke an indictment." He lifted a stack of legal briefs an inch thick and gestured to more distributed throughout the table.

The smell of photocopies irritated Duncan, emanating futility. "What do you suggest?"

"*Our* strategy is to keep you out of the spotlight, let the furor around your circumstances subside, then negotiate favorable terms for each of these cases. With enough time, people will lose interest, and your persecutors will give up."

Although his words preached defense, his tone gave offense, suggesting that he, not his client, would dictate the script. "It's been two years," Duncan said.

"Which is not long in matters such as these. Many litigations take a decade or more."

Duncan studied his advocate's chalk stripe suit, whose sheen reflected its Italian fabric and whose fit its custom tailoring. Once, not long ago, Duncan appreciated such finery, but lately he'd lost interest in peacock displays, preferring the casual comfort of wash slacks and open-collar shirts. The polish his attorney reflected may have impressed juries, but to voters and the media of the state it suggested elitism. Just the week before he'd read an editorial accusing him of hiding behind "the legal progeny of the Pinkertons." How could such a representative chart a course to redeem him in the eye of the public?

"I can't wait that long," Duncan said.

The attorney leaned forward and clasped his hands as though in entreaty. "You say someone contacted you. Who was it?"

Duncan searched for her name, or the name of her organization, but recalled only innocence. "A woman representing a nonprofit."

"What else do you know of her?"

"That she champions the falsely accused."

Dreifort nodded judiciously and rapped his hands once on the table. "She could be a Mata Hari sent to undermine you."

"Isn't that a bit... cloak-and-dagger?"

"Not in the political world you inhabit. You made many enemies during your career, all of whom are looking to capitalize on your... misfortune."

"Inhabited. Past tense. I'm no longer playing spy versus spy."

"But your enemies are."

Duncan exhaled and sought some escape in the expanse of the gardens, the lake, and the horizon. Instead, he felt confined by the window that framed them. "Fine. I'll ignore her. As I do the daily barbs from the muckrakers. But I need something from you in exchange."

"What is that, sir?"

"Progress. I need to see that we're nearing an end to this... inquisition. There's nothing more I can tell you, no one else you can interview, that will shed light on my time in office. We need to move past it, to get it off the front pages and into the record books. Whatever the outcome, I need resolution."

Dreifort reclined in his plush chair. "I won't promise that. We can't prevent the government from investigating you, nor private attorneys from suing you, much less control what is reported in the media. We can only respond to what they do. We react, we defend. We don't dictate the pace of play."

"And I can only forbear for so long."

CHAPTER 5

AFTER THE BRIEFING, DUNCAN ESCAPED THE downtown on Lake Shore Drive, which offered endless water views and relieved the tedium of driving. Usually. Even with little midday traffic, the hubbub of weaving cars irritated him. Had he known that he'd spend a year of atonement for every year in office....

He studied the lake, which appeared calm and flat, missing the usual chop from the winds that bedeviled the city. Along the beach, people jogged and biked, walked their dogs, and played Frisbee. How he longed for such freedom, to frolic in public unmolested. As governor, he'd bristled at the security that accompanied him everywhere, yet now that he'd shaken loose of it, he still felt confined.

He dialed the radio to WFMT, where the announcer spoke with a slow cadence and long pauses in between chamber pieces, so he finished the trip in silence.

His destination, Charlie Trotter's, was the hot new restaurant, getting ecstatic write ups in the *Tribune* and even *The New York Times*. Reservations booked two months in advance, yet his wife, Josie, had secured a table on short notice by playing on his former influence. At least someone in the family still could.

The place had reconfigured a brownstone in Lincoln Park, a neighborhood more known for pricey Victorians than tony dining. A broad awning ushered visitors inside, where even at midday white tablecloths glowed under dim lighting. The rest of the interior hinted at extravagance: mahogany moldings, cherry wood parquet floors, and a wine cellar accessed by a ladder.

Josie sat prim and poised at a table by the front window. She still favored the business suits and bouffant of her former office as first lady, an homage to her hero, Margaret Thatcher. By contrast, he felt underdressed in his chinos and polo shirt. On seeing him, she rose and offered a cheek to kiss as though they were acquaintances.

"Good to see you," she said without irony.

Once he'd sat down, he checked the room. A few people had noted his entrance, and one—a middle-aged man in a three-piece—nodded to acknowledge him, but all of them quickly returned their attention to their meals. At bastions for the upper classes, people respected the privacy of public figures, even scandalous ones.

"It's so exciting that Chicago is finally getting restaurants with sophistication," Josie said.

"Second City no more," he said.

The menu ran only a page but featured ingredients he'd never considered: poussin, squab, veal cheeks, profiteroles. Quite a departure from the city's signature dishes of hot dogs, pizza, and ribs. As someone who'd earned his fortune in packaged meats, Duncan found the choices a bit grasping, trying too hard to impress. If asked, he couldn't even define the place's cuisine, so he ordered something familiar: sausages, albeit stuffed with salmon, shrimp, and scallops. For dietary reasons, Josie chose a salad of duck breast, papaya, and walnuts.

Once the server departed, an awkward silence rose between them. After a year's separation, it felt strange sitting across the table from his wife, who'd demanded time alone to process all that had happened. Since then they'd met sporadically, and always in a public place, to keep the conversation civil.

"So what have you been doing with yourself?" she asked.

He shook his head. "The usual."

"No new job? Hobbies?"

"Just meeting with lawyers."

She sighed and fiddled with one of her earrings as though it pinched. Rather than the pearls or precious stones he expected, this hoop contained only a golden chaff of wheat, a design by the city's native architect, Frank Lloyd Wright. Many years before, just after they'd married, Duncan had chosen it for her birthday at a time when it was the only thing he could afford at the gift shop of the Art Institute. Good to know she hadn't packed up every remembrance of him. Then again, he still wore his wedding band, which had carved a lasting indent on his ring finger.

"And what do our advisers have to say?" she asked.

"The same. They're working on our defense."

"Before they finish, Aden will have served his entire sentence."

Duncan nodded. Perhaps by consenting he could avoid the usual fight.

"There must be some cause for appeal," she said, "something they can use to get him out on bail. There's no reason for him to spend so much time in custody when we know that ultimately he'll be exonerated."

At trial, police and prosecutors described how the Cochrane family had deceived them, hiding their son at boarding school and misdirecting the investigators toward other suspects. Aden declined to testify in his own defense, and his father, when forced to take the stand, had to invoke the Fifth Amendment right against self-incrimination.

"They're doing their best," he said. "The judge on his appeal is... unsympathetic."

"Then find another judge. Can't your friend Ron help?"

"I doubt it. He's not sympathetic either."

"You must know someone in the DA's office or on the Court of Appeals who owes you a favor."

He exhaled and culled his mental Rolodex, which had thinned greatly since he'd left office. "Let me think about it."

She unfolded her napkin and settled it in her lap as though she'd committed to stay for the meal. "Have you visited him recently?"

"Just yesterday."

"How did he seem?"

He studied her face for some clue about her impressions, but it remained oddly neutral. "The same."

She sighed deeply. "He's going to waste. The only thing he works on is his muscles."

He nodded. "We discussed that."

The waiter's arrival interrupted them. Delicately, he carried two ceramic spoons containing melon balls wrapped in prosciutto, with a thin sauce pooled beneath. Though only a single bite, the flavors of salt and fruit mixed as though paired by nature, making Duncan long for more. Perhaps this nouvelle cuisine wasn't all hype.

"I've been looking into new schools for him," Josie said.

"Schools?"

"Colleges. Once he gets out, he's going to need an education."

Duncan thought of the boy's sullen silence just the day before, his resistance to even a class in jail. "Don't you think it's... premature for that?"

Josie dabbed her mouth with a napkin and rearranged it in her lap before answering. "We need to prepare for his release. I don't want him sitting around idle."

Did she intend that as a dig against him? He let it pass. "What have you found?"

"I'm thinking of a private, liberal arts school—somewhere away from here, maybe the East Coast. Of course, we'll need to be discreet in where we place him."

"Even once he's released, he'll need to stay in state."

"Not if he's exonerated."

Duncan nodded and stared toward the kitchen. Apparently, quick service wasn't part of the restaurant's appeal. "Have you found any colleges that would accept him?"

"Why wouldn't they?"

Duncan searched for words. "We don't have the same... clout we once did. Our name won't guarantee his admission. Maybe the opposite."

She stared at him unrelentingly. "Stop all this pessimism. Look where it's gotten you. You act as though you're retired, padding around in resort wear. Two years ago, you commanded all of Illinois, and now you're afraid to step outside."

"I am retired," he said.

"You're too young."

"I've worked since childhood. First in my parents' store, then twenty-five years as hog butcher to the world, not to mention four years as head of state. I've earned enough for us both to live comfortably. Why persist? There's nothing left for me to prove."

In her frown, he saw remnants of the woman he'd married thirty years prior, one who'd left her family's farm in upstate New York to test herself in the wider world. They'd grown into prosperity and prominence together, with her keeping the books for his meat-packing business while he was in the field selling. At the slaughterhouse, he'd given her an office where she'd be out of the way, but she always made excuses to come onto the cutting-room floor when a customer arrived. Once, she'd visited a buyer who'd fallen two months delinquent, despite carrying Lindsay into her eighth month. She'd refused to leave his office, threatening to give birth on his desk if necessary, until he paid. Later, he told Duncan that no woman outside of his mother had intimidated him so.

"What *are* your plans then?" she said.

The arrival of their lunch saved him from responding.

The sausages flouted all of his expectations, fragrant of the ocean, with a salty savor that meat could never equal. Not that he preferred the seafood to a typical filling, but perhaps he'd missed an opportunity earlier in his career. How clever to stuff an animal skin with something other than animals.

When he asked Josie about her salad, she called it "divine," though to him it appeared little different from any other mix of lettuces and toppings. Even this she ate European style, holding the fork exclusively in her left hand, a legacy from their trip to France years before.

They remained silent, practicing a détente that his parents had demanded at the dinner table. No heated words nor expressions of discontent should distract from the food, they said. No wonder he ended up in butchery. However, the tradition had not survived in his own family. Once, he and Josie could discuss their children with pride and optimism. Now, every comment was tinged with regret or accusation.

"What about you?" he said. "What's new in your life?"

She detailed a half-dozen activities—tennis dates with other political wives, volunteering at the League of Women Voters, rummage sales at the North Shore's most important Congregational church, even charity work with the Chicago mayor's office—none of which surprised him. However, they proved two things: she remained busy, and she remained connected. In her list, he heard a repudiation of his own isolation, proof that even a fallen hero could rise again. Maybe he was too sensitive. She'd always kept a full schedule, even when raising three young children. Why would she change?

"Sounds fulfilling," he said.

"For now."

He didn't ask what she planned next. Instead they compared notes on mutual friends—whose children had been accepted to the Ivy League, whose were engaged or expecting—until the waiter offered a dessert menu. Rather than the traditional cakes or pies, Trotter's featured unconventional ingredients in unlikely combinations: Cranberry and Walnut Tart, Pineapple Tarte Tatin with Ginger-Hokkaido Squash Ice Cream, Rosewater Crème Caramel with Primrose Sauce and Black Pepper Tuiles. During their meal, Duncan had been eyeing the last course at some neighboring tables with little recognition. Now that he saw them described in words, he understood why.

Craving something familiar, he ordered Chocolate Macadamia Nut Cake with Coconut Froth and Sugar Cane Ice Cream, while Josie opted for a trio of citrus fruits with foam overtop. Apparently, every confection needed some fizz.

Just as he'd received a coffee with real cream, she fixed him with a stare.

"You haven't said what you'll do about Aden."

"About him?"

"How you'll protect him from your prison edifice."

He recalled their son as he'd appeared a day before, bruised and dispirited. Based on their conversation, he guessed that she hadn't seen him in that state, or she would have used it against him. He gambled that the boy would heal before his mother's next visit.

"You know, I think he's holding up surprisingly well. Yesterday, we discussed how quickly his life would turn around once he's released."

"Which is why that needs to happen soon," she said.

He nodded and sipped his coffee, which tasted as smooth and rich as any he'd tried, without the usual bitterness.

"So, what's your plan?" she said.

"I'll contact some friends."

"Who?"

He glanced about the room, where her raised voice was drawing the attention of other patrons. With his chin inclined to them, he said softly, "Some people who know far more about incarceration than either of us."

CHAPTER 6

BY THE TIME THEIR MEAL ENDED, Duncan chafed to escape. No matter how tasty the food, he had soured on the conversation, which reflected his own discontentment. His return along Lake Shore Drive, where an hour prior he'd felt agitated by the activity around him, now offered relief, the sun glinting off the water suggesting some escape on the horizon.

However, one of Josie's comments still nagged at him: that he behaved as though retired. It echoed his own sense in recent months that he'd allowed his lawyers and advisers to sterilize him, to prescribe a role that was so limited, so isolated, that he could not find himself in it. He thought of their latest prohibition on speaking in public. After years of hearing his every word recorded, repeated, and analyzed, it felt wrong to maintain such anonymity. And truly, what had it earned him but more of the same? His banishment from public life felt ever more permanent.

With a clear calendar for the afternoon, Duncan elected a detour. At the S curve by Oak Street Beach, he exited the outer drive and headed west toward the Newberry Library. In contrast to its big public cousin downtown, this private collection offered small, quiet, isolated rooms full of obscure scholarly journals and artifacts.

He found a parking space across the street and retrieved his disguise from the glove box—a Cubs cap pulled low and sunglasses—then hustled inside. Toward the back lay the archives with the microfiche. Only there did he pause to recall the name of the organization he wanted to research. Innocent Prisoner Program? Something like that. Should have given more attention to it.

He approached the reference desk, where a young woman in a loose sweater and slacks watched him attentively. With his head lowered, he asked in a minimum of words for her help in scouring the periodical index. He felt awkward hiding so, particularly by wearing a hat indoors, which his parents trained him never to do.

She ignored his lack of grace and quickly located a reference to the Innocence Inquiry in a recent edition of the *Tribune*, then helped him skim the microfilm to the correct page. There he found a description of the group, which affirmed what the advocate had said ("nonprofit lobbying for judicial reform") and a reference to several cases it was following.

Again he needed the librarian's help to locate clippings, but she exhibited skill far beyond the youthful naiveté she affected. Within minutes, she found the story he wanted. Across the front page, the *Tribune* blared, "Home Breaking Killer." The story highlighted many gory details: "retired couple bludgeoned in their bedroom," "killer lived just down the block," "desperate search for a dose."

Even reading about it left Duncan feeling revulsion for the suspect and the crime. Someone had invaded the home of a nice retired couple and beaten them to death, all for a hundred dollars' worth of jewelry and electronics. Days later, police arrested the suspect, who admitted his guilt under questioning.

Why involve himself in such a case? The advocate insisted on the man's innocence, but all of the evidence affirmed his guilt. He'd left behind a radio at the crime scene, and worse, had confessed to the police. No do-gooder optimism could contradict that.

Duncan respooled the microfilm and returned it to the librarian, who tilted her head so her blonde ponytail shook. "Did you find what you were looking for?" she said.

"Unfortunately so." He met her gaze briefly and tried for a smile but felt himself grimace instead.

Her expression shifted to reflect his, with a perplexed sadness, but no sign of recognition. "Is there something else I can help you locate?"

He shook his head and turned to leave, but got only as far as the doorway before she spoke again.

"Governor?" He turned to face her with a measure of dread at having been discovered, but she smiled genuinely, revealing the dimples of youth.

"You may want to review the files down at the courthouse. They'll have more details about criminal cases. In some you can even read the transcripts from the trial."

He studied her face, which could be pretty under the right light. Though her hair and clothing were more demure, she reminded him of his own daughter, Lindsay, who would have been about the same age, had she survived.

"Thanks. I'll do that."

CHAPTER 7

INSTEAD, HE HEADED TO THE SECURITY of his apartment. Two public appearances on the same day were enough.

Despite central air, inside it felt sticky. The southern windows, which offered such expansive views of the river and the downtown, also slow roasted the building, so that by late afternoon he could smell the heat like baking bread. One disadvantage to living without curtains.

After shedding his sport coat, he circled the living room looking for direction but found none. Owing to the building's circular design, all the rooms elongated into trapezoids, projecting out to the city at large, the opposite of what he needed. Then he noted the sports section of the newspaper and checked the start time of the baseball game.

To the amazement of all city residents, the Cubs were playing competitive ball that season, only a couple games out of first. During the winter, they'd rebuilt their rotation through trades for Dennis Eckersley and Scott Sanderson, giving them a lineup worthy of the majors. Then, rather than the usual mid-summer fire sale of marketable assets, they'd acquired another starting pitcher from the Indians for a utility outfielder. Native Chicagoans dared not speak of a pennant, much less a World Series flag, not after centuries of futility, instead counting the team's relevance after the All-Star break as blessing enough.

With first pitch half an hour away, Duncan lingered by the plate glass window. At midday, the roads and sidewalks clogged with people. Most walked in pairs or groups: men in suits chatting, women with children, couples arm in arm. Even forty floors up, he felt their intimacy.

He stepped onto the oval balcony so he could hear the sounds of the city: the rev of engines, the exhalation of wind. A gust off the lakefront whistled through the iron railings and trembled through the floor below him. When he first moved in, the building's sway would awake him in the night, reminding him of his solitude, but now he hardly noticed it. He'd accepted the solidity of the concrete shell around him, despite its vulnerability to the larger forces of nature.

His son inhabited another concrete structure, one with no view and no privacy. At night, did he feel alone, or did he find companionship with the other inmates—a joke or a game of cards? More likely a fight, to judge by the damage.

Duncan returned to the kitchen phone and dialed a number he knew by heart. On the second ring, an anonymous woman's voice greeted him, "Markham offices."

"May I speak to Ms. Markham?"

"Just a moment, Mr. Cochrane. Let me see if she's available."

Some Muzak intervened, a Beatles tune, the melody familiar but the lyric elusive. He filled in the missing words. "...you know I believe and how...." Just when the rest came to him, the tune stopped.

"Hi, Dad."

Duncan recalled how Glynis appeared when he'd last seen her months before: serious and polished, with her nails and hair professionally done, plus a new wardrobe of silk blouses and knit skirts—no longer the perpetual college student lacking makeup or purpose. "Is that my daughter? Since she changed her name, she's all but renounced her family."

Through the phone, he heard a door close before she answered. "You know why I took this name."

"You never put it into words."

She sighed. "I'm starting a new practice, and I don't need the family... legacy following me."

My *legacy,* he thought, but kept it to himself. "Anyway, it's nice to hear your voice."

"Is that why you called?" She sounded impatient, the message implicit: stop interrupting my work.

"I was wondering when you'd be coming down to visit?"

A silence on the line suggested never. "Not soon. Trying to build a business is—"

"I know. I did it once. Believe me, I understand. But you need to take *some* time away for yourself, your family."

Again, she sighed, this time so loudly she clearly meant it to be heard. "You mean Aden."

"He's part of your family." Another silence, this one conveying her distaste for the topic. He moved toward the couch, but the phone cord wouldn't reach, so he sat on a bar stool by the kitchen counter. "I think he'd benefit from seeing you. He seems... despondent."

"He should be. He killed his sister. My sister."

"I know, I know. But at some point we have to accept that, and so does he."

Silence.

"Have you visited him lately?"

"You know I haven't."

"You should. You'd hardly recognize him. He's... hard to reach."

"That's his baseline."

"Not to this degree."

In the background he heard typing. Was she trying to work during their call?

"It's too far to stop and say hello, Dad. Madison is three hours away. It'd take me all day just driving there and back."

"You must be able to take *some* time off."

"My clients need me. My *real* clients."

Duncan had wound the phone cord about his finger so tightly that it was cutting off the circulation, but when he removed the wrap, its imprint remained.

"I know you're not inclined to forgive him. Believe me, I understand. I felt the same way. For years. But we can't forsake him. He's still family, and in not so long he'll be free again. We need to ensure he returns a better man."

In the pause that followed, he noted that the typing had stopped. "We've discussed this, Dad. I can't treat a relative," she said. "It would be unethical."

"Not treat, just visit."

"I don't see how one visit is going to help. He'll still be a convict."

"He's not a convict. He's your brother." He stopped himself, his tone growing more strident. He wanted to keep this civil, productive. "Surely you feel some... concern for his wellbeing, if only professionally?"

"I know what you're trying to do: convince me to see him so I'm frightened enough to get him a therapist. If that's what you want, why not just request one? After all, you ran the place."

"I ran a state, not a penal colony, and I don't govern any of it any longer. Anyway, I've been checking, and it appears there's no mental health treatment in any of the prisons here."

"You didn't plan any while you were building them?"

"It was enough of a struggled getting them funded, let alone more services."

He stood and walked a circle as wide as the phone cord would allow. "I know one visit won't change him, but he needs to know we still care."

"What about his lawyers? They could request an evaluation."

"They're afraid of anything that might draw publicity. Other than filing papers."

Outside, a pelican landed on the railing to his balcony and stared, voyeuristically. It must have gotten lost on its migration.

"You're sure you can't get away, even for a day?" he said. "Make it part of a trip to see the family?"

She sighed again, this time more deeply. Through the phone, he heard her flip through something and imagined her checking a busy calendar.

"I'm free this weekend."

"Visiting is weekdays only."

"It's all I have."

"Fine. That'll be fine. I'll... call in a favor."

He paused a beat. "Will you be staying over?" He glanced around his empty apartment, with only a couch for visitors. "There's many good hotels nearby. I'll make you a reservation."

"No need." She waited a beat. "Do me one favor. Don't tell anyone I'm coming."

"Anyone like who?"

"Mom. You know how she gets."

He sat again on the barstool. "I know. I'll keep it between us."

CHAPTER 8

LATER THAT DAY, DUNCAN LAY ON the couch in his apartment listening to the Cubs game. He preferred the radio to television, letting his imagination create the images, even though he found the play-by-play man, Harry Caray, a shameless digresser. Rick Sutcliffe was going for his ninth win in ten starts, yet in the seventh inning the big redhead had faltered, allowing two runs and cutting their advantage in half. Duncan pictured the fans, sunburned and restless in the bleachers, sweating through the eighth. Middle reliever George Frazier had protecting the lead, giving up not a single base runner, but he was no closer, and Lee Smith had pitched three of the past four games.

Duncan had opened the patio door to allow in some fresh air but caught the scent of dead fish off the lakefront. In summer, Alewives washed up by the thousands along Lake Michigan's sandy shores. Clean up crews bulldozed them every day, yet by morning another slaughter appeared. Nonetheless, their smell faded, along with the sounds of traffic and people below, as the game wore on, everyone in town transfixed by the prospect of a winner at Wrigley. As the Cubs took the field in the bottom of the inning, Caray urged listeners to get out of their seats and cheer on the boys. In his typically muddled style, he butchered the names of the opposing players while whipping the faithful into a religious fervor.

A knock at the door interrupted. No one came to Duncan's apartment, ever. Few people even knew where he lived, and the building's security kept out most of those who did.

He rose from the couch, feeling stiff after several hours of tense listening, and staggered to the peephole, which showed a woman with pale skin and light blonde hair tied into a bun. The distortion of the rounded glass made her difficult to recognize, but something in her set mouth triggered déjà vu.

"Who's there?"

"Governor, I'd like to speak with you a minute."

Her voice too rang familiar, a basso out of keeping with her age and gender. Against the chain lock, he cracked the door to see her face in full view. "Regarding?"

"The Innocence Inquiry. Have you reconsidered our request?"

Of course. The woman from the diner downstairs.

The radio crackled with an elevated cheer. Had the game ended already? "I haven't time right now," he said.

"Could we meet later in the week?"

"No, look, I don't want to lead you on...." He regretted the word choice, given the intimacy of the setting, but continued anyway, "...I've checked into your project, and I can tell you I'm not interested."

"And why is that?"

Unaccustomed to such interrogation, he paused to find the words. "Because the evidence is conclusive. The man you're defending confessed."

"Under duress. Chicago police tortured him for hours. Without that, there'd be no evidence to arrest him, let alone win a conviction."

"That is... regrettable, but I'm still not interested."

"Governor—"

"Please don't call me that."

"I mean it with the utmost respect."

"Still, I don't hold the office anymore, so it's not fitting—"

"How would you prefer to be addressed?"

"I'd prefer to end this conversation. I really have nothing to—"

"Mr. Cochrane, joining our cause will benefit you as well as the accused."

Another cheer from the radio, this one louder than the first. Duncan strained to hear more but made out only the lisping monologue of Harry Caray on some tangential story.

He could close the door on her, push her and her cause away and hope she didn't return, but his parents had trained him not to treat people so, and she'd acted polite, if pushy, during both their meetings, so instead he invited her inside. He thought of turning down the volume but hadn't the chance. She talked for five minutes uninterrupted about the righteousness of the effort and the state's abuses of power. By the end he almost believed her until he recalled the details of the news story, how the victims had been fatally assaulted in their own apartment by a burglar they'd caught.

"I still don't see how you can be convinced of this man's innocence when he confessed. What would impel someone—"

"Have you heard of bagging?"

"Bagging. As in groceries?"

"It's a technique used by the police. They place a typewriter bag over the suspect's head until he can't breathe. Oftentimes they beat him while he's hooded. The treatment has induced many people to admit to all sorts of things they didn't do."

"Still, I can't imagine someone confessing to such a hideous crime if—"

"During the Inquisition, people pleaded guilty to all manner of crimes—even when they knew it would result in their execution—just to end the torture."

Duncan inhaled and noted a subtle floral scent from her, then wondered what odor his apartment carried. Probably used sweat socks. Instead of an aroma, he noted the broadcast, which had subsided to polite conversation between the announcers. Surely the game had not ended already. More than anything, he wanted to return to its escape. Like anyone under interrogation, his best option was to finish it quickly. "What exactly is it you want from me?"

"Your help in obtaining more evidence—"

"As I told you before, my name carries little weight any longer."

"But if you acknowledged the mistakes of your administration, the excesses of your judicial policy, it would convince people to reexamine them."

"Even if I agreed with your... characterization, I don't see how I can—"

"To start, we ask only your help in discovery. Mr. Flores told us that his questioning was recorded. If we could obtain copies of that tape—"

"I have no influence over the Chicago police."

"But you know people who do."

"I've retired from public life."

She glanced about the empty apartment, and again he felt ashamed at his living conditions, more like an aimless bachelor than a former head of state. "I've just moved in," he said.

She nodded and looked past him to the view of downtown. "Don't you owe it to the people you represented to ensure that the right men are locked up?"

Was she referring to his son? He studied her face for judgment or contempt but instead saw the zealotry of righteousness. Much like his estranged wife, she persisted until he relented.

"If all you want is a copy of the tape, why not hire a lawyer and sue the city for it?"

"We've tried." She paused to inhale, for the first time displaying the emotion behind her persuasion. "The truth is, we're running out of time. The deadline for a habeas petition is a year after trial and it's coming up next month, but all we have is the testimony of a condemned man. We need proof. Otherwise, Mr. Flores may never get to challenge his conviction. His last appeal would be to the governor—the current governor."

Duncan thought of his successor, who displayed little interest in crime or justice, and of his recent visit to a state penitentiary. "If I agree to help you get the tape, you must keep my involvement confidential."

"It would be far more powerful—"

"That's not negotiable."

She folded her hands in her lap and stared at them a moment before replying, "very well." She handed him a business card reading:

Catherine Fontanelle, Advocate
The Innocence Inquiry

A fitting title.

In the background he heard Harry's signature call "It might be... it could be... it IS! A home run! Holy cow." Did that just happen, or were they reliving some highlight? Even with the sound down, he couldn't have missed such a moment.

"Why don't you meet him?" she said, and laid a hand on his forearm to focus his attention.

"Who?"

"Mr. Flores. If I can arrange a visit, would you agree to speak with him?"

He stared at her face, with its translucent eyes and pale skin, looking for a way to say no, but finding none, instead said, "Yes."

He ushered her outside and closed the door firmly behind, then returned his full attention to the game, but he'd missed the end. Harry was performing the coda to another victory, proclaiming the arrival of a new era. "Sure as God made green apples, someday the Chicago Cubs are going to be in the World Series."

If only Duncan had such faith.

CHAPTER 9

WHEN HE AWOKE BEFORE DAYLIGHT THE next morning, Duncan felt a brief panic. Despite climate control, damp sheets wrapped his legs and ensnared his arms, making it difficult to extricate even his hands. Once he'd freed himself, he reached for the clock expecting to see the familiar digits 2:34. For months after his daughter's death, he'd alerted each night at precisely the same hour, minute, probably second, reliving her cry for help. Instead, he saw that the hands had passed five, nearly his time for revival.

He lay in bed plotting his day—three appointments outside his safety zone—and recalling images from the day past. The monotone of Aden's voice, the swelling of his face, the lethargy of his being, all lingered in Duncan's memory. He needed to restore hope to his son.

Then Duncan thought of another man who rose early to tend the souls of the downtrodden.

***

St. Dominic's lay a few miles north of Duncan's apartment, near the towers of Cabrini Green, one of Chicago's largest housing complexes. Though modest in scale and ornamentation compared to the cathedrals of downtown, the church's solid brick façade looked lavish by the standards of its blighted neighborhood. Its sea-green doors offered sanctuary from the crime and poverty and despair that permeated the nearby tenements.

Inside, the nave loomed dim and smoky, with a lingering aroma of incense and mildew, suggesting decay more than deliverance. Even the bricks showed their age, with chips in the walls and floors worn smooth like river stones. A man knelt before the altar, arrayed in the patchwork denim cloak that was his emblem. When he'd finished his prayers, the penitent rose and startled to see an old friend and accomplice.

"You snuck up on me," he said, advancing up the aisle like a superhero, his cape billowing behind.

Up close, he looked every bit the enigma that Duncan remembered, a layman who spoke and acted like a priest, who the locals referred to as Father Frank, but who travelled among sinners and professed a criminal past. His looks, too, contained a mystery, with dark skin and eyes that could have indicated many origins. His black hair had grown since they'd last spoken, falling to his shoulders, but a gold stud still glinted from one ear.

"I didn't want to disturb you," Duncan said.

"This house is made for the disturbed." Father Frank led Duncan to a pew and sat an intimate distance from him. "What brings you back to *this* neighborhood?"

"Advice. About my son." He hesitated, unsure how to begin, but his confessor waited. "You must know what's... become of him."

The father nodded and smoothed his vestments as though preparing for a lengthy explanation.

"Lately he seems... " Duncan searched the dim murals and sooty windows of the sanctuary for the right words, "not himself."

"How's that?"

"It's hard to describe. He's been distant ever since puberty. Not that that was so long ago, but... now more than ever."

"How long's he been down?"

"'Down' meaning depressed? Hard to say."

"'Down' meaning incarcerated."

"Six months."

"What's his bid?"

Duncan needed a moment to process the lingo, which flowed from the reformed prisoner like a native language but to his ears sounded foreign. "Five years."

"A nickel." The father nodded and lower his head in thought. "He's still processing."

"Pardon?"

Father Frank shook his head as though to escape an unpleasant memory. "People think the first night being locked up is the worst—gang rape and all that. It's not. Don't get me wrong, it's bad, especially for fresh fish, but really the weight of the place falls on you a few months in—before you're institutionalized, when you're still reminiscing about your old life. You get assigned your cellie, your job, your schooling, whatever's going to be your program. You adapt. Until you realize there's no appeal, no salvation coming. That's when a lot of guys lose faith. They've been going on adrenaline so long that when it finally runs out, they're exhausted."

"I can relate."

The father smiled knowingly but did not reply.

"So how do I pull him out of that funk?" Duncan said.

"You don't." Father Frank paused, letting his words echo through the empty vault. "Your boy's got to find the light for himself."

Duncan nodded and looked toward the rose window above the altar, which in the dim light looked kaleidoscopic. "There must be some way I can help him, get him assigned to another prison or enrolled in some program."

The layman shook his head. "That only delays enlightenment. He's got to find his own path to the truth."

High above them, a bell tolled seven, reminding Duncan of his own passing time.

"I'm worried about him, about his... soul. He seems weary, despondent."

"Deep down, a lot of people are. We put on a convincing façade, but we can't fool ourselves."

"Then what do you recommend?"

"I can tell you what worked for me: God. I discovered His love when *I* was on the inside and looking for an escape. Since then, I've never despaired, no matter how dire things got."

Duncan nodded, though he took little solace from the advice. Ever since his daughter died, he placed no faith in an almighty who allowed such things. As governor, he'd made a show of religion—attending services at a Presbyterian Church—but like so many of his interactions the words meant little to him. "What about something... practical?"

The layman lowered his head—in prayer or thought, Duncan couldn't tell which—and stayed that way for an uncomfortably long time. "If he's truly in peril, you could get him put on suicide watch."

"He's not suicidal."

"He don't have to be. A lot of times guys land there cause of what's happening with them: they just got sentenced to a long bit or they got hooked up for the first time."

"I thought that's what protective custody was for."

"P.C. ain't secure, it's less *in*secure."

"So suicide watch is basically what, solitary confinement?"

"Of a sort, only it's not punitive, it's protective."

In some ways Aden fit the model—not many prep school kids landed in prison—yet the boy had always possessed a sullen charm with his peers, an ability to twist his rebelliousness into coolness. Perhaps when surrounded by true miscreants, he realized his own conventionality. "You can request that?" Duncan said.

"Most can't. Something bad has to happen for a body to land there. A fight, a violation. *You* probably could, though."

The innuendo, that he possessed powers and connections from his time in office, echoed the assumption of Josie and Catherine, of so many people really, who didn't recognize how far he'd fallen.

"I wish I still wielded such influence."

"You do," the layman said. "Here in the neighborhood, people remember how you risked yourself to protect them. Nothing you did before or since could undo that."

Duncan smiled at the memory of his time living in Cabrini to catch a sniper, then he recalled the deaths that accompanied his stay, the people he couldn't save. "Thanks for the advice." He offered his hand for a shake, which Father Frank took in both of his as though readying to pray.

"Before you go, let me give you one more insight. Once you get special treatment, it's tough to reintegrate. You get branded as weak, vulnerable, and after that guys prey on you. Sometimes—and this contradicts what I preach to the kids here, but prison follows another morality— sometimes you got to fight your way through, prove you're not afraid. Maybe it's the Lord's way of testing us. I don't know, but to follow his teachings requires a lot of fortitude."

CHAPTER 10

FROM THE SANCTUARY, DUNCAN TRAVELLED BACK toward the relative safety of downtown. In the distance, skyscrapers welcomed him like an anonymous mob, but he bypassed the turnoff to his own high-rise and rattled across the LaSalle Drive Bridge over the Chicago River and into the Loop. Police headquarters lay a couple miles farther south, beyond the luxury apartments and Fortune 500 companies. It occupied an entire city block, a brick box as stolid and silent as the people who worked there.

Due to his loss of rank in the state's bureaucracy, Duncan had to wait in the lobby while the desk clerk, a young cadet whose uniform sagged off her shoulders, paged a friend of his on the force. Two years before, as governor, the police would have escorted him anywhere in the building without impediment. Now he sat on hard wooden benches next to winos and derelicts. None of them recognized him, so he took the opportunity to study their indifference. Each occupied a tragedy of his own, preoccupied with the injuries and injustices that had brought him to this waiting room. One who smelled like a campfire muttered to himself as another who masticated non-stop stared with hunger at the desk clerk. She dutifully ignored them all. Perhaps the former governor mattered no more than they did.

When Detective Gino Peruzzi finally strode into the lobby, he shook his head at the scene. "Sorry you got classed with the underclass," Peruzzi said. As he led Duncan past the reception desk, he said loudly, "People without character can't tell it when they see it." The clerk only glared after them, either indifferent or disdainful, Duncan couldn't tell which.

They ascended to the tenth floor, where the cops were divided into corrals, banging out copy like news reporters. Interspersed among them were citizens of every stripe dictating their tales to these glorified scriveners, who copied the details with no show of credence or enthusiasm. A few of the cops watched the man who'd once commanded them, probably wondering if he'd finally be getting his comeuppance for lying about Aden's guilt, but most remained intent on their busywork.

Since Duncan had last seen him, Peruzzi had escaped their rank to a small office, which offered the privacy of a thin door and odor of stale coffee. The sergeant sat and gestured for Duncan to do the same opposite him in a stiff, wooden chair no better than the lobby's bench. "What brings you to purgatory?" he said.

"First, detective, I want to thank you for seeing me without an appointment."

"It's sergeant now," Peruzzi said, and pointed to the name plate on his desk. "Anddon'tmentionit." Despite his promotion, the cop retained his habit of rushing whole sentences into a single word.

"Now that you're a supervisor, I'm sure you've got a lot on your docket."

Peruzzi gestured to the poundage of papers that cluttered his desk and said, "Tellmeaboutit. Nobody warned me when I joined the pencil pushers that the only daylight I'd get to see is through this window." He pointed behind him to a small double hung with frosted glass, which let in a dim light.

Duncan studied him for signs of aging that might require such a reassignment. He noted the shadow of a double chin and a few strands of gray on his sideburns. Otherwise, Peruzzi looked as compact and lean as before, with his hair slicked back off his forehead and his sport coat fitted close to his chest.

"I need some information from you," Duncan said, "for a case I'm working on."

"Didn't know you'd become a gumshoe."

Duncan felt embarrassed by his gaffe. "I misspoke. A case that interests me." He let the term hang in the air between them and decided it sounded more accurate. "I've read about a technique called 'bagging,' and I wanted to know more about it."

Peruzzi let the term hang in the air without reply. Its silence accentuated the other sounds filtering through the thin door: the clacking of typewriter keys, a cry of anger from one of the cells, a woman's elevated voice in the bullpen. Then Duncan noticed the detective's heels bouncing like a boxer awaiting the bell, releasing his restless energy. Such an office must have confined him too tightly, which gave Duncan hope that he could wait out the interrogator.

"Where'd you hear that term?" Peruzzi said neutrally, though his stare betrayed arousal.

"From a colleague."

"The brass banned that technique years back. If you're hearing about it now, it's got to be from an old case."

"Not that old," Duncan said.

The cop stared at his witness as though trying to intimidate him. "Still, nobody uses it anymore."

"How *was* it used?"

Peruzzi kept his gaze steady, though he continued to vibrate from the feet up. "For interrogations. When a suspect wouldn't cooperate."

"And what specifically does it involve?"

"No offense, governor, but I'd rather not get into the details. It's an outmoded style of investigation, like walking around with a magnifying glass."

In the past, Peruzzi had always spoken plainly, even when it worked against his purposes. Here, the cop was clearly hiding something. "You can't give me an inkling?"

The detective hunched forward, putting enough weight on his feet to still them. "The name pretty much says it all. Basically, it's putting a bag over somebody's head so they think they're suffocating. It didn't hurt anybody, but it scared a lot of 'em."

"Could it induce someone to confess falsely?"

"Since I never tried it myself, I can't say." He sat back again, restarting his nervous legs. "Look, I can tell by your questions that you're aligned with those do-gooders who want us to treat crooks like misbehaving kids. Yougotttaunderstand, this town averages two homicides a day, and that's just murders. You can't even imagine how many rapes and robberies and assaults come across my desk." He gestured to the mound of folders that covered every inch. "Plus, we got this new drug coming our way: crack. You heard of it?"

Duncan shook his head.

"You will. It's all over New York and L.A. Can't take long for it to spread here. WhatI'msayingis, we can't sit tight waiting for the bad guys to confess. Sometimes we need some inducements to get them to do the right thing."

"How many police used it?"

"It's not like it was ever part of the training manual. It's more... improvised, when things aren't going so good."

"Did many of your colleagues know about it?"

"Knowing about it and using it are different things."

Duncan should have thought better than to interrogate a cop with far more skill in verbal combat than he possessed. Instead, he called on the tactics he'd learned in business. "Funny thing is, I believe our interests here are more in alignment than you realize."

The detective waited for him to continue, keeping time on his invisible bass drum.

"We both want killers to go to jail. *I* was the one who passed the three strikes law and built the prisons to hold all the new inmates. And you know why I did it."

Peruzzi raised his eyebrows empathetically.

"Regardless of what happened with my son, I want the right people punished for their crimes. I can tell from your answer that you don't approve of abusing prisoners any more than I do. Now, unlike the 'do-gooders' you mentioned, I don't want to punish cops for doing their jobs. I just want to know that the people we're locking up are the ones who need to be locked up."

The detective again leaned forward to close the distance between them and lowered his voice to a level no one outside the room could hear. "If I thought we were busting the wrong guys, I'd be with you, a hundred percent. But I'm not. Most cops here, they may not always do things the official ways, but they do their jobs. They want convictions, and they get tired of seeing crooks walk because we don't have overwhelming evidence of what we see every day."

To deescalate things, Duncan sat back in his chair. "How about this: convince me you're right. You don't have to say anything now, but promise me you'll examine your files for this one suspect. If you tell me there's nothing suspicious, I'll take your word. Only, be thorough about it. You don't have to involve anyone else or hurt any of your confederates, but do a proper investigation. Once you're satisfied, I'll be satisfied."

The detective frowned but stilled his heels. "It may take a while. Tobehonestwithyou, I don't have the time right now."

Duncan wrote Harry's name on a scrap of paper and slid it across the desk. "Whenever you can make time."

Peruzzi nodded, picked up and paper, and deposited it in his shirt pocket.

"Yougotit."

CHAPTER 11

OUTSIDE THE POLICE DEPARTMENT, THE SUN had topped the fence of buildings downtown, warming the street and gleaming off their glass façades. Duncan had paused to extract his sunglasses when a touch on his elbow startled him: a woman both young and dowdy.

"Governor, I thought that was you," she said.

He studied her face—which lacked makeup or grooming, with lank hair and a pair of big eyes magnified by tortoise-shell frames—but made no connection to it. From her cheap clothes and inky hands, he presumed she worked at one of the local newspapers.

"What are you doing here?" she said.

"Attending to some personal business."

She rose only to his shoulder, so he looked overtop her, trying to recall where he'd parked.

"Is it about your son?" She opened a slim tablet and jotted something in illegible shorthand.

"Another matter," Duncan said and walked east into the blinding sun.

She followed at his elbow. "Are you still hopeful he'll be freed soon?"

He quickened his pace, using long strides to distance her, but she kept up with a clumsy gallop.

"Are you in contact with him?"

"Of course."

"How is he doing? In prison, I mean."

At a cross street, he paused but saw nothing familiar. All the buildings looked the same, towers of steel and glass. "As you'd expect." He waited for a walk signal, hoping a new vantage would stimulate his memory.

"I'd love to interview him, get his perspective on things. I could make him more sympathetic, less of a cold-hearted killer."

"Which is how you all portrayed him."

"Only because we never saw any other side. You kept him hidden even during his trial."

Finally, the light changed, and Duncan tried to rub her off by weaving through oncoming pedestrians, but she pursued with the desperation of her looming deadline. At the opposite corner he paused again and scanned the block but couldn't spot his BMW. The downside of sport coupes.

"I tried once to get in to see him, but he walked away as soon as he heard I was a writer."

"Reporter," he corrected. "Your job is to report what people say. And the answer is no."

She lay a moist hand on his arm and left it there. "What about a few quotes from you?"

What new brand of scribe was she? He'd adapted to pushy, impertinent questions, but not to being pursued. Previously, he'd deployed security to fend off such pestering, but along with his office he'd lost their protection. "Who employs you?" he said.

"The *Sun-Times*."

That explained it. Since Rupert Murdoch had acquired the city's tabloid, it had degenerated to muckraking, with full-page headlines for every scandal. Duncan had stopped reading it after seeing weekly stories disparaging himself, his family, his tenure, and his boy. He strode back toward the police department, taking strides so long that they reverberated up his spine. At worst, he could hide there until she gave up.

"With all your connections, I'm surprised your son got convicted at all." She smiled with hunger or delight, he couldn't decide which.

"It's nothing to do with that," he said.

Several beat cops observed their approach as he jaywalked to the department's front entrance, but none moved to intervene. Typical.

"I really must be going," he said and walked past this sanctuary toward the adjacent block. At worst he could find an El stop and escape her that way.

"Don't you think you've kept silent long enough?" she said. "You have nothing to lose by sharing your story with people."

"If only that were true."

"What about an interview with you, one on one. Tell people anything you want."

He stopped midstride, forcing other pedestrians to step around him. A prickly heat irritated his scalp, and his breath came in hot pants. "What will it take for you to leave me be?"

For a moment she looked startled, but that quickly turned to eager optimism. "A quote. One I can use tomorrow. Something worthy of a headline." Her longing contorted her features into a menacing squint.

"Very well." He scanned the street for inspiration but found only regular people disinterested in his suffering. "I remain... optimistic about my son's future. He's a promising young man who erred, but who should not be defined by that one mistake."

Dutifully, she scribbled his words, then glared at him, awaiting more.

"Enough?" he said.

"Just," she said, and left him standing alone, unsure how he'd get to his next meeting.

CHAPTER 12

COMPARED TO THE FAMILIAL VISITS WITH his son, death row felt like a fortress. Two guards led Duncan and Catherine through a half-dozen security measures—checkpoints, sliding doors, metal detectors, watchtowers with armed sentries—before they arrived in a segregated booth. With each layer of security, the rooms grew colder and darker, more isolated from the natural world.

Their destination offered no distractions, with blank walls and gray paint, a space distinguished by its lack of ornament or comfort. Not even dirty vents decorated it, leaving only Catherine's lilac body wash to fill the vacancy. Fittingly, the booth opposite their own sat empty.

After sitting on a pair of hard metal stools, Duncan felt stunned to silence by the mistrust shown to them. No special treatment for the ex-governor here. He could only imagine how the institution treated regular visitors. A draft on his bare arms made him shiver.

Finally, Catherine spoke. "Can you imagine living in such a place?"

"I'd rather not."

"The men here are locked away by themselves twenty-three hours a day. They eat one hot meal. They bathe once a week. They're not even allowed contact visits with their spouses. Many lose all sense of society."

"Those that possessed it before they arrived."

"It doesn't feel cruel to you, treating another person so?" Her pale blue eyes implored him to sympathize, but he felt more pity for *her* than the inmates—until he thought of his own son isolated in such a cell.

"Not compared to what they did to land here."

They discussed the proper treatment of killers and what constituted cruel and unusual punishment until a door buzzed opposite the glass. A man entered the other cubicle, moving with the wobbly grace of a penguin—his hands chained at the waist, feet linked to each other—until he fell onto a stool across from them.

Through the thick glass that separated them, he appeared smaller and paler than Duncan expected. His jumpsuit bagged off his narrow shoulders, and his skin looked jaundiced in the fluorescent light. Only his dark eyes and skin suggested his Latin roots. He nodded to his visitors deferentially, then stared at his hands, which he kept folded in his lap.

Duncan searched for a phone to connect them and finding none said, "How do we communicate with him?"

"Speak loudly," said Catherine. She turned to the inmate and said, "Hello."

He nodded again but said nothing, so she leaned toward the solid glass and shouted, "How are you?"

The man shrugged and said, "Okay," his voice so muffled that Duncan had to watch his lips to understand him. His face betrayed neither joy nor anxiety about the visit.

"This is no way to communicate," Duncan said. He looked behind them to the door where they entered, but the guards had disappeared. He nodded to a camera mounted in the ceiling. "Can they hear everything we say?"

"I'm sure." She turned back to their guest and smiled. "Mr. Flores, do you know who this is?"

The man glanced at his visitor and shook his head.

"Former Governor Cochrane, who ran this state when you were arrested."

The inmate looked unimpressed, but he kept his thoughts to himself.

"He's here to help us," she said.

Duncan noticed pinholes at the corners of the glass and leaned into them. "I'd like to hear more about you."

While Flores sat quietly, Duncan tried to guess his age, which appeared close to his own, nearing a fifth decade. There the similarities ended, as this man appeared to lack all pride, slumped in his seat, his head lowered. Finally, after at least a minute of silence, the convict shrugged. "Like what?"

"Where do you live?" Duncan said.

"Addison Station."

"I've never heard of that neighborhood."

Catherine lay a hand on his arm. "He means the train stop."

"The El platform? You live below the El?"

Flores nodded. "In a closet."

He appeared small enough to hide in such a cavity. "What do you do?" Duncan said.

Again that bashful shrug. "Sleep mostly. There's not much you can do here."

"I meant on the outside, for a living."

"Collect bottles and cans." He nodded as though a simple phrase could summarize a life.

Duncan studied him, this time for deceit, but he noted only modestly. How could this small, demure man have killed two elderly people in a botched robbery?

"Ms. Fontanelle tells me that you're innocent."

The little man nodded.

"Yet you confessed. Why would you do that?"

Flores stared into his lap, shamefully. "They made me."

"Who, the police?"

Again, the abashed nod.

"How?"

"They wouldn't let me go." Flores raised his eyes long enough for Duncan to detect some emotion, a sorrow that transcended even his current circumstances.

"How do you mean?"

"They locked me in a room, covered my head so I couldn't see or breathe, left me handcuffed to a chair till I signed their paper."

"Surely you knew what it would mean, admitting to such a thing." Duncan swept a hand to take in all around them. "A lifetime of incarceration." He purposefully left out death.

"I wasn't thinking about that."

"What were you thinking about?"

"Making it stop."

Once more, Catherine touched his arm to intervene, causing an involuntary tingle. "By the time he signed his confession, the police had interrogated Mr. Flores for thirteen hours. Under such pressure, many men will admit to anything."

"Did you know what you were signing?"

Flores bowed his head and shook it.

"Did you read it?"

And again, that ashamed shake of the head.

Catherine whispered to him, "His literacy skills are very poor. The man received only a third-grade education in Mexico."

Duncan sighed and fought against his own desire to escape this small cell, though he'd been locked away less than—what—half an hour? "I still don't understand why the police would detain you in the first place. Other than living near the crime scene, why were you a suspect?"

"Drinking."

"When? The night of the killing?"

"When they took me in."

"And when was that?"

For the third time, a touch on Duncan's arm distracted him. Catherine explained, "The police first interviewed him two days after the event. Initially, he told them he'd been asleep inside his closet at the El stop, but they claim he passed out after committing the crime."

Duncan turned back to the little man. "How does being drunk make you a murder suspect?"

"I'm different then."

"So are many people. Most don't end up here."

The familiar touch interrupted again, irritating him. Why would she not allow the man to speak for himself? "Apparently, Mr. Flores undergoes a personality shift when he's under the influence of alcohol, a real Jekyll and Hyde transformation."

Duncan studied the little man, who did not move. "Is that true?"

Eyes downcast, Flores nodded.

Duncan asked several more questions about Flores' life prior to his arrest but got only shrugs and nods as explanations.

***

Once they'd reentered the warmth and daylight beyond the prison's high walls, Catherine stopped and turned him with a hand on his elbow.

"So, what do you think?" she said.

He looked about them at the sea of farmlands surrounding the prison island and inhaled the fresh air, which carried the smells of barnyards and hay. "For someone facing execution, he doesn't exhibit much—what—emotion?"

"He's given up. The state has condemned him to die and rendered him helpless."

Duncan chose not to take the comment as an insult. "I still don't understand why the detectives would identify him as a suspect."

"They needed someone to blame, and he was an easy target."

Duncan shook his head, unable to believe that even the Chicago police would act in so self-serving a fashion. In his experience, they practiced more indifference than malice. "What about his trial? Didn't his lawyer object to the confession?"

"She tried, but it's difficult for jurors to believe that a man would falsely implicate himself."

Duncan sensed her efforts to sway him with his own skepticism, but he didn't want to argue in the parking lot of a prison. "Was there nothing else that implicated him? No physical evidence, no witnesses?"

"Nothing. His confession condemned him."

Duncan nodded and stared at the high walls of the institution, which confined information as effectively as they did convicts. "Even so, I cannot involve myself publicly in this case."

Disappointment twisted her face, as though she channeled all of the sorrow of her clientele. "But there's much you could do privately."

"Not as much as you imagine."

"Anything that brings light to this hidden injustice would help." This time when she touched his wrist, she let her hand linger.

"Let me talk to some people."

***

During the long drive home, the sun shifted the colors of the fields from yellow to gold to brown. The rural scene provided relief from the prison's high walls and the skyscrapers of downtown. It also offered Duncan time to process what he'd seen and heard away from the distraction of Catherine's touch. He could not reconcile the accounts he'd read of the crime with the modest, restrained man he'd met. Could such an unfortunate beat two people to death? Probably not. Then again, a killer had deceived Duncan before.

CHAPTER 13

TWO MEN SIT ON THE CEMENT floor of a small room, drinking from a plastic bag, some orange liquid fluorescent and bubbly. They act jovial, laughing, passing the bag between them despite their confinement. Nearby a train passes, roaring over their dialogue and shaking the room from floor to ceiling, but they are unfazed, shouting above the din and celebrating its departure.

"To safe passage," says one.

He wears the surgical scrubs of an inmate, and immediately Duncan recognizes him as Harry, except that he is no longer confined to a cell but rather returned to his closet beneath the El.

The other man is scrawny and scraggly, with a thick beard and a whirl of hair, but despite his aged appearance, Duncan knows his son. This doppelgänger tries to stand but is too drunk to support his weight, falling backward into a puddle of sewage and debris.

"To the future," he toasts, empty-handed.

***

Duncan awoke with a jerk then lay still, caught in a state of half consciousness, irrational and unsettled, arguing with himself and the men, threatening to call the police on them, warning them of the dissolute path they had chosen. By the time he fully roused himself, he felt too agitated to risk such a dream again.

Instead he rose early for a nostalgic trip.

***

A favorite stop in his old neighborhood was Walker Brothers Pancake House, which sat only blocks from Duncan's former home along the lakefront. A tradition on the tony North Shore, it had dispensed comfort food to the privileged for a quarter-century. On weekends, the wait for tables took up to an hour, and people brought their newspapers to the lobby, but weekdays usually required no such patience. Duncan barely had time to take in the smells of grilled bacon and sausage before being seated.

In his old environs, people left Duncan unmolested. CEOs and VIPs did not impress the restaurant's clientele, who typically included such families. Still, he requested a table at the far corner and turned his back to the other patrons.

When the waitress arrived, he studied her face for recognition but saw only pert naïveté. Her flawless skin and almond eyes suggested a privileged life. Probably a Northwestern student, which provoked in him a paternal admiration. Without looking at the menu, he ordered a German pancake and large coffee, then picked up the newspaper he'd brought with him.

A quick survey revealed no news about him but several echoes of his past. The governor, his successor, appeared in a front-page photo at *Taste of Chicago,* the city's homage to unhealthy eating, where brats and ribs and Italian beef could be combined in a single meal. He looked as out of place as a bird at a dining table. Despite the heat and humidity, he wore a three-piece suit without either hat or sunglasses. Instead, he squinted into the camera, his nose hooking grotesquely, as he bit into a slice of deep dish. The image brought back memories of Duncan's own time as ceremonial celebrant, when he made up to a dozen appearances a day. That aspect of the job remained constant no matter who held the office.

Truth was, after denouncing him daily on the campaign trail, Governor Vukovic had retained many of Duncan's old policies, including his sentencing reforms and his prison buildup, even as financial wonks warned that Illinois could not afford it. In response, the politician blamed his predecessor for the state's spending excesses, a fair tactic and one Duncan had employed as well. Still, he hated to hear this preening peacock, who'd disgraced him during the race, deriving credit from his policies.

After finding no answers in the news, Duncan resorted to eavesdropping. By a slight turn of his head, he listened to the other diners—retirees and matrons, mostly, with a sprinkling of young families. Their conversations hovered over familiar topics—the accomplishments of adult children and the politics of local churches—reminding Duncan of a time when such things preoccupied him as well.

When his own children were school age, the family often ate at Walker's. Aden liked the apple pancake, which was so syrupy it should have been called a pie, while the girls usually opted for the more traditional eggs and ham. Even then Josie chose something light out of concern for her figure, oatmeal or fruit in a cup, a waste of a good indulgence.

The place hadn't changed much since those times. Same menu, same oak booths and moldings, same stained-glass windows and lamps. Even alone, he took comfort from the familiarity. When the food arrived, he squeezed lemon over the pancake, dusted it in powdered sugar, and cut into the high crust to reach the airy center. As delectable as he recalled, mixing tart and sweet in a delicate puff. He ate without pause, then sat back to recall his schedule for the day. A meeting with an old friend for a game of golf and perhaps some advice. Odd how good it felt to have an agenda outside his own tedium.

Before he finished his coffee, the waitress returned to refill it. She reached for his empty plate, brushing his arm with her dress. "You enjoyed it?"

"Immensely."

She smiled, showing her perfect teeth. "Is this your first time?"

"First in a while."

"We're glad to see you again." Her innocent face showed intrigue but not recognition.

"And I you." He felt a pang of guilt at indulging such a flirtation with her. Probably just angling for a better tip, but still. "My daughter Lindsay once worked here, but it was years ago."

"What's she doing now?"

Duncan sought a neutral explanation but found none aside from lies. "She passed away."

The girl looked stricken, distorting her youthful beauty.

"Eating here brings back pleasant memories of her," he said.

She looked comforted but lingered by his table, likely seeking a graceful exit.

"You remind me a bit of her."

Which elicited a smile from her. "How?"

"Your optimism. You greet everyone with joy."

"There's enough dour news in the world," she said and nodded to his paper. "Better to focus on the positive."

"Well said." He stood and lay a hand on her shoulder. "Thank you for everything."

***

Outside, the sun had emerged from the cloud cover to warm the streets, forecasting a hot day. Cars ground toward downtown, bound for work, but Duncan saw only possibilities. Then, a headline caught his attention. In a newspaper rack next to the restaurant, he saw his own name commanding the front page of the *Sun-Times*:

Cochrane
Calls Son
'Promising'

Like that, all optimism drained from him.

CHAPTER 14

AFTER HIS UNSETTLING BREAKFAST, DUNCAN DROVE across town to his next appointment, hoping for a reprieve.

The links at the North Shore Country Club offered as much privacy as any locked room. Beyond the clubhouse, rolling green hills extended as far as Duncan could see in three directions, with trees and ponds more sylvan than an urban park. A warm breeze ruffled the leaves and carried the call of birds.

Ron Turner waited by the putting green in a tracksuit and running shoes more befitting a jog than a round of golf. Hard to judge if his getup forecast confidence or discomfort.

They'd known each other since college when they teamed up on the infield of Northwestern's baseball team. Since then, they'd lost touch after graduation and regained it when Ron joined the governor's staff as legal counsel, then lost it again when Duncan fired his old friend over a betrayal of trust. Now as a judge on the court of appeals, Ron offered the best—really the only good—advice Duncan received about how to handle a shameful family secret.

Ron understood family dysfunction, perhaps because he grew up not among country clubs but rather on the city's impoverished South Side, where wayward sons and dead daughters were commonplace. He was the first to tell Duncan that such scandal could not be suppressed. As a young black man, he'd learned firsthand the power of the criminal injustice.

Despite his incongruous dress, Ron shouldered his bag easily and walked gracefully toward the first tee. He retained the lean build of his youth, and the easy confidence, warming up with pleasantries. Duncan too felt a familiar ease at reuniting with an old friend who forgave all grudges. Perhaps these two aging athletes could reclaim a bit of lost glory.

However, on the first drive, Ron skipped his shot down the fairway only a hundred yards, while Duncan shanked his ball into grass that reached his knees, sending him on a hunt that lasted ten minutes. By the time they'd triple-bogeyed the hole, both men were cursing audibly.

At the second tee box, Ron said, "Remind me why you brought us here."

"Advice."

Ron scanned the course, which featured a narrow fairway angling toward a sand trap. "Quit while you're behind."

Duncan ignored the sarcasm and watched his partner's stroke, which had the fluency of a robot, with rigid knees, elbows akimbo, and a clipped backswing more worthy of a putt than a drive. Still, Ron kept the ball on the short grass while Duncan's again found the rough.

"I'm researching a case—a capital one," Duncan said as they strode down along the greenway, which felt as soft underfoot as a mattress.

"Why?" Ron said.

"A friend asked for my help."

"If the accused has reached death row, it's too late for your help. Unless you expect to regain your old office and offer him clemency."

"Not likely, but I need to try before the state condemns him."

"And you want what from me, an overturned verdict, a new trial?"

"Just guidance."

Duncan outlined the case—a man falsely accused, forced to confess, now facing death—and his own hopes for a reversal.

"So you're filing a direct appeal or a habeas corpus petition?"

"The latter—I think."

"The difference is significant."

"To a lawyer, perhaps. To a politician, what matters is innocence. As I understand it, we have to file within three weeks or the window on appeals will close, leaving only an unlikely pardon from my successor."

"Then it's most likely a habeas case. In federal or state court?"

"I... I'm not sure," Duncan said, feeling the fogginess of sleep loss. "I just know we have a deadline coming."

"You'll want to clarify all that. The courts are equally unforgiving of tardiness and vagueness."

"Can I finish before you kibitz?"

Duncan noted irritability rising in him but suppressed it. No sense alienating his confidante. As he explained the specifics of the trial, Ron lined up his second shot, which moved his ball fifty feet closer to the green with a bouncing two iron. By contrast, Duncan sprayed himself with sand only to imbed his ball deeper into the bunker.

"What is it about this game that you like?" Ron said.

"It's the sport of my ancestors."

"The same ones who wore skirts and brewed moonshine and fought a losing battle with the English for generations?"

"The same."

Duncan's second attempt at a wedge cleared the bunker, then ricocheted off a tree and bounced halfway back to them.

"Doesn't seem you inherited their sporting genes," Ron said.

"Lack of practice. As governor, you don't have a lot of time for recreation."

They walked slowly toward their balls as Duncan explained what drew him to the case, how improbable a suspect Harry seemed. Ron listened intently but said nothing. After several minutes and a hard-fought double bogey, the judge said, "What race is your man?"

"Hispanic, I assume. Why do you ask?"

Ron paused at the third tee to survey the hole, which rose and hooked to an invisible green. "How many dark-skinned people do you see around here?"

Duncan glanced about the course as though taking a census.

"Not counting the gardeners and caddies," Ron qualified.

"Stop. This isn't Augusta. There're many Afro-American members."

"Nobody uses that term anymore except for rich white people at private clubs."

"One of whom helped us get a tee time on short notice."

Ron lined up his third drive, swung through it tentatively, and watched it piddle fifty yards up the fairway. Despite the early hour, his underarms darkened with sweat. "Seriously, half the guys who land on death row, it's not because of their crimes. It's because they're poor minorities at the mercy of the state. Their defense never hired an investigator, slept through their trial, didn't call any witnesses, or gave up without cross-examining the cops."

"You know this because...."

"I read the transcripts. The legal system dresses them for the gallows with indifference. By the time they reach my courtroom, they're so stripped, they've got no clothes left."

"That's not my concern in this case." Duncan squinted into the low sun to line up his tee shot, wished he'd brought his hat and sunglasses from the car, decided to ignore the bend halfway up the fairway, then overshot the turn and landed among the trees. "This man's— advocate, I guess you'd call her—claims he was abused by the police."

"Was he?"

"According to him."

Ron shouldered his bag heavily and walked without comment.

"You're not surprised," Duncan said.

"The role of the police is not to protect and serve. It's to preserve the social order."

"Meaning?"

"If this man is from the underclass, then the police would think nothing of condemning him. It's how the powerful maintain their power."

"That's taking it a bit far."

"How do you explain the '68 convention?"

"You mean the protests?"

"I mean the police riot in Grant Park, all the uniforms busting the heads of hippies and yippies while the Democrats picked their next leader a few blocks away, watching the violence on TV while protected by more local cops."

"That was one isolated incident."

"But look who got prosecuted! Not the police. The Chicago Seven."

To keep the conversation civil, Duncan resisted counterpunching such a political jab. "So you believe the police are routinely abusing suspects?"

They paused beside Ron's ball as he aimed to bisect the dogleg in the course but instead sliced his ball into the same forest as Duncan's. "After you've heard enough stories about police misconduct and corruption, it's hard not to think there's some truth to them."

"How could I confirm it in this case?"

They rooted through the tall grass at the course's edge, without success, until a shout from behind echoed over the landscape, disrupting the quietude with a judgment as ominous as an oracle. "You mind if we play through?"

Duncan turned to see two figures waiting at the third tee, observing their suffering. "Go ahead," he yelled. He and Ron stood in the shadow of the trees and watched the men arc their drives to the middle of the fairway past the elbow, accomplishing more in one shot than their predecessors had in three. Though well past retirement, the men played with an efficiency that shamed the governor. As they scooted past in a golf cart, they waved collegially. Ron stood silent, watching the pair with cold remove until they stood by the green, well out of earshot.

"You see that?" he nodded to their betters. "That would never happen in poor neighborhoods."

"What, golf?"

"Playing through. Nobody willingly cedes a basketball court or baseball diamond, not given how hard it is to capture *any* ground. You have to beat them off it. Sometimes literally."

"What's courtesy have to do with our discussion?"

"It's not courtesy, it's privilege. Your people expect fairness, mine assume inequity."

Duncan glanced at his friend to see if he was deliberately goading him. He saw an earnest glare, which he found even more irritating. "I came to you for legal advice, not a civil rights lesson."

"Before challenging the legal system, you have to understand how unequal the odds are."

"I understand the odds. I *don't* understand how to beat them."

The lawyer stared after the interlopers as he spoke. "The first thing I'd do is read the trial transcripts. They'll tell you if the defense offered any resistance, and it might include your allegations of abuse, if the public defender was worthy of his meager salary."

"I've never heard that lawyers were underpaid."

"For cases like this, there's not enough money to compensate them."

Once the two show-offs cleared the green, Duncan hacked through his ball, returning it to the fairway along with a large divot of grass, which released the aroma of peat. How good a Scotch neat would taste. He glanced back toward the clubhouse, but a stand of boxelder obscured it.

"What else?" he said.

"Get tapes of the interrogation."

"There are none."

"That's unlikely. The police always want proof, even if it's coerced. It's a hedge against recantation."

Ron's ball lay so deeply imbedded that the grass obscured it. He considered his options among the clubs, selected a nine iron, and missed the ball entirely.

"Want a mulligan?" Duncan said.

The attorney looked about him for witnesses, then kicked his ball out of the rough.

"Where will I find all this?" Duncan said.

"I can get you the trial record. For the other...." He shrugged. "Use your connections."

"You're one of the few who remain."

"Invite them here. Nothing like a round of futility to motivate people."

With shots more effective than impressive, they reached the green, where they three putted, then paused for a breather. Already Duncan felt the humidity clotting his lungs. A mockingbird's fickle call persuaded him to rest. For duffers, nine holes constituted a workout. "You think I'm doing the right thing?" he said.

Ron nodded. "After all the new powers you gave to the prosecution, you owe the defense a fair trial."

"*My* lawyers have advised me to lay low."

"As a defendant, you don't have that option. You've got to fight back."

The fourth hole offered a water hazard, a pair of sand traps, and a sloping green, all in a par three. After surveying the course, Ron picked up his bag and turned toward the clubhouse.

"You don't want to keep playing?" Duncan said.

"Maybe your people enjoy frustrating themselves, but mine have enough frustrations without inventing more as sport."

CHAPTER 15

WHEN DUNCAN RETURNED TO HIS APARTMENT, the red light on the message machine summoned him. The recording proved lengthy, with several scratchy sections he could not interpret, but he gleaned that his lawyers were unhappy about something he'd said, and that the attorney general was making political hay with it. The clock read 11:57, just in time for the midday news, so he flipped on his TV.

The broadcast led with the arrest of a pipe bomber who blew up his own car, followed by a report about the Cubs winning streak. At least Duncan didn't qualify as the top story. Then the anchor described his gaffe with the newspaper, and Edwin Muskegee appeared. The AG dressed as flashy as ever, with a pink shirt, plaid suit coat, and a paisley pocket square, but his face looked fleshy and pale, spawning his nickname, the Muskie. "Given Mr. Cochrane's recent incriminating statements, I shall recall him to testify before the grand jury regarding his role in concealing his son's guilt." The anchor returned to summarize what most of Illinois already knew: that his son remained incarcerated and he unemployed.

Duncan turned off the set, picked up the phone, and dialed the number from memory. After speaking to two receptionists and sitting on hold for several minutes, he reached his lead attorney, who sounded breathless, as though he'd run across the room to answer the call.

"We need to talk. Can you come by today?"

Duncan sighed. Another afternoon wasted, not to mention hundreds of dollars in fees. "If it's about the prosecutor's threats, there's no need. He's just grandstanding for the cameras."

"Let's hope, but we need to ensure that we don't give him grounds for indictment."

More legal melodrama. Duncan should have finished his game of golf, lunched at the club, maybe bought a round of drinks, and enjoyed his day of leisure. "I'll see you in an hour, then." He hung up without giving the other man a chance to negotiate the time.

***

Dreifort met Duncan in his private office without any of his junior staff to distract them (and run up the cost). The room proved as lavish as a royal chambers, with rosewood shelving, oriental rugs, and silk furnishings. As in a museum, the climate control blew a dry cool, causing Duncan to shiver. The advocate showed him to a pair of antique Eastlake couches whose straight backs made for uncomfortable conversation. He poured tea fragrant of mint and set out a plate of sandwiches cut into squares with the crusts removed. Then the attorney reached into a manila folder and extracted a copy of the day's *Sun-Times*. "Tell me how this story came into being."

"I was shanghaied," Duncan said.

The attorney sipped his tea and added a squeeze of lemon. "Please explain."

"The reporter cornered me outside the police department and followed me until I gave her a quote. Typical yellow journalism for Murdoch, creating scandals out of nothing."

The attorney took a delicate bite of his sandwich and chewed it contemplatively. "If scandal was her goal, she succeeded. The attorney general picked up on it hours after publication."

"Muskie? He's just grandstanding. Still bitter that I kicked him off the Remedahl case two years ago—for similar behavior. Wants to boost his Q rating at my expense."

"Be that as it may, our defense right now is tenuous. As we discussed previously, the case law around parental evidentiary privilege is inconsistent. When you declined to testify before the grand jury, you did so on the premise that you are not obliged to incriminate your child. However, that defense will not hold if you speak out now publicly."

Although he'd skipped lunch and his stomach growled for the hors d'oeuvres, Duncan avoided the food in hopes of ending the meeting quickly. "You don't know Muskie like I do. He's not capable of anything so difficult as an indictment. Most of his cases involve crooked car dealers and negligent nursing homes. Easy targets."

The attorney set his teacup on the table and leaned back into the cushions. "Actually, I know Edwin quite well. We attended law school together at U of C many years ago, and from what I see of him, he hasn't changed. He's an opportunist, always looking to capitalize on the weakness of others. In class, he delighted at correcting other students, demeaning them until they capitulated to his arguments. He marshaled that talent into a lucrative private practice and has used it ever since to secure the highest legal position in the state. He's not someone with whom we should trifle."

Duncan shook his head, seeking the words to explain. "This isn't about the law. It's politics, payback. By tomorrow, he'll file away this case and forget it."

"Regardless, we can't afford any more misquotes. I have to insist that you avoid the media under all circumstances. Anything you say could be used against us later. Any publicity hurts our chances for a dismissal, on all our actions. Judges may not admit to it, but they read the papers, and they're influenced by public pressure."

Duncan frowned and studied the law books surrounding them, which all showed flawless leather spines and gold lettering. How many of them had even been opened, much less studied? "I can't see what difference it makes what I do. These scandals persist if I'm in hiding or in the open."

Dreifort refilled his teacup but did not taste it. "Mr. Cochrane, you have two active cases already, including a civil suit alleging false imprisonment, and your son's appeal. We don't want to top that with state criminal charges for obstructing justice. You hired us to speak on your behalf, in court and in the public theater. Let us do our job."

Duncan looked toward his broad desk, which held only neat files, not a single paper protruding from them. "Fine."

"Meaning you will avoid appearing or commenting publicly?"

"Yes."

The attorney studied him an uncomfortable time before continuing. "In two days, we have a deposition for your civil suit. We'll need to prep your testimony to prevent any more... inaccuracies. Do you have time today for rehearsal?"

"Right now, I've got little else but time."

The attorney walked to his desk to buzz his secretary. As he reached for the button, Duncan interrupted. "Just so you're aware, I am helping out a friend on that other case."

The attorney paused, hand hovering over the intercom. "What case?"

"The one I told you about before. There's a man in Menard named Harry Flores. I'm helping an advocate prepare his appeal."

"Menard. You mean on death row?"

Duncan nodded.

The attorney retreated from his desk to sit opposite his client. "*How* are you helping them?"

Duncan inhaled his impatience and scanned the broad office for the proper words. Finding none visible, he indulged in a square of cucumber sandwich. The cream cheese and dill proved too sour for his taste. He craved something more savory, meaty. "We believe that he confessed falsely after being abused by the police. We're seeking new evidence to corroborate that."

The attorney fixed him with a stare worthy of cross-examination. "What evidence?"

"Transcripts. Police reports. Whatever we can find."

"And your role in this is what?"

"They'd like me to be out front, but I've explained that I can't be the spokesman. I'm just calling some old friends to assist us."

"Friends meaning former colleagues?"

"Just friends now."

The attorney sighed and reached for his teacup, then withdrew his hand. "Mr. Cochrane, I fear that I have failed to convey to you the gravity of your situation. If we lose *any* of these cases—worse, if you provoke any more legal actions—you could be facing ruin: bankruptcy and imprisonment are both possibilities. Your friends cannot shield you from the justice system. Taking on a lost cause such as a capital case can only further imperil your own standing. I frankly don't understand why you would voluntarily risk your security in such a way."

Duncan shrugged. "I guess you'd call it an obligation. As one person phrased it, I created the machinery of the prison system, so it's my duty to keep it running correctly."

"This friend is another of your former colleagues?"

"We've known each other since college."

The attorney leaned forward but not to take a sandwich. "Be circumspect, in the extreme, even with friends. Do not discuss your cases, any of them, with anyone. We cannot afford to have those people subpoenaed."

"We don't talk about me."

The attorney sighed and studied the governor. "I was told that you liked going off script."

"Told? By who?"

"Before we took on your business, I interviewed many of your former staffers. They warned me that you're difficult to manage, prone to... improvising, I believe is the word they used."

Duncan smiled. "It's how I got elected. People get tired of politicians who play it safe."

"Only you are no longer a politician. *You* are a defendant. Never forget that."

***

For hours thereafter, junior staffers grilled Duncan about his deposition. Acting as scout team, they quizzed him on every aspect of his daughter's murder case, from the police investigation, to the arrest of a career criminal, to Aden's evasions. Typically, they uncovered nothing new, nothing that hadn't been publicly reported many times already. Still, the attorneys acted worried, as though negligence might cost them a large, year-end bonus.

***

Once he left the office, Duncan craved something more satisfying than being chided by his advocates. A block away, a public square offered refuge and, more important, vendors, so he fitted himself with a fedora, lowered his head, and strode there, avoiding eye contact with other pedestrians. As he expected, several food sellers ringed the block, banging their lids, releasing the scent of pizza, pretzels, and tacos. At the far end he spotted a familiar awning and headed for it.

Six years before, he'd owned the city's largest producer of brats, sausages, and hot dogs, supplying all the major league sports teams and many corner vendors. Since he'd sold the business, the name had changed, along with the recipe of spices, but the new owner had kept the distinctive brown and yellow awnings that he'd designed. At times like these, such familiarity offered comfort.

Duncan ordered one "drug through the garden," then watched the vendor layer it with mustard, relish, onions, peppers—everything but ketchup. Already he could taste the savory goodness, which carried on the steam, but he enjoyed the ritual of its preparation almost as much as the consumption of it. The merchant focused on his cuisine, ignoring the customer in front of him until he'd sealed in the flavors with waxed paper. All at once, he recognized his old boss and was struck dumb until Duncan nodded in acknowledgment and said, "Well done."

He retreated across the concrete square, which shimmered in the late afternoon sun, and settled into a bench beside Chagall's mural. The mosaic stretched almost the length of the plaza, wrapping four sides of a pedestal with thousands of colorful tiles depicting a mélange of images: birds, fish, flowers, donkeys, and people, all floating in an ethereal universe. Duncan studied the wall as he consumed his treat, which proved as salty and satisfying as when he'd made them. In the artwork, he searched for some meaning in the random creations but found only isolated figures. Maybe that's what cities were, a bunch of disconnected stories inhabiting the same space.

Still, one man had created this piece, presumably with some unifying idea in mind. A god-like man. During his time as chief executive, Duncan had enjoyed moments of insight into how things worked. Now he needed someone with a broader perspective than his own, or his legal team's, who despite all their training could only see the problems before them. He needed someone who understood politics at least as well as he understood people.

***

The reporters converged as Duncan's car approached his building, filming him through its tinted glass, shouting questions to him through its closed windows, blocking his path home. A couple he recognized, including that pest from the *Sun-Times*, yet they behaved as though he were some scoop never before told. He waited a minute, maybe two, for the building's security to shoo them away, then slow rolled to his condo's parking garage.

"Been here all day," said the garage's attendant, "just for a shot of you."

Upstairs, he called his former chief of staff, Kai Soto, who'd guided him through so many melodramas, and set a date for the following day. Perhaps his old aide could save him yet again.

CHAPTER 16

THAT NIGHT, DUNCAN DREAMT OF A pack of creatures unidentifiable even in moonlight. They snarled and yipped at him, passing so close he could feel their hot breath, but never touched him, yet as soon as he evaded one, another attacked from behind, repeating the scene. Several times he woke himself, only to lapse back into the same nightmare once sleep returned. By the time he rose, he could not shake the dread it aroused.

Ordinarily, he would have driven to his meeting except that the news posse awaited him outside. Taking the train bore equal risks, but he could escape the building undetected through a back entrance. He followed a subterranean path beside the Chicago River and emerged a block away onto State Street. To his relief, no one filmed or stopped him during his walk to the station.

He descended to an empty subway platform, with few commuters heading out of town mid-morning. Years had passed since Duncan last commuted so. As governor, he'd always required an escort, but after a term being penned in by security, traveling like a regular citizen appealed. He'd forgotten the smell of steel and the sound of a saxophone amplified by the vault.

Even underground, Duncan left his sunglasses on, reducing everything to shapes and shadows. That in itself should have drawn attention since most Chicagoans reserved their shades for the beach. The conceit felt much too Hollywood, but with so few people around, no one noticed. Still, the squeal of metal and the gust of wind that signaled the subway's arrival brought relief.

On the train, he stared at the black walls of the tunnel and listened to the screech of the wheels, which made conversation impossible. The car smelled of motor oil and baby powder, but not unpleasant. Once it emerged from its underground lair, the train rumbled through a corridor of low-rise buildings, giving brief glimpses of the lake front at cross streets. After the Fullerton station, a race between the red and brown lines played out next to him. Odd that their parallel motion gave the illusion they weren't moving, even as he felt the sway of the cars. Somewhere lay a metaphor for his own life, though he preferred not to pursue it.

He exited at Addison where, from the raised platform, he saw people gathering in front of Wrigley Field two hours prior to first pitch. Despite forty years of losing seasons, the Cubs packed the stands, even mid-day and mid-week. To those who called for lights atop the stadium, he asked why? The ban on night games afforded Chicagoans an excuse to take a day off work.

Unlike those fans, Duncan planned stops other than the concessions stand. He descended to the street and walked north along Sheffield, paralleling the tracks. At the trial, police hypothesized that the victims following this same path on their last night. Across from the outfield, several apartment complexes held bleachers atop their roofs with a private view of the game. People assembled there as well, hanging from the railings while sipping beers and shouting predictions to their neighbors. Such a genial part of town. Not the sort that usually witnessed fatal robberies.

Past the ballpark, the block resolved to low-rise buildings of brick or greystone, middle-class dwellings for working people. The ash trees sprinkled the sidewalks in purple petals while providing a green canopy over the street, shielding him from the morning sun. Cars rolled past slowly, in no rush to their destinations. Pleasant now, but how would it have felt on a brisk winter evening, with the winds howling off the lake?

A block west he found the right building, rising three stories, blockish and solid, little different from dozens of others along their street. He stared at the top-floor window but saw no evidence of the crime. In his old home, Duncan kept a light burning in Lindsay's bedroom windows for months after her death, inspiring people to pause or stop. However, even that memory had faded with time.

At the security door, he rang the bell to apartment 302, then waited a minute with no reply. At 10:00 on a weekday, why would he expect different? Nonetheless, he tried two other flats without success, then connected to a man in 201 through the intercom.

"Yeah?" said a gruff voice.

"Good morning," Duncan said, trying to sound friendly. "My name is Duncan Cochrane. If I may, I'd like to speak to you about the death of your neighbors two years ago."

"Duncan Cochrane? Like the ex-governor?"

"The same."

"The hell you say."

A pause. Perhaps Duncan should not have identified himself so. Then a window scraped open above him, and a man leaned out. To make it easier, Duncan removed his hat and sunglasses.

"Sure as Al Capone!" the man said.

He buzzed open the door and—before Duncan had climbed halfway to the second floor— peered over the railing. From his messy hair and bathrobe, the man appeared to be either a layabout or to have just awoken. Up close, he looked clean but fatigued, with a pillow crease on one cheek and a scent of menthol rub. "Sorry about the getup. I work the night shift at Dominick's. I just conked out. What are you doing in this neighborhood?"

"Catching a game," Duncan said and tipped his cap.

"I though you said you wanted to know about the murders here?"

Duncan nodded, trying not to lead his witness.

"Truth is, I don't know much. Just moved in a year ago after the super before me quit. I heard they arrested somebody used to hang around the El station."

Again, Duncan nodded, this time to conceal his disappointment.

"It's crazy to think something like that happened right here."

A train clattered by close enough to be heard even in an interior hallway.

"Sound carries here," Duncan said.

"You know it. You oughta hear some of the stuff goes on above me...." The guy smiled wistfully, then thought better of it. "Not that I'm trying to listen."

"Is there anyone else in the building who lived here at the time?"

The guy frowned and poked out his lips. "Most of the tenants left after that, except one. Downstairs in 102 there's an old woman been here since the fifties. She's kind of a shut in. You never see her, but she's always around."

Duncan thanked him and turned to go but paused halfway down the stairs when the man spoke again. "Oh, yeah, governor. Sorry to hear about your kid being locked up. That's gotta sting."

"It does."

"I did a little time myself once for a DUI. It's not as bad as people make out. He'll get through it."

Duncan nodded and descended another step, then paused. "So, you were able to get work despite your... record."

"No sweat. Only thing I can't do is drive. But in *this* town, that's a relief."

He disappeared behind the banister, and Duncan walked to the first floor with an odd feeling of relief. At the rear, he found the plate for 102 and knocked. When no one answered, he considered going outside and ringing the doorbell. Then the floors creaked inside the unit, and a quavering voice asked, "Who is it?"

"Good morning, ma'am. I'm investigating the death of your neighbors, Mark and Eleanor Mulvaney."

He waited long enough to question his tactics before the locks clicked and the door inched open, releasing the tang of brewing coffee. The face that greeted him had shriveled with age but retained a clear-eyed surprise. From her expression, Duncan assumed that she recognized him despite his disguise until she asked, "What did you say you wanted?"

"I understand you lived here when the crime occurred, and I'm curious what you recall."

She clutched the collar of her muumuu, which festooned her from neck to knees in a bright floral pattern. "Oh, that was a terrible thing. They were such nice people. He'd just retired, you know, and was looking forward to the best part of his life."

"So you knew them?"

"Not well. We'd see each other on the stairs. We were neighbors, not friends."

Duncan nodded to hide his disappointment.

"They arrested that poor man from the train station for it."

"You knew him also?"

"I'd see him every day on my way to work. He's lived in this neighborhood for years, almost as long as I have."

"Did he ever threaten you?"

"Oh, no, he was very quiet. Hardly spoke at all. He'd sit with his cup out, looking sad, but he never disturbed anyone. That's why we let him stay. If he'd been loud or aggressive, we would have asked the police to remove him, but he never bothered anyone. Even the CTA employees tolerated him. Everyone knew he lived under the station, but we all accepted it. He was one of us."

"I've heard he liked to drink."

"Who doesn't? There's nothing wrong with an adult beverage now and again. But I never saw him looking sloppy, if that's what you mean. At worst he might fall asleep while panhandling." She paused and stared past him wistfully. "I worried more that he'd die of exposure than kill someone."

"So you don't think he committed the crime?"

"If he'd been a thief, we would have known it. Can you imagine surviving that many winters without heat or even a decent coat? He endured so much for so long, I can't imagine what would push him to crime. No, if he'd stolen to support himself, he wouldn't have lived the way he did."

Duncan wanted to record her name and testimony but feared it might put her off. "Did anyone ever try to help him, find him a job or a better place to stay?"

"I doubt it. People lost that charity after the Depression. Back then, we looked out for each other, even strangers. Now we only care about ourselves. Like these corporate raiders you hear about on TV, trying to keep all the money for themselves."

"So what do you think happened to the Mulvaneys?"

The old woman paused as though she'd never considered the question. "I heard the robber broke in through the back door. The fire escape there is open to anyone." She cracked open her door and gestured down a hallway, which held a wall of bookshelves overflowing with thick texts. With so much in the way, Duncan couldn't see the exit, but he'd glimpsed enough of these walk-ups on the El that he could picture the design: a wooden stairwell that residents used for barbecues and parties but that satisfied the fire marshal. "Really, anyone could have gotten in that way. How many times we asked the super to build a secure fence in back, but he said people would just hop over it. We've got that silly security system in front, which does nothing—even you managed to get in without my buzzing you—but out back there's nothing."

"Did you hear or see anything that night?"

Her wide eyes, which needed no glasses, fixed him. "Someone running down the rear steps. By the time I got to the back door, he'd disappeared into the alley. If the cheapskate who owned this building had put in a light back there, I might have made him out, but with those bitty streetlamps you couldn't recognize your own kin."

"Is there anything else you can tell me?"

She thought and shook her head. "Only that you don't need to disguise yourself like that, governor. People can still recognize you under a baseball cap. You must have seen Humphrey Bogart in *The Big Sleep*. Even with a fedora and sunglasses, you always knew it was him."

"Yes, ma'am," he said and left.

***

Despite her scolding, Duncan retained his cap and sunglasses as he entered the stadium and climbed to the press box, which included a segregated area for dignitaries isolated from spectators and reporters. Still, he sat back from the open window to hide himself and waited silently for his date to arrive. Just across a thin wall, he heard Harry Caray prattling on about the team and their chances that year, and he noted to keep his voice down.

During batting practice, Leon Durham and Ron Cey tried for power, routinely sending balls to the warning track, but Ryne Sandberg possessed a sweet swing that could deposit one in the bleachers without strain. On the infield, the young second baseman moved with economy and grace, fielding odd hops and gunning throws to first as though they put no stress on him. Duncan liked to think he'd possessed such qualities as a young man though he rarely felt so now.

From below came the smell of beer and peanuts and the sounds of vendors hawking them. It reminded Duncan of his early days in business, when as the chief supplier of all hot dogs to the ballpark he visited frequently with friends or clients. That too sparked nostalgia, though he'd gladly relinquished that task as the company grew.

"I hardly recognized you," said a voice behind him. "Glad to see you've come out of hiding."

Duncan turned to see his former campaign manager, Kai Soto, framed by the open door. The young man looked different from their last meeting a year back. Now that he worked for the city's new mayor, Kai had cut his hair to above the ears, and he put into storage the mod clothes that marked his style in the state capital. Chicago was a conservative town, and to survive among the Irish establishment, this Japanese kid from the West Coast needed to conform.

"My low profile is for your benefit," Duncan said softly, conscious of the press across a thin wall. "Don't want you to be seen carousing with an infamous ex-communiqué."

Kai shook his head and offered a hug to his old boss. "Voters don't dwell on old scandals. Who even remembers the Black Sox?"

"I wish you could convince my lawyers of that."

"They should know. This town has tolerated graft and corruption for generations. How else could Richard J. Daley win six terms as mayor despite overwhelming evidence of his crookedness."

"Nice to be classed in such company."

"Don't take offense. Politics got us these seats." Kai gestured to their private booth.

With the game about to begin, they settled into their seats and focused on the action. In the top half of the inning, Dennis Eckersley used his high leg kick and sidearm delivery to retire the side. Then the home team scratched together a run on a walk, a productive out, and a sac fly. Throughout, Duncan kept his eyes on the field, but he talked over the action. Kai agreed that the Cubs were exceeding their abilities and that some return to normalcy was overdue, but he could endure a few more weeks of winning.

During the break between innings, Kai turned to face his old boss. "All kidding aside, seeing you here is a great surprise."

"I don't want to taint your career any more with my scandal. Bad enough you got dragged before the grand jury."

Kai waived away the apology. "I had nothing to tell them."

"Still I appreciate your loyalty."

"And I'm happy to see you at a game. For a guy who's disappeared from public, this is a very public setting."

"After a lifetime of losing, I couldn't miss the Cubs' moment of glory."

"I hope your reemergence is a preview of things to come."

"That's why I wanted to talk to you. I've been thinking about taking on a more—to use your word—*public* role." He explained the advocacy group that wanted his help and the evidence of false confession, trying for a neutral tone.

In response, Kai nodded and smiled until he mentioned the police department's role. "Since we're enjoying the mayor's private box, let's give Chicago's finest the benefit of the doubt for now," he said.

A knock on the door interrupted them. Kai opened it cautiously to find a hot dog vendor with his box of goodness at the ready. He acted accustomed to dignitaries, merely nodding to the men while inquiring if they'd like anything. Even from several feet away, Duncan could see the steam rising from the container and smell the flesh simmering. He hadn't intended to indulge his penchant for simmered pork on a second consecutive day, but the game wouldn't be the same without one.

By the time he'd received the food, the second inning had commenced with a cheer from the crowd when Eck struck out the leadoff man on a slider. Duncan took more pleasure from his meal, which tasted salty and savory, although it lacked the usual retinue of condiments. For relish and onions, he'd need to hit the concessions stands below, which seemed an undue risk. Instead, he slathered his dog in mustard and downed it in a half-dozen bites, then continued the conversation. "I've already spoken to a couple of our old allies. They both think I should jump in, but my attorneys are telling me to keep my involvement underground. They say I'm risking indictment if I surface right now."

"Who are you talking to?" Kai said.

"Ron and Father Frank."

"Getting the band back together, eh? Planning a reunion tour?"

"More like a high school reunion. See who's gotten fat or divorced."

Kai patted his belly, which appeared as flat as ever, and took a large bite of his hot dog. "In all seriousness, why not? You're not going to win any more applause standing off stage. May as well walk into the spotlight, let people hear your voice."

Kai's penchant for theater references remained. Apt for a pitch man who saw everything in dramatic terms.

"You probably heard the attorney general yesterday," Duncan said.

Kai waived off the suggestion like an umpire would a failed pickoff. "That's just self-aggrandizement."

"Which is what I said, but my advocates disagree."

"Lawyers like to hear themselves talk. All lawyers. The truth is, they do little more than that."

Duncan paused as Ryne Sandberg came up to bat. He took two close strikes, fouled off a pitch, then stroked a single into shallow right. "That kid's got talent," he said.

"Too bad it's wasted in Chicago."

The next two batters couldn't advance the runner, so the Cubs returned to the field holding only a one-run lead.

"What about your new boss," Duncan said. "You think he'd care?"

Kai leaned back to be out of sight to those below, then answered in a low voice. "As you know, this mayor comes from a different neighborhood than the pols you and I fought. He's not one of the boys from Bridgeport. I'd say he's much more sympathetic to young black men who were abused by the system."

"Because he's one of them?"

"Because he's spent a career fighting for them."

Duncan watched as Eck walked the first two batters he faced. A hush in the stands told him that other fans anticipated the same result that he did: another failure. "You don't think getting involved would hurt my public image?"

"I don't think you have a public image anymore."

"And I'm coming to prefer it that way."

"Then why join this advocacy group?"

After two balls, the catcher called for time and conference with Eck on the mound, giving Duncan time to think. "Because I can't accept condemning innocent people. That was never my intent. I wanted to catch criminals, not patsies."

"That's very... selfless of you."

"I spent enough time in the governor's office worrying about myself, my legacy. Now I just want to help people."

"You don't think you did that as governor?"

"Not enough. So much of what we did was self-promotion, trying to get reelected."

"Your stay in public housing was a campaign ploy?"

"Not that. You know what I mean."

"You mean catching the woman who was poisoning Remedahl?"

"You're twisting my words."

"I'm trying to get you to see what's in front of you."

In front of them, Eck induced a double play, leaving a man on third but two out.

"I don't want to become... a distraction from the real issue. I want the focus to stay on this case, not my role in it."

"I doubt that's possible. Wherever you go, people will remember you, the good and the ill."

"These days, it's the ill that makes the papers."

"The scandal sheets don't represent public opinion."

After running the count full, Eck surrendered a solid single up the middle, scoring a run and tying the game. Like so many in the crowd, Duncan responded with a curse, albeit a quiet one.

Once the Cubs retired the next batter and the teams switched sides, Kai stood and explained that he needed to get back to work.

"I'd hoped you could stay till the end, advise me what to do," Duncan said.

"This game's nowhere close to over."

***

By the time Duncan returned to his condo, the sun hid behind the skyscrapers to the west, and most of the news crews had abandoned their watch. He rose to the twentieth floor, buoyed by a winning rally in the eighth, and by Kai's advice. Not one person bothered him at the game, or on the train, nor the street. True, he remained in disguise, but the old woman at the apartment complex had seen through that instantly. Perhaps no one cared anymore.

On the answering machine, a light blinked insistently. If the message came from the advocate, he felt ready to commit to her, maybe even to a public acknowledgment of his participation. He pressed play and instead heard a deep male voice.

"Governor Cochrane. This is Warden James from Stateville Correctional Center. Sorry to disturb you, but I wanted to tell you myself. Your son is in our infirmary. We found him unconscious on the floor of his cell this afternoon. If you want to know more, I'll be at my desk until six tonight, but I wouldn't suggest that you visit until tomorrow as he's currently resting."

Duncan checked his clock, saw it was past the appointed hour, and called anyway. The phone rang a dozen times before he gave up and tried the main number, then the infirmary. All went unanswered. Then he placed another call to his daughter.

"It's your father. You remember I said that Aden needed your help. It's urgent. Can you come tomorrow morning, early?"

***

Duncan felt too anxious to sleep, instead pacing laps in his apartment, then trying unsuccessfully to read, and finally staring out the window at the skyline. With each activity, his mind got the better of him, summoning visions of hospital beds and prison cells. After several hours of agitation, he decided the best cure might be not rest but exertion, so he descended to the gym and started his workout early, hoping to fatigue himself to exhaustion.

CHAPTER 17

FOLLOWING A SLEEPLESS NIGHT, DUNCAN AROSE before dawn, sped past the few early-bird journalists assembled in front of his building, and drove to Union Station, where he picked up Glynis. She'd taken the first train down from Wisconsin and, despite the early hour, she looked put together, with her clothes pressed, her hair cut into a bob, and a healthy tan on her cheeks.

The freeways proved empty at that early hour, with most cars heading into town. By the time they reached the cornfields of the countryside, Duncan had set the BMW to cruise control. He cracked the window to keep himself awake until the odor of cow manure wanted inside the small compartment.

During the hour drive, they talked of insignificant things—her new apartment and his renewed interest in baseball—but not about the reason for their visit. She retained her adolescent habit of answering questions about herself with equivocations, as though rebelling against an overbearing parent. Still, she exhibited more ease—with herself or him, he couldn't decide—than he'd witnessed for some time. She even wore a perfume hinting of jasmine, an evolution from her unwashed hippie aesthetic in grad school.

Two guards escorted them through the long, bright halls of the prison, which reflected the glare of fluorescents off their white walls and polished floors. Typical for the institution, it smelled of chemical pine, as though someone had just cleaned, though the tiles felt tacky underfoot. Along the way, a chain gang leered and whistled at the sight of a woman. Unlike her sister, Lindsay, who often drew stares, Glynis hid her femininity under loose clothes and minimal makeup. Duncan sensed her discomfort at the attention and looked to the guards for some correction, but the two strode along as though deaf. No wonder inmates never reformed.

They bypassed the examination rooms where Duncan typically saw Aden and entered a common area with a dozen hospital beds, where the smell of bleach covered something even more nauseating, vomit and other bodily fluids. A doctor who often hosted Duncan's visits manned the door like a sentry. He bore the shaved head and handlebar mustache of an inmate, but with a subtle cologne that undercut the hard image.

At the far end of the room, Aden lay in a narrow bed, eyes closed, tubes dripping from one arm. His hair, normally neat and slick, whirled into a nest, and his forehead showed deep bruising. Initially, his eyes remained shut, but when Duncan lay a hand on his arm, they sprang open. He glanced from his father to his sister, whom he had not seen in more than a year, then frowned in greeting.

"What happened?" Duncan said.

Aden shook his head. "Don't remember."

"The authorities told me they found you passed out in your cell."

"I guess." The young man turned his head askance as though embarrassed.

Even with a sheet covering him, Aden looked thinner than Duncan recalled from their visit just a week before. Against his will, Duncan flashed back to waking his son after drinking bouts, when the teenager groaned and pretended to have caught a cold, though he typically recovered quickly from those maladies.

More questions—about his diet and his pain—drew more evasions, leading Duncan to ask bluntly what he suspected, "Who attacked you?"

Almost imperceptibly, the boy shrugged.

"Was it the men you told me about, the ones you were fighting?"

Aden shook his head.

"What's the last thing you remember?"

The boy paused in mock thought. He smelled off—of iodine and sweat, as though unbathed—and hardly moved below the neck. Finally, he said, "Reading the paper."

Even prison walls could not keep out news of the attorney general's threats.

Exasperated, Duncan looked to his daughter, who stared at her brother's arms. Without socks to cover them, Duncan could see a row of parallel scars like the rungs of a ladder climbing toward his elbow. "Could you keep him company a moment?" Duncan said.

He walked to where the doctor sat, reading a medical text. "I'd like to know what happened," Duncan said.

The doctor nodded and without moving said, "You'll have to ask the warden."

"Where is he?"

The physician pointed toward the corridor they'd just traversed. Since the turnkeys who'd escorted him had disappeared, Duncan showed himself to the boss's office, which sat unguarded.

"I got your message last night," Duncan said. "What more can you tell me?"

The warden stood to shake hands, offered Duncan a chair, and closed the door before sitting opposite him. He was a small, trim man with a cop's mustache and a blazer that fit him as though off the rack. Still, he sat with his legs crossed at the knee, an effete gesture for someone acculturated to such a hard place.

"Our investigation is ongoing," he said.

"Do you know who attacked my son?"

"At this stage, we don't believe another inmate is culpable. All the men locked down several hours prior, and our videos don't show anyone entering or exiting the location after count."

"Then how do you explain the state he's in?"

The warden clasped his hands around his knee and pulled himself forward as though about to deliver some confidence. "It appears that your son injured himself while drinking."

"Drinking?" Duncan noted the irritability in his tone and tried to suppress it. "How could he have been drinking? This is a prison, not a bar."

"The men brew their own wine here—pruno—from items on the commissary."

"What are you feeding them, grapes and yeast?"

"You'd be surprised how easy it is to make. Some fruit juice, a slice of bread, and some candy will ferment in a plastic bag within a couple days. Think of a bottle of O.J. that you forgot to put in your fridge. After a couple days, it turns acidic. It's basic chemistry."

"Why don't you stop all this... brewing?"

"We do. We shake down the cells every few weeks. Typically, we confiscate dozens of bags. It's foul stuff, I tell you. You wouldn't believe the smell—rotting fruit concentrated in plastic."

Duncan felt his anger swelling toward irrationality and exhaled to release it. "I still don't understand how Aden could have gotten into such a state."

"Our best guess is that he started a batch right after our last search and drank it all at once. When we found him, his BAC was .27, nearly triple the legal limit to drive. It would take half a dozen shots of liquor to reach that."

"That doesn't explain his head. How did he get so bruised?"

From a file atop his desk, the warden withdrew a crinkled paper. In blockish pencil, it read:

A snort, a spliff, a fifth
Is punishment enough
No need for chains or locks
Their bonds a paradox

Toilets loud as jets
Oranges dry as sand
Flip flops on your feet
Socks upon your hands

You drifted till you brutalized
You made your first kill now
You drank until you're paralyzed
You did your first bit now

Let your ego dye
A red-eyed demise
Let your hope retreat
From the hubbub on the streets

Once the people disgust
A breach of trust
Since then you live without friends
While the public condescends

They banished you too near
To calm their hateful fears
Of men who battle selves
In isolated grief

How can they reform
What they do not esteem?
How can they redeem
What they will not touch?

Let your ego dye
A red-eyed demise
Let your hope retreat
From the hubbub on the streets

"I don't understand," Duncan said.

"We found this in your son's cell," said the warden.

"And?"

"It suggests suicidal thinking."

"My son is not suicidal, and even if he were, why are you treating despair like a crime?"

"Because attempting suicide *is* a violation of the prison rules. It's a killing, like any other."

Rather than suppress his frustration, Duncan channeled it. "This is just... nonsense. I understand this isn't a detox center, but you must keep a closer watch on my son than this. I don't know how much you know about Aden's... history, but alcohol abuse plays a big part in why he's here."

The other man nodded impassively, giving away little. "Addiction is an ugly thing when you see it up close, and here we see it every day. You have to be pretty desperate to consume prison wine, but many men here do exactly that."

"There's got to be some way you can keep him sober."

"My Cochrane, surely *you* understand the scale of what we do here. We house over a thousand inmates, with more coming every day, half of them drunks. We're double-bunking all but the most anti-social, and even then we're short of space."

"What about the two new prisons that just opened?"

"They'll be filled to capacity the day they open." He paused to collect himself. "I fully supported your sentencing reforms—still do—but none of us anticipated *this* many convicts this *soon*. I've been in law enforcement twenty-five years, and I've never seen such a surge. Violent crime rates have doubled since I started."

"Is this your way of saying you can't help my son?"

The warden sat back in his chair and drummed his fingers on the armrests while in the hallway an inmate called for "my public pretender," leaving an echo hard to ignore. Finally the jailer said, "Based on this incident, we could place him on suicide watch. That would isolate him from other inmates. It would also make it far more difficult for him to brew another batch. There's nowhere in those cells to hide a full plastic bag."

While he pondered the options, Duncan examined the warden's office. It showed a typical lack of character for a cop, no personal items or photos, the only decor a pair of framed handcuffs that must have constituted some sort of award. With no windows and a drafty ventilation system, the place felt closed and cell-like itself. Plus, it bore that same vague odor of decay that permeated the prison although the vents held no debris.

"He's not suicidal," Duncan said.

The warden sat back from his desk. "If you want to assure his safety, I'd recommend we pretend that he is."

"That's the best you can offer?"

"For now, it is. If you could persuade your son to speak to us about what happened, that would help, but so far he's been unresponsive."

"You must experience that commonly."

The warden shrugged his agreement.

"So how do you typically investigate cases like this?"

With a sign, the warden explained that most prison violence remained unsolved. "Unless we get some cooperation from the inmate, all we can offer is more punishment."

***

During the drive home, Duncan couldn't contain his frustration. "I build them two new prisons and fund the guards to staff them, yet they can't even keep watch over one inmate. If I didn't know better, I'd think they were neglecting Aden on purpose."

"Even in a hospital, it's tough to protect people from harming themselves," Glynis said.

"I don't believe for a minute Aden did that to himself. He's being targeted because of me, and the staff there don't want to protect him."

"Did you see the cuts on his arm? They look just like the girls I treat who self-mutilate."

"What would compel someone to cut himself?"

"Abuse usually. A lot of the ones I see were molested by a parent."

"You think that Aden's being abused by other inmates?"

"That's one possibility."

"What's the other?"

They tunneled through corn and soybeans so tall that they blocked the view of anything but the sky and road ahead, which continued as straight as the prison halls.

"Aden's always had a self-destructive bent," Glynis said. "It could be he's doing it out of guilt or shame or despair at how his life has turned out."

"Then how did he get those bruises on his forehead?"

"Battering his head into a wall."

"That's crazy."

"Yes, and crazy people do exactly that."

A crop duster buzzed low overhead and banked into the sun, startling Duncan. "He did seem rather... down the last time I saw him."

"Which is why you wanted me to come here in the first place."

"So you think he's depressed?"

"He's got a lot of typical symptoms: slow, unresponsive—"

"He's probably medicated."

"Did you see how subdued he acted when I walked in? All he did was flinch. You'd think we'd never met."

Duncan watched the plane retreat then turn for another pass. "If that's the case, then what? The warden suggested putting him on suicide watch."

"So long as they watch him, but I'd worry about him being ignored."

"Isn't the whole point of suicide watch to *watch*?"

"They typically check people every hour, at least in the hospitals I've seen. I don't know how you train them here."

The way she said 'you' made it sound as though Duncan were personally responsible for every regulation of the prison system. "Whether he's doing it to himself or having it done to him, just keeping him in isolation won't work for long," Duncan said. "We need to monitor what he's doing."

"He's got another, what, two years on his sentence? Can you enforce that for so long?"

"I can't, but someone I know can."

CHAPTER 18

AS THEY NEARED THE RAIL STATION, Duncan urged his daughter to stay the night, but she claimed a needy client awaited her first thing in the morning. More likely she'd endured enough of the family scandal. Six years ago, she'd fled to Wisconsin and minimized her contact with her parents. Why would she change her mind after being called in to consult on another sibling crisis?

Before she stepped from his car, she gave Duncan one sentence of advice. "You can't ignore Aden's problems any longer." She left without explaining, but Duncan heard an indictment of his every response to Lindsay's death, which mustered only damage control.

He forgot about the media surveillance at his building until he reached the cross street, then continued driving to a nearby garage and walked to the back entry. By the time he stepped into his apartment, depression gripped him. What had he done to so alienate both of his children, and how could he redeem himself in their eyes from a place of such powerlessness?

He contemplated this until a knock at his front door startled him. He peered through the peephole, only to see a young man wearing a bicycle helmet and goggles.

"Yes?" Duncan said.

"Package for you," said the deliveryman. He hefted a box the size of an orange crate from the floor so Duncan could see it through the spyglass. Still wary, Duncan asked him to drop it outside his door and waited for the man to depart before retrieving it

The return address indicated the court of appeals. For once he felt uplifted by a message from lawyers. True to his word, Ron had enclosed a transcript of Harry's interrogation, trial, and sentencing.

Although he'd yet to resolve his own turmoil, Duncan began reading.

***

Hours later he rose from his couch feeling stiff and dour. He'd skimmed not even half the pages, but already he understood that the law had condemned Harry from the start. One day after the murder, the building's superintendent had pointed the police to him. When confronted by detectives, Harry appeared "intoxicated" and "combative." They detained him for resisting arrest—without any indication of what justified his detention—and questioned him until he confessed. No record of his interrogation existed other than the detectives' own notes, which started with his claim to have little memory of the night other than drinking and passing out. Then, hours later, revelation and a signed confession. At his trial, defense lawyers never questioned this turnabout, nor cross-examined the cops about the circumstances of it. With that as the primary evidence, the state's attorney won a conviction.

As Catherine said, no physical evidence tied him to the crime. The police never found a deadly weapon, a bloody piece of clothing, a bit of the stolen jewelry. The closest thing was a battered transistor radio that they claimed the killer had left at the scene, attuned to a Spanish language station. Instead, Harry's own testimony condemned him.

The police classed the case as a burglary gone sideways. The Mulvaneys had returned home from a night at the theater and surprised an intruder. A rolled-up play bill lay on the hall table. The front door sat ajar. His body fell in the bedroom, hers in the entryway, suggesting he'd gone to investigate the break-in.

The DA had made a great plea for the jury's empathy based off the victim's intelligence—a precocious ability to disassemble and fix any gadget—yet he'd never attended college and spent his career as a salesman. If he were so bright, why had he confronted a criminal? Probably because the Chicago cops were too busy collecting patronage to bother with a call from the neighborhoods. Only the well-connected along the Gold Coast received prompt service.

Among the hundreds of pages, only the crime scene photos compelled a conviction: Mark Mulvaney toppled on his bedpost, his head crushed on one side; Eleanor Mulvaney sprawled by the front door, her blood spattering the walls. Littered around them lay lamps and clocks and doodads, all suggesting a violent fight. Another picture showed the back door propped open and leaves drifting throughout the house, confirming that the killer had fled down the rear steps, just as the lone witness had told Duncan. One closeup stayed with him: of the Mulvaney's family photo smashed to bits.

Difficult to imagine Harry clubbing two people to death, not only because of his size and temperament, but because the killer had so mistimed things. Police claimed that he saw the couple take the El downtown and broke in thinking they would be gone, yet they'd left hours before, and the killer brought a weapon with him. Even drunk, that behavior made little sense. Plus, why would Harry turn to burglary after so many years of survival without? Although he had a dozen prior convictions, none involved even a felony: mostly trespassing and drunkenness. Unless he were a master criminal who'd evaded detection, he could not have hidden such instincts for so long.

From his time in office, Duncan recalled the stats about crime in Chicago: a hundred thousand thefts every year, the vast majority nonviolent. As he'd drafted his crime bills, beat cops bemoaned the volume of such cases, which overwhelmed them. With that many criminals operating, how could detectives have located one suspect so quickly, or gathered enough evidence to arrest him?

More than anything, Duncan wanted to shine a light on this case, get others to look as closely as he was, yet Catherine had spent months trying for public attention and getting little. When she approached reporters, they dismissed her as a bleeding heart.

Attracting the media was never a problem for Duncan. The problem was the *kind* of attention, as the throng below attested. He could imagine the spin that the *Sun-Times* would put on this, or the *Champion*, the city's Afro-American daily, which had first published Aden's confession. Even the conservative *Tribune* had mocked his fate.

He needed someone more sympathetic, more interested in evidence than scandal. A tough find in the city of broad shoulders. Then a face appeared to him, of a young woman with dark eyes that saw through him but did not turn away from his imperfections.

***

At her suggestion, they met beside Buckingham Fountain, which animated the night with multicolored lights and geysers. People surrounded them, taking pictures, splashing in the waters, shouting to each other, tourists mostly, too new to the city to notice a local celebrity. Mist from the jets helped dispel the day's lingering heat. Still, Duncan walked his companion along one of the paths radiating into Grant Park, out of range from the noise and the jostling. Behind them the city lights shimmered like fireflies, while in front of them cars blurred past along

Lake Shore Drive. In the distance the great black expanse of Lake Michigan blended with the night sky, adding a breeze that felt cool and refreshing.

Two years had passed since they'd last spoken. At the time, she'd helped him catch a sniper in the infamous Cabrini Green housing complex. Superficially, Whitney looked different, with short hair replacing a round Afro and a linen suit instead of hip-hugger jeans. Probably angling toward a job as anchor. People in their twenties changed so much more rapidly and effortlessly than those in middle age, with careless disregard for the expectations of others. Still Duncan instantly recognized her caramel skin, pert nose, and plump lips.

The way she walked beside him, close enough that he could smell melon on her skin, told him she had not forgotten their previous time together. Unless she behaved so with all her sources, feigning intimacy to promote disclosure. No. He'd met enough of the manipulative press to know the difference between engaging and beguiling.

She started by asking about his wife and children, then about what he'd been doing since he'd left office, but she kept her notebook and tape recorder in her bag, signaling this was small talk. Duncan preferred such a warm-up to the frontal attack that most reporters used. For someone so young, she exhibited precocious decorum.

"You're probably wondering why I called," he said.

She stopped and turned to face him, brushing against his arm.

"I've become involved in a... project, I guess you'd call it. One that should interest you."

In as much as he could condense the story to a few minutes, he briefed her on the criminal case against Harry, suggesting his doubts about the evidence without voicing them. Throughout, she listened silently, nodding to encourage him, but leaving hidden any sign that she was recording this mentally. When at last he paused, she asked, "What's your role?"

Such a simple question, yet not one for which he'd crafted an answer. Staring into her youthful, optimistic face, he couldn't think of one. "As adviser."

"So you're off camera?"

"For now."

She nodded and tilted her head as though visualizing the piece. "It's a much stronger story with you in it."

"I'm not... I can't comment publicly. Not at this point."

She extracted a tablet and jotted a few lines. Despite being hurried, her script had the precision of calligraphy. "I could talk to your friend, the advocate, or maybe the inmate, if you could arrange an interview."

He thought of the regimented treatment he'd received on death row. "Perhaps."

"With that, I might get ninety seconds in the middle of the five o'clock broadcast." She reviewed her notes and shook her head. "But with a comment from you, it would most definitely lead."

He looked to the shifting lights of the fountain, where a geyser topped the skyline and sea horses rose from the waters. "That's not possible."

"But if you want publicity—"

"Not that kind."

"What about unattributed? Call you a 'source close to the investigation.'"

"I can't see what that adds to your story."

"Only credibility. To persuade my editors. There's no way to trace it back to you."

"Credibility in anonymity—I like the sound of that. Rather a good description of my life at present."

He watched her jot a few more words in the notebook and scanned the text upside down. The heading read "deep throat." Once she'd finished scribbling, she looked to him with curiosity. "I don't understand why you're so reluctant to play a public role. Your term may have ended badly, but that didn't turn off all the people who loved you prior."

He met her gaze, which probed for intimacy, and turned away. "Better for everyone. I'd just get in the way now."

She shook her head sadly. "You were the one light in a blackout. Since you left, all we see is shadows of government."

"You flatter me too much."

They walked toward the darker reaches of the park, into a stand of elms where few people travelled at night despite its proximity to downtown and the outer drive.

"You were a great interview. You'd say more in a minute than most politicians did in a career."

"My minute expired."

"People call the station all the time asking what happened to you. We've even talked about doing a 'blast from the past' feature."

"Please don't."

She transfixed him with her almond eyes. "Just promise me that if you change your mind, you'll call me first."

"You only."

CHAPTER 19

TWO MEN ENTER A STORE LINED with shelves of liquor. They circulate through the aisles, stuffing bottles of cheap wine and beer into the pockets of their overcoats. Their hands are gnarled and filthy, leaving smudges on everything they touch with their fingerless gloves. One carries a transistor radio playing some jaunty tune worthy of a merry-go-round or an organ grinder.

Together they approach the cash register where a young woman stands alone. She has the blonde ponytail and sun-kissed skin of Lindsay, except her clothes are frumpy and her expression dour.

"Just these," says one man, filling the counter with his stockpile.

Duncan recognizes the man as Harry, who dips his head in shame before her.

Instead of answering him, she turns to the other man, who wears a stocking cap and sunglasses. "You know better," she says.

The drunk stares at her mute, then removes his shades to reveal a face that is old and grizzled. "Forgive your fellow man," he says.

She stands stiff and unmoving until he draws a handgun and points it toward her head.

"Aden... " she says.

Before she can complete the thought, he fires. The gun produces the faint pop of an air rifle, but it knocks her to floor, where she lies clutching her throat. There is no blood, only a divot in her larynx, but still she gasps for breath. As she convulses, her sibling steps over her body to extract several more bottles of alcohol from the shelves behind the register.

Outside, suddenly, wait the police, their light bars strafing the interior, their sirens drowning out the music. In response, the two men crack the seals on their best bottles and guzzle them as though savoring their last drink together.

***

Duncan jerked himself awake, sweating, panting, tense, and rolled from his bed. He walked a couple laps around his apartment to revive and calm himself, then lay awake for hours, too anxious to sleep, too fatigued to rise.

Just after dawn a loud knock summoned him. He crossed the hard floor in bare feet and pajamas to peer through the peephole at two state policemen. After covering his groin with one hand, he opened the door on the chain.

"Sir, we'd like you to come with us," said the younger of the two, a man with freckles and bristly red hair.

"Go with you where?" Duncan said.

"One of our detectives would like to speak with you."

"What detective?"

When the youngster hesitated, his partner, a Hispanic with a stocky build and a prison yard stare, said, "Will you get dressed please, sir."

He looked familiar though in the uniform Duncan couldn't distinguish one state cop from another. Dozens had guarded him during his time in office, yet in contrast with these two they tried not to draw attention to themselves.

"Not until I know where you're taking me, and to whom," Duncan said. He removed his hand from his crotch to cross his arms over his chest, trying for toughness despite his sleepwear.

The senior officer stared impatiently before saying, "Detective Malloney."

The name echoed through Duncan's memory for a time before striking a familiar chord, which reverberated through many chambers. Several years before, he'd spoken to a native Irishman whose casual confidence had struck him as insolent even then. The man had treated the governor as he might a peer, leaving his suit coat unbuttoned, leaning against a door jamb, probing him for information while offering none in exchange. Now emboldened by Duncan's fall from grace, he'd dispatched two lackeys to drag in his superior like a common criminal.

"What exactly does he want to talk to me about?" Duncan said.

The elder officer inhaled his irritation before saying, "I'm sure he can explain that to you. Now, if you'll just get dressed, we can—"

"I'm not coming with you until I understand what this is about."

The man broke from Duncan's gaze. "It's not our place to say."

"But it is your place to wake me up and order me about. Two years ago, your job would have been to protect me, not interrogate me."

The younger of the two studied the floor as he spoke. "Sir, this will be much easier for all of us—"

"Much easier for you, perhaps, but hardly for me. Wait here."

Duncan closed the door and phoned his lawyer's home number. After hearing the word police, the attorney said, "Do nothing. Say nothing. I'll be right over."

Duncan started a pot of coffee and extracted a box of English muffins from the cabinet. He threw one in the toaster for himself, then returned to the policemen. "Come in," he said.

The two exchanged a glance, with the elder looking resentful and the younger uncertain, then stepped just inside the threshold.

"My lawyer is on his way. We'll wait for his arrival before we decide whether it's necessary for me to follow you."

The two men remained standing in a military at ease, looking anything but.

"I don't have much to offer you, but I'll share my breakfast if you're hungry."

The Hispanic cleared his throat before saying, "As you know, sir, we're not permitted to accept gifts from the public."

"It's not a gift, it's a pastry."

When the muffin sprang from the toaster, Duncan moved to the refrigerator for butter and marmalade. With only a dribble of coffee ready in the pot, he sat at the kitchen counter and watched it drip while crunching through the sweet treat, which tasted dry and stiff despite the additives.

"Is Captain Simpson still in charge of this investigation?" he said.

"Yes, sir," said the Hispanic.

"So you two came here all the way from Springfield?"

"All the way, sir, which is why we need to leave *now*."

"Long drive for such an errand. Your boss must have a lot of questions for me."

"I wouldn't know, sir."

"I bet you know a lot more than you're saying."

When the coffee pot began to wheeze and sputter, emitting a burnt pungency, Duncan rose to pour himself a cup, then found he'd made enough for two.

"You sure neither of you want some?" he said. "I've never met a cop who didn't like coffee."

The youngster stared at his feet as though fighting a craving while the Hispanic studied the apartment as though jealous. Of what, Duncan couldn't guess. Compared to the governor's mansion, his condo offered the comforts of a prison cell. Then he noted the man's wedding ring and thought of the low salaries deputies made, barely enough to sustain a family even in the inexpensive downstate.

"Sir, when will your lawyer get here?" he said. "If it's going to be long, I'll need to report back to my superiors that we'll be delayed."

Duncan added milk and sugar to the brew, found it too bitter, then added more before responding. "I'm not sure. I had to disturb him at home—much as you've done to me—and I don't precisely recall where he lives. Somewhere in the western suburbs, I think. It could take a while for him to get here, given the morning traffic."

With an exasperated shake of his head, the Hispanic stepped into the hallway, leaving the younger man to guard the witness.

"I don't think I've met you before," Duncan said. "You must be new to the job."

The man kept his head lowered as he said, "Started last summer, sir."

"How do you like it so far?"

The young man shrugged bashfully. "It's interesting."

"I find that hard to imagine. Standing guard over politicians always struck me as tedious."

In the silence following, something squeaked in rhythm with the young officer's gentle rocking. Initially, Duncan attributed it to a loose floorboard until he noted the concrete beneath them. Perhaps that's why the man studied his shoes so relentlessly. To relieve the tension, Duncan said, "I think you'll find that the pleasure in the job comes not from the duties themselves but from your role in the greater good. You're one small member of a huge assembly that keeps this state running. Try to remember that."

"Yes, sir."

A knock interrupted. Duncan nodded for the uniform to open it, then studied his guests for clues as to their next move. The Hispanic stepped inside, closed the door, and locked it before looking at his old boss. "We've been directed to remain here until you're ready."

"So I'm under arrest?" Duncan said.

"Only wanted for questioning."

"In that case, you two should get comfortable. This could take a while."

***

By the time his lawyer arrived, Duncan had showered, shaved, and changed into his daywear—khakis, a polo shirt and docksiders. In contrast, the attorney had chosen a cashmere sport coat with matching shirt, tie, and Oxfords—a nice getup for someone who claimed to be hurrying.

Once they'd established that Duncan was under guard in his own house, the attorney stepped between his client and the officers to ask, "What is the purpose of this detention?"

The men repeated their mission to bring him into Detective Malloney.

"Is it regarding the case against Aden Cochrane? Because if so, my client will have nothing to offer that he has not stated already."

The Hispanic played the dutiful messenger, forswearing any knowledge of the cause.

"Ignorance cannot excuse an illegal detainment. Your superiors should realize that they cannot compel someone to speak against himself or his family, particularly someone who is currently threatened with indictment from an overzealous attorney general." Despite a flaccid body, the attorney stood imperiously firm, all but challenging them to dislodge him. "Unless you intend to arrest and charge my client, he's not leaving with you. You had better ask your superiors if that's their design. If so, I will need to know the charges, and I will accompany you to speak on his behalf."

The Hispanic excused himself again and used the hall to radio his superiors. In his absence, the attorney nodded for Duncan to sit and again positioned himself as an obstacle. When the cop returned a minute later, he looked relieved. "Detective Malloney said he doesn't need to talk to you right now. He'll let you know when he does."

The attorney stood to see them out. "Before you return, make sure you establish the grounds for such an interrogation. I think you'll find the Constitution is rather unsupportive of false imprisonment."

For once, Duncan appreciated his advocate's domineering tone. Until, that is, the lawyer turned it against his client. "*This* is the risk of appearing in public."

Duncan stood to clear his breakfast dishes and refill his cup with cold coffee. "It's just a scare tactic, the AG's way of harassing me. The state police know I'm untouchable. They want me to keep quiet. It's their version of a brushback pitch."

"Regardless, those men are a threat to your liberty. You should not have allowed them into your home."

"I couldn't very well have them wait in the hallway. How would that look to my neighbors or the media, seeing a cop linger outside my door for hours?"

The attorney walked a lap around the apartment and stopped beside the box of court records from Ron. He skimmed an open folder sitting on top before saying, "The police are always gathering information. All *this,*" he threw down the folder, "will certainly get reported back."

"That has nothing to do with my son."

"It has *every*thing to do with why they want to speak to you. They're sending you a signal to keep quiet."

"Message received."

"Is it? Because when we spoke about this a week ago, we agreed that you'd stay out of the news. Only to have a quote appear in the next day's paper."

Duncan thought back to his activities of the night before, which in retrospect felt not just clandestine but dangerous. "Since I've got you here, do you mind offering an opinion on something else?"

CHAPTER 20

DUNCAN EXPLAINED HARRY'S QUICK APPREHENSION, LENGTHY interrogation, and sudden confession. He detailed the poor representation at the trial and the absence of a coherent defense: letting all the questionable statements of the investigators pass without challenge, never objecting to the brutal interrogation tactics.

Then he explained the imminent deadline for appeals, now only three weeks away, after which... what? He wanted to get the details right, but hadn't the language, so he referenced the only word he could recall—habeas, which he knew meant hold in Latin, or was it body?—and appealed instead to the lawyer's sense of justice, denying a condemned man his legal rights.

Throughout, the attorney sat immobile at the breakfast table, neither speaking nor moving, taking it all in as a judge might the testimony of an expert witness. At the end of his discourse, Duncan asked what it would take to get Harry new representation.

"That's exactly the kind of advocacy you should avoid," said the attorney.

"Don't worry, my role is strictly behind the scenes."

"Apparently not if the police are raiding your house."

"They have no interest in this."

"Not yet, but if you go public with accusations of misconduct, you should anticipate that they will."

Like the departed patrolman, Duncan studied the floor abashedly until he noted that his advocate's socks did not match. In his haste, the dandy had selected one navy and one black stocking. Evidently his calm exterior concealed a troubled conscience.

"What if I kept the files at your office?" Duncan said.

"Why would you wish to do so?"

"I'm looking for an attorney to take on his appeal."

"We're not qualified."

"So no one at your firm handles criminal law?"

"Certainly. Our clients are not immune from prosecution—much like yourself, I should add. Not of that variety, though."

"What's the difference?"

The attorney sipped his cold coffee without expression. "Death penalty appeals are a specialty all their own, one with which most advocates, and I fortunately, have no experience. Typically, they're assigned by the court to young attorneys who are willing to work for civil service wages."

"But you have someone capable?"

"Mr. Cochrane, unless you're asking us to take this on pro bono, which is unlikely, I need to warn you that cases such as this are tremendously consumptive of time and money. Capital appeals often take years and rarely prove successful. Is this really what you want to pay us to do?"

"I pay you for a lot less important work."

Dreifort stood and walked to the window, where the sun gleamed off the Chicago River. "Nice view," he said. "I can see my office from here." He paused and turned a few degrees. "And the attorney general's."

"I've noted that myself, only I don't see the relevance."

He kept his back turned to his client but shook his head. "I worry that you're becoming distracted from your own wellbeing. As I have tried to impress upon you prior, your legal situation is precarious as is. To take on another action such as this...."

"So you'll do it?"

Slowly, he turned to face his client. "I know someone who may. I'll contact her." He turned to face Duncan. "Provided that you desist from any more publicity seeking. I don't want the firm to become associated with lost causes."

"Other than me, you mean."

"Your joke is apropos as we have a deposition in just two hours." The attorney appraised his client's preppy attire. "I trust you'll be ready."

CHAPTER 21

MANY PEOPLE DESCRIBED J. STONE HUDSON as a champion of civil rights, but Duncan had read more about his bombastic press conferences than his victories over official oppression, so he'd asked his own attorney what to expect.

"Do not underestimate him," Dreifort had said.

"Meaning what?"

"His publicity stunts are a front. At heart, he is a true radical. The man has defended members of the Black Panthers, the Weathermen, Rising Up Angry. He even consulted on the appeal for the Chicago Seven."

"So he's a patron of liberal causes."

"I would term him an agitator. He will attack you as a representative of state oppression. He may call you a dictator or a tyrant. Do not be provoked. Answer his questions concisely and rationally, but do not let your emotions guide you. He wants to upset you into misspeaking."

"Sounds like most of my interviews as governor."

As Duncan poked through the traffic of the Loop toward Hudson's office, following his own attorney's luxury car, he tried to forget the warning. Then he stalled along Wells Street in the shadow of the Sears Tower, and his mind returned to it. For distraction, he switched on WFMT, which usually played something soothing and classical, but today noted the police presence at Duncan's building that morning, which brought back Dreifort's final advice:

"Above all else, know that there is nothing honorable about him."

***

Hudson's office occupied an old warehouse near the train station and the stock exchange whose industrial origins still showed, with exposed ducts and raw concrete walls. The lobby rose three stories to a metal roof, amplifying every noise—a chair scraping the floor sounded like tearing sheet metal. Meanwhile, the a/c blew heavily, ruffling everyone's hair. Not what Duncan expected from a prominent advocate, but it did suggest a working-class toughness.

By contrast, the conference room where they settled felt closed and stuffy, without windows or ventilation to relieve the lingering odor of tobacco. Along one wall hung a framed copy of the Constitution next to a photo of demonstrators at the Democratic Convention being beaten by Chicago police. Hudson waited at the head of a broad, steel table, as long and angular as a scarecrow, attired in a pinstriped burgundy suit and caramel shoes that had been highly polished. His getup reminded Duncan most of a revivalist minister trying to impress the Lord with his haberdashery.

"Governor," he said formally.

Next to him sat Oges Hoxter, dressed in street style with a leather seaman's cap and matching coat ringed by an imitation fur collar. Freed of captivity, the man looked less threatening than Duncan recalled, with the freckles and gangly build of a teenager. To him Duncan ascribed the earthy essence that permeated the room. The convict did not rise or speak, instead smirking at the sight of his opponent.

Hudson fiddled with a reel-to-reel recorder, then shoved a microphone uncomfortably close to Duncan. With exaggerated effort, the advocate pressed two buttons on the machine then watched it grind into motion before nodding to himself.

He started by narrating the time, date, location, and parties present, noting that Duncan had chosen to be represented by his own counsel, rather than one employed by the state—as though he'd entrust his freedom and prosperity to the very agents who were trying to incarcerate him.

Then Hudson explained the proceedings: a deposition for a civil suit against "the former head of this state" and "parties unknown" who'd "conspired to falsely imprison" his client for reasons unspecified. His rhetoric sounded rehearsed, as though he was trying to impress a jury with his righteousness even though none would ever hear the recordings. Once he'd finished his opening statement, he turned to Duncan and stared at him dramatically.

"Governor, please tell me how it is that you first became aware of the gentleman I'm representing in this cause of action."

Following the script that his own attorney had prepared, Duncan detailed the break-in at his house six years before when he awoke to find his daughter Lindsay unconscious in a bedroom just down the hall from his own. She couldn't speak or breathe due to a broken larynx, which the medical examiner ascribed to a blow to her throat. She died minutes later, asphyxiated in her own bed. Throughout, Duncan kept a flat tone, suppressing the emotions that attended the memory through years of practiced recitation with the police and the press.

"Governor, we're all familiar with your family tragedy. My question was how you became aware of Mr. Hoxter."

Duncan glanced at the convict, who showed his typical agitation, drumming his fingers on the tabletop in a five-note pattern ending with a heavy backbeat—BrrrAT.

"Several months later, the local police told me that your client was arrested for a similar crime nearby."

"And why would they connect this other allegation to the reputed break-in at your house?"

"Not reputed. My daughter died."

The attorney leaned forward, flaring his gangly arms into a diamond. "You're evading the question, governor."

"You'll have to ask the police that."

"So you have no knowledge of how my client became a *suspect*?"

Against his will, Duncan recalled the months that police spent stumblebumming around Lindsay's case, trying and failing to connect Oges to her. "I *suspect* it's because he has been locked up a dozen times at least for everything from burglary to intoxication."

"But I never kilt no one," Oges said. His fingers settled for a heartbeat before resuming their rhythm.

A touch on Duncan's elbow kept him from responding. "I believe the focus of this deposition is on his latest stay in prison," Dreifort said.

"We will attend to that," said Hudson. "First I wish to establish the degree to which the governor is aware of the state's persecution of my client."

"I know only what the police have told me," Duncan said.

"So you have relied on the testimony of the men who have for years unlawfully harassed and detained Mr. Hoxter."

"Your words, not mine."

The advocate leaned forward, putting all his weight on his spindly arms. "What words would you use to describe such a history?"

Duncan resisted uttering the phrase "career criminal" and tried to block out the relentless drumming—BrrrAT, BrrrAT—while he searched for phrasing of his own. "I would say that he has a lengthy history of malfeasance."

"I'm not the one spent the last four years lying to people about who kilt his child," said Ones, leaning forward in his chair until his attorney restrained him with a hand on the shoulder.

"Malfeasance, is that what you'd call it?" said the advocate. "Then how would you explain my client's incarceration for five years based on nothing more than failing to live up to the terms of his release, a crucible from which he was only recently freed?"

Duncan stared at the wheels of the tape deck, which wound in hypnotic rhythm, urging him to sleep, and wondered if his words would be audible over the constant pounding from Oges. "Due to his lengthy criminal record and his involvement in assaulting another woman in her bed, your client was given a parole violation. *None* of which involved me."

"So you say, but as the sovereign of this police state, was it not within your ability to command all those who worked in its penal institutions, from the schools to the factories to the jails?"

"You ascribe far too much power to my office."

"But governor—"

"As you're aware," Dreifort said, "Mr. Cochrane has not held that office for more than two years."

"Today, however, we are focused on his activities while he occupied the seat of greatest power in this state." Hudson paused to compose himself. He'd brought no notes, nor did he write anything, relying on memory and rhetoric, like a fire and brimstone preacher. "Governor, to what degree were you aware, at the time of my client's arrest, of the lack of any credible evidence connecting him to the events at your private residence?"

"I am aware that he was never charged with the crime."

"And yet he was publicly named as a suspect in the case."

"Not by me."

"By your night sticks," Oges said.

"By the agents of your regime," corrected his mouthpiece.

"Again, I do not control the actions of every police officer employed in this state."

"But you do control the prisons, do you not?"

The incessant drumming—BrrrAT, BrrrAT, BrrrAT—grew louder, but Duncan didn't want to reveal his irritation, so he turned to face only the attorney. "I *did*."

"So you're familiar with the panopticon where my client was held captive."

Duncan strained to maintain a polite tone. "If you mean the Stateville Correctional Center, then yes I am."

"And are you familiar with the conditions therein?"

"As I'm sure your client has told you, I visited him once to see how he was faring."

The inmate snorted his disdain but commented only with his restless hands.

"And what were your impressions?" said the attorney.

Duncan glanced at Oges, who acted as antsy and disrespectful as during their last encounter, slumping in his chair like an insolent movie gangster. "He appeared to be quite at home there."

"Due to *you,*" said Oges.

The attorney leaned forward to regain the governor's attention. "You're familiar with the term 'panopticon'?"

Again Duncan strained for a polite response. "No."

"It references a semi-circular layout that maximizes the authority's ability to observe and control people without being seen themselves."

Duncan turned to his own attorney for a whispered conference before responding. "Since I haven't toured the prison, I can't refute or confirm your description. All I saw of it was the visitor's room. However, I can say that the two penal institutions constructed during my tenure do not employ such a structure."

"Was he not placed there so that you and your minions could keep watch over him?"

The drumming accelerated like the hoof beats of a climactic Western chase. "Could you ask your client to desist from that... racket?" Duncan said.

Oges broke his paradiddle for a heartbeat before resuming the rhythm at a slower tempo and louder volume. "Them's a habit I picked up in the joint to block out all the noise in them cellblocks."

"From my understanding, you've developed a number of bad habits," Duncan said. "Nonetheless, you are no longer in a prison yard."

"That is precisely our point, though," Hudson said. "The state's means of correcting behavior was designed to inhibit my client's capacity for self-determination."

Just in time, Duncan recalled the lessons of his Presbyterian father. "I prefer to believe that all men are accorded free will to make choices for good or ill."

They continued thus, like two birds in aerial combat who never collide, until Hudson drew himself up to his full height and stared down his witness. Duncan responded in kind, inhaling to broaden his chest.

"Now, governor," Hudson said, "your own son is currently incarcerated by this same authority, is he not?"

"You know that he is."

"And is he subjected to the same punishments and deprivations as other inmates?"

"He gets no special treatment."

"At what security level is he housed?"

"Medium, I believe."

"Despite his conviction for murder."

"Manslaughter."

"He was convicted of killing your daughter, is that correct?"

"Unintentionally."

"A crime for which my client was originally suspected."

"As I stated before, your client was detained for other offenses."

"Parole violations, you said."

"Yes."

"And yet Mr. Hoxter was housed in the state's highest security facility, one where the men receive only an hour a day of sunlight, and where they may speak to relatives only once a week."

Duncan spread his arms to allow some ventilation there, but the airless room offered no relief. "I did not set the conditions of his detention."

"And yet you are allowed to visit your son at any time you wish."

Though his attorneys had prepped him for questions about Aden, it irked him to hear them delivered by this histrionic actor. "No."

"You saw him just two days ago, outside of the usual visitation hours."

Duncan stared at the advocate, who responded with a salesman's false smile. How could he know such a thing? Only by bribing someone inside the prison to act as informant. When he glanced at his attorney, Dreifort nodded for him to answer the question without acknowledging its impertinence.

"It wasn't a visit. My son had been taken to the infirmary. I was checking on his injuries."

The attorney gave an exaggerated shake of the head and laid his hands on the table. "So because your son drank himself into a stupor, you were permitted to see him unchecked, without guards or restraints."

"No."

"Your son was not inebriated at the time of his injury?"

"I don't know."

"That was the conclusion of the prison staff, was it not?"

"To my knowledge, their investigation is ongoing."

"And where is he now?"

"My son? He remains incarcerated."

"But *where* in the prison is he detained?"

"Solitary confinement."

"You mean protective custody."

"I mean in a cell by himself."

Duncan's attorney touched his elbow, a silent signal that the interrogation was getting to him, yet how could it not?

On seeing the gesture, Hudson smirked and continued. "The two are not synonymous, governor, as my client can attest."

"Them's the double truth," Oges said in between drumbeats.

"Pardon me," said Duncan's attorney. "Could you please remind Mr. Hoxter that he is not the one giving testimony today?"

Hudson ignored the request and continued staring down his star witness. "Your son is receiving special protections from the prison."

"Not to my knowledge."

"Did you ask the staff there to watch over him?"

"No more than any other inmate."

"Yet he has a private room and a full-time guard."

"Since I left office, I have no power over his housing."

"Governor, you realize that you are required to tell the truth in this proceeding?"

"Which I am."

At last, the advocate reached into a bag beside his feet to withdraw a legal tablet with notes, which he shook for emphasis. "I have sworn testimony from several prison staff attesting to his preferential treatment."

"Who?" Duncan said, with no effort to contain his contempt.

"I am not prepared to reveal their names at this time."

Dreifort reached across the table for the tablet. "You *are* required to share all evidence with us in discovery."

"As was the state in its case against my client, yet it did not."

"That's outside the bounds of your case."

"Hardly."

Dreifort withdrew his hand but maintained a solemn glare.

Duncan leaned forward to interrupt their debate. "I feel like we're dancing around the real question here."

The attorneys stared at him as though unable to read the subtext they themselves were writing. "You want to know if I engineered your client's detention to protect my own son. Is that it?"

For the first time, Hudson smiled while Duncan's own counselor responded with a frown. "If that's your question, the answer is no, I didn't. I let the police do their jobs. They identified your client as a suspect based on his own actions, not mine."

A quiet fell over the room filled only by the steady drumbeat of time passing. "Is there anything else you wish to ask my client?" said Dreifort.

"Oh, yes, many more things," Hudson said. "Why, do you require a break?"

"For the restroom."

***

Compared to the interrogation chamber, the bathroom felt cool and fresh. Still, Dreifort turned on one faucet before speaking to his client. "For privacy," he said. "At this point, I would recommend that we settle."

"For what? That man knows nothing more than what that... jailbird told him."

"On the contrary, he knows a great deal about your son's detainment."

"There's nothing invidious about visiting my son."

"True, but this lawsuit is not about facts, it's about appearances, and to an outsider it might appear that you are using your power to your family's benefit. Again."

"I'd hardly call locking up my own child a benefit."

"Nonetheless, with all the scrutiny you're receiving from the grand jury, not to mention the attorney general, we cannot afford to have this released to the public."

"Why would it?"

Dreifort smiled. "Everything that J. Stone Hudson, Esquire says is scripted for the press. That man is a shameless self-promoter whose greatest joy is to appear on camera. The safest course is to negotiate a settlement in exchange for a non-disclosure agreement."

"Why should I pay to silence a liar?"

"For the same reason you're paying me: to protect yourself."

The continuous sound of running water proved almost as irritating as Oges's drumming, so Duncan reduced it to a trickle and leaned in close to his attorney.

"Say that I do settle. Then what? How do I assure that none of this gets leaked by the same people who leaked it to them?"

"Odds are, Mr. Hudson paid handsomely for that information, far more than any journalist could offer."

"That's not much reassurance."

"It's the best I can offer."

Duncan stepped away to relieve himself and recalculate. Long ago he'd learned that any situation could be inflamed by the intrusion of lawyers. Every hour he disputed the case was costing money, possibly more than he faced as a penalty for losing. Perhaps a quick ending was his best option. Once he'd washed and shut off the faucet, he turned to his counsel, "See how much they'll accept."

As they reentered the conference room, Oges leaned back in his chair, legs akimbo, one hand by his crotch, suggesting power and majesty. He smiled knowingly as Dreifort explained the conditions for a resolution without ever naming a sum, but Hudson only shook his head and frowned.

"Governor, I'm afraid you don't understand," he said. "It's not money we're after. It's a confession. Without an acknowledgement of the state's abuses, no sum will satisfy us."

CHAPTER 22

DURING MANY MORE HOURS OF NEGOTIATIONS, Oges and his mouthpiece never strayed from their insistence on a confession. Duncan refused, so they parted without progress.

"They're suing the state also and need your admission to back their claim," Dreifort concluded afterward. His parting words for Duncan foretold more cross-examinations to come.

***

From the law offices, Duncan drove out of town on a trio of freeways named for politicians—the Eisenhower to the Dan Ryan to the Stevenson. Illinois liked to honor its pols with memorials, especially its native son, Abe Lincoln, whose name affixed to a road in every town. Would Duncan ever receive such recognition? Probably an alley at best.

The turnpike dropped him just outside the criminal courts for Cook County, another possibility for honorarium. There he climbed to the upper floors where the judges presided. By 3:30, most had heard enough lies for one day and retired to their chambers. Inside one, he found a black woman with short, straight hair, arranging files on the desk.

"Can you tell me where to find Judge Baker," he said.

The woman paused and glared at him. "You've found her."

She looked too young for the job, with flawless chocolate skin and a sturdy frame. Plus, she dressed in casual clothes—jeans and a checkered blouse—more befitting a school function than a courtroom.

Illinois elected its judges, but it still took political savvy to earn the party's blessing. Typically jurists ran unopposed once they'd been vetted, yet most spent years making the necessary connections. How had this woman attained such a position so quickly? He scanned the office for photos of her with local dignitaries but saw none. Perhaps she represented a new generation of designees, ones chosen more for their qualifications than their associations. Neither of the city's last two mayors—a woman and a black man—represented the Machine, breaking the generational Irish hold on City Hall.

To avoid further embarrassment, Duncan omitted small courtesies and asked directly if the judge recalled Harry's trial.

"Quite well," she said. "I never forget a capital case. I take it as my duty to give them my full attention."

From her tone, Duncan couldn't tell if she had taken offense, so he ignored any he'd given and explained his reason for asking. By the time he'd finished, she regarded him with a mix of deference and disdain, perhaps owing to his status as fallen dignitary. Apparently judges, unlike cops, felt no need to hide their feelings under questioning.

"And what precisely do you wish from me?" she said.

Again he scanned her office, looking for some way to connect with her. Its decor proved far more extravagant than typical for a civil servant, with Turkish rugs and African sculptures. Then he noted a pair of framed photos on her desk: an adolescent girl holding a violin and a boy in a baseball uniform.

"My girls played in the orchestra when they were young," he said. "Flute and clarinet. Well, too. I always wished that they'd stuck with it, but by high school they'd found boys...."

She smile indulgently. "And your son?"

Duncan replayed her words, seeking some tone of condescension or condemnation, but her expression remained neutral, that of one parent talking to another. Next, he pictured Aden with his guitar, thrashing out power chords from his punk records. "He preferred more... contemporary music."

Rather than risk further revelation, he asked her again for her recollections of the trial.

"Normally, Mr. Cochrane, I would take umbrage at a member of the public questioning my work, especially one from the executive branch." She paused and gestured for him to sit opposite her in a pair of leather chairs that faced each other. "However, in this case...." She paused.

"I recall clearly that the verdict rested on a confession from the defendant. The prosecution offered little other evidence of his guilt besides the suspicions of the police and a few neighbors. Still, an admission of guilt usually persuades jurors, as it did with Mr. Flores."

"You had doubts?" Duncan said.

She sat erect and proud, with a look of judgment more fitting for a courtroom. "One always has misgivings at sending a man to his death."

She extracted a mint from a dish on her desk, as though to cleanse the bad taste left by the case. "Nonetheless, twelve citizens agreed on the verdict, rather quickly as I recall."

"Even though he confessed under duress?"

"As your question implies, the defense argued coercion, but a signed statement undercut that explanation."

"From a man who can't read."

She settled her hands again in her lap and fixed him with a stare. "Bear in mind that I'm speaking to you now as a courtesy—"

"I appreciate that," Duncan said quickly. "It's just... upsetting to think an innocent man could await execution. That was never my intent when I passed tougher sentencing laws."

"Which took away most judicial discretion. Under your guidelines, any conviction carried mandatory minimums."

"Even death?" he said, genuinely confused.

She paused as though recalling the statute. "No, not in capital cases. However, when a jury recommends that punishment, judges typically listen."

She raised one hand and left it hanging in the air, a professor leading a pupil to an obvious conclusion. "I'm afraid your reforms will handicap your new cause."

"Indeed." He studied the dense walls of law books as though he could glean an answer from their spines. "In your experience, what would it take to overturn a verdict such as this?"

She cocked her head and smiled. "It's not often I'm asked how to overrule myself. I assume you're referring to a habeas petition and not a direct appeal?"

He nodded, thankful that she'd supplied the legal jargon.

"In my experience...." She laid her palm flat again. "It's not enough to suggest that the condemned may have suffered a prejudicial investigation. There's a standard in such appeals called harmless error. In essence, it means that a violation of a defendant's rights is not in itself sufficient cause for the courts to vacate his conviction. The violation must be substantive enough to elicit grave doubts about its effect on the outcome."

"In this case, there were no such grounds. I would not have permitted the trial to reach a conclusion had I observed such. Rather, to win a reversal, you'll need an alternative explanation of the facts."

"Meaning?"

"In layman's terms, you'll need to prove that someone else committed the crime."

***

By the time he fell into his couch, Duncan felt too tired to change out of his suit, yet he dreaded even a nap, fearing more self-flagellating dreams. He flipped through the TV channels absently, hoping to find the Cubs score and forget all the false charges of the day.

Instead, he saw his cause on ABC's local news, which detailed its efforts to "exonerate" an innocent man. Not exactly what he'd said, but close enough. Whitney appeared to narrate the details, including the allegations of police abuse and false confession. In her diction and tone, she maintained a professional remove, yet when she mentioned a confidential source, a subtle smile crept in. True to her word, she kept the ex-governor's name to herself, but she did splice in a quote from Catherine Fontanelle about the Innocence Inquiry.

A minute after the report ended, his phone rang. Fearing an onslaught of other media, he let his machine answer, then picked up at the sound of Catherine's voice.

"Wonderful," she said. "You've done more good for us than a dozen volunteers over the last two years."

"You exaggerate," Duncan said.

"Time to celebrate and plot our next steps," she said. "What are you doing?"

"Tonight?" Duncan felt the fatigue of the day pulling him to the couch. "Staying home."

"Can I come over?" she said. "I don't want to waste this moment."

He scanned his apartment, which showed no thought of visitors. "Sure," he said. "Briefly."

***

Before she arrived, Duncan changed into jeans and a striped Oxford, then cleaned his living area, moving the old newspapers and mail into the bedroom. The result looked bare—a couch, dining set, and television—so he searched the fridge for some hospitality. There he found only a cheap bottle of wine and half a brick of cheese, so he put on a pot of coffee and waited.

When her knock came an hour later, Duncan felt a nervous energy rise in him that he could neither understand nor suppress. Probably that he rarely hosted guests. He opened the door to see her looking more made-up than before, with a flattering midnight blue dress and a wave in her bobbed hair. She embraced him briefly, giving him a whiff of lilac, then stepped inside without invitation. She walked a lap through the main room and paused by the windows, which offered an unobstructed view of the skyline, lit up like stars in the urban sky.

"Coffee?" he said.

"I'm too wired. That would keep me up half the night."

She moved to the couch and sat at one end, her hand extended along the back rest as though to welcome him. He shut off the brew without pouring himself a cup, then sat opposite her with his hands clutching one knee.

"I'm already getting calls from other reporters," she said. "They all want to run stories. That's why I'm so late, setting up interviews for tomorrow."

"Excellent," he said.

"None of this would have happened without you. I spent literally months trying to get someone—*any*one—interested. Not even WGN would carry the story. They said a bunch of do-gooders had no credibility."

"Kind of ironic that *I* would lend your group credibility."

"Not at all. You still hold great sway with certain people."

He did not contradict her, instead looking to the silent TV that had carried their news.

"Just imagine the kind of attention we could draw if you went public."

He resisted looking at her. "No."

"It could be the difference between success and failure."

"You said that you were already fielding calls from other outlets."

"Stories, yes, which will highlight our cause, but we still need legal help."

"I've asked my... advisers to look at the case. If they find something, I'll let you know."

"That's fantastic."

He studied her rapt expression, her penetrating blue eyes. Up close, she looked more feminine than he recalled, with taut skin that accented her sharp nose and jaw. "Was that all you wanted?"

She continued to gaze at him with unnerving intensity. "We need something more."

"More?"

"Something big, to hold people's attention." She leaned toward him. "We need *you*."

He stood and walked to the kitchen to pour himself the coffee. "A friend suggested we need an alternate explanation."

"For Harry's confession? Isn't torture explanation enough?"

"She said we need to find the killer."

"That's just one person's opinion."

"A judge with experience in death penalty cases."

"Which is why we need *you*—to exert some pressure on law enforcement."

He returned to sit opposite her. "I'm not available."

"What are you afraid of?"

"I'd just prefer to keep my private life private for now."

She threw out an arm to take in the empty apartment. "I'd call it reclusive."

"You sound like my wife."

She fell back into the cushions and pulled a pillow to her chest. "I didn't know you were still married."

"I am."

"Does she live here?"

"She visits."

"Why don't I see any evidence of her?"

He sipped the coffee but still found it too hot. "What do you mean?"

"Maybe if I looked in your bedroom, searched the closets, I'd find a couple of her dresses, some of her makeup, but this room has not even a photograph to prove her existence."

He looked to the windows so he did not have to face her. "We're separated—for now."

"That explains your solitude."

"I'm hardly alone." He continued staring outside. "I've got a city of three million people watching for me."

She lay a hand gently on his arm to draw back his attention. "I should probably go. I can tell you're not ready to join us fully."

He turned to face her and saw disappointment in her thin mouth. "Just a minute ago, you were telling me how much good I've done for your cause."

"And you have. But you're not ready to commit, and we need people who are."

She removed her hand and headed to the door, then paused at the threshold. "Think about it tonight, and I'll call you again tomorrow."

After she'd left, he could still smell her scent: lilacs perfuming the night.

CHAPTER 23

CAFFEINE KEPT DUNCAN UP HALF THE night, and even after he finally dozed on the couch, his dreams jumbled with thwarted sex until he awoke feeling both aroused and exhausted. As he showered and dressed, he wondered if this sudden stirring of his libido signaled some change or merely a rekindling of instincts long suppressed. He remained a married man and felt a sting of guilt at his impulse for infidelity yet also the thrill of new flirtation.

Unable to reconcile these contradictions, he suppressed them by turning his car stereo to patter about the Cubs. He no longer needed a map nor a watch to gauge the trip south from Chicago, yet he amped the sound to keep himself alert. Despite the infinite sameness of the crops, row upon row of corn and soybeans taller than his vehicle, he knew he was drawing close to the prison when the radio signal faded.

However, inside its walls, the guards directed him to an unfamiliar wing, one accessible only through the yard. They walked across a broad concrete court where inmates played handball and basketball. Many stared after this visitor in civilian clothes, but none said anything until a young Hispanic with a scar creasing one cheek called out "El Jefe." Then the men whispered to one another and pointed until their target disappeared down a long, white hallway.

When Duncan asked why they were headed to the farthest corners of the prison, the guard—a young fellow with acne and a wispy mustache—said only, "following orders."

They passed a half-dozen unmarked doors and through a stench mixing piss with lemon before stopping outside a metal slider. The door motored open, revealing another hall with more doors evenly spaced every few steps. Duncan peered inside a couple of the small windows to see forlorn faces watching his passage. At the far end of the corridor, another metal slider led them to a small chapel. The prayer room looked nearly as bare as the halls, with a handful of benches facing a music stand set atop a narrow podium. It offered no stained glass, no banners, no bibles, no prayer books. Only a cross painted on the far wall and some red cellophane on the skinny windows suggested devotion. The few lights had been dimmed, leaving the center of the room in crimson shadows. Unlike most sanctuaries, which bore a scent of wine or incense or candle wax, this one smelled only of dust and sweat.

Aden waited in the front row but did not turn until after his father had sat beside him. Even in fresh scrubs, he looked weak and bedraggled, sagging into his clothes. He still radiated something menthol despite having shed his bandages and tubes.

"Why are we meeting here?" Duncan said.

"There's no visiting in solitary," Aden said.

"I was told you'd be... under watch." He didn't want to use the word suicide.

Aden shrugged. "Same difference."

If not for the boy's aversion to all institutions, Duncan would have thought he'd caught his son in the midst of prayers. He stared at the bare altar, his hands clasped in his lap.

"So how are you feeling?"

The boy shrugged.

"Any better?"

"There is no better in here, only more of the same."

"You know what I mean. Are you still thinking about... harming yourself?"

"Is that why you put me on lockdown?"

"The warden did. For your own protection."

The boy shook his head. "Following your dictates, no doubt."

"We—your sister and I—were concerned about you."

"Why?"

"You've lost weight."

"There's nothing to eat here but dry oranges and toast."

"Do you need me to put some money on your commissary?"

"For what, toothpaste?"

Duncan looked about the empty room for inspiration. "Do you ever come here for services?"

The boy shrugged. "Sometimes."

"Are you... interested in religion now?"

"It's something to do. This place is even worse than p.c. Twenty-three to one isolation. The only guys I can talk to are guards. We have feeding and bathing alone. I take yard by myself. All I can do is read."

"That sounds... edifying. What are you reading?"

Aden shrugged again. "Whatever."

Duncan studied the bruise on his forehead, which in the tinted light looked even more vibrant than before, with a sunset of red, brown, and yellow. "When did you start drinking again?"

The boy shook his head and turned his face away.

"I thought rehab had cured you of that."

"You're never cured, Dad. More like in remission, waiting for the cancer to return."

Duncan reached out to grip his wrist, then remembered the ladder of cuts there and laid his hand instead on top of Aden's forearm. "Nonetheless, you can heal."

When the boy did not reply, he tried again. "I don't think I ever told you this story, but... I was arrested once, too. As a child. I stole a baseball mitt from the local Sears. Of course, I got caught. At ten, I wasn't too crafty. The police took me home to my parents, who scared me more than jail. I know with their grandkids they were doting, but to me Pop and Ma were Old World Presbyterians. They believed everything you did reflected your odds at salvation.

"Anyway, to atone for the sin, they made me work in our family's grocery for a month. The butcher shop. Said I needed to learn what it took to make leather. I'd go there every day after school, scooping up entrails and collecting hides. For the first couple nights, I'd scrub my hands with turpentine to remove the scent of blood. Didn't work.

"Probably why I went into meat packing...."

For the first time, Aden smirked. "Too bad no judge offered me that deal."

They sat together in silence for a time, staring at the big cross that decorated the wall. Try as he might, Duncan could find no solace in the symbol, which felt so at odds with their surroundings. Through the warmth of Aden's skin, he began to understand the despair that gripped his son. How could one maintain any optimism in such a place?

"I thought that putting you in here would keep you safe," Duncan said. "I understand now what a mistake that was."

Aden shook his head. "Stop trying to protect me from myself."

Gently, Duncan pushed up the socks that covered his son's arms so that he could see his wrists. In addition to the faint scars, he found a new wound: a tattoo running the length of the forearm, in dark blue ink, the borders still red with irritation. Duncan leaned forward to see it clearly in the dim light while holding the boy's arm still. In elaborate cursive, it read "ratione autem liberamur."

"How did you get that?"

The boy shrugged.

"Did you join a gang?"

The boy snorted and shook his head, sadly. "They wouldn't have me."

"Good. That's nothing to play at."

Duncan wet his fingers and tried to rub it away, but the ink did not even smudge. "What does it mean?"

The boy shrugged and withdrew his arm. "I read it in a book."

"What book?"

"Doesn't matter."

Duncan lifted his other forearm, which remained unadorned, then checked his neck and face to be sure. "Is it your only one?"

"So far."

"Good. Make it your last. You don't want your time here inscribed for life."

The boy continued to stare away from him at obtuse angles.

"I don't understand why you'd do that to yourself."

"As a reminder."

"Of what? This place? Why remember this place? Once you leave...." He couldn't conclude the thought, feeling both too fatigued and agitated for clarity. Truthfully, he couldn't think of anything that would diminish his son's suffering. To his jailers, though, he had plenty to say.

He looked behind them for the guards, but with the door closed he couldn't even hear footsteps in the hallway, only the rattling breath of the a/c vents. He stood, then wondered how he was supposed to get out. "I need to go, but I'll be back in a day or two. In the meantime, promise me you won't... deface yourself any further."

The boy sighed his indifference.

"Aden, please."

"Fine."

Duncan studied him for signs of sincerity, but through many years of practice his son had learned to disguise his true intentions.

"Like I told you last time, this won't last forever. It's only a short phase of your life."

Duncan walked to the door, tried the lock, then pounded on it, sending a metallic echo out into the vast network of hallways. Shortly, a key scraped in the lock and light flooded in from the entrance. Before he exited, Duncan turned back to his youngest child, who sat as still as before, facing away. "See you soon," he said, but the boy did not reply.

***

On his way out, Duncan stopped at the warden's office. The door sat closed, but he banged on it twice, flustering the young guard who accompanied him. When the prison head flung it open, he appeared both angry and shocked, but on seeing his former boss he composed himself.

He was listening to jazz, something somber and slow, Miles Davis perhaps, but so low it was mysterious.

"I want to know how my son got the tattoo," Duncan said.

"We don't allow ink in here."

"Then how could he get so disfigured?"

The warden shook his head wearily and smiled to himself. "Inmates are crafty, governor. He must have stolen a pen while he was in the infirmary."

"And carved into *himself*?"

The warden studied him before saying, "Possibly."

Hard to imagine etching into one's own skin. When Duncan was in the military, most soldiers took a heavy dose of alcohol before subjecting themselves to the needle. "Your security must be awfully lax," he said, "to allow such transgressions."

The warden fixed him with a hard stare worthy of the prison yard. "This institution houses some of the state's most incorrigible inmates. We keep multiple murderers and serial rapists and gang leaders. Still, in the decade I've worked here, we've had no escapes, no revolts, and no deaths. If now and again somebody gets away with defacing himself, I'd say we're doing a solid job."

They remained standing in the doorway, with the warden's arm barring entry while the guard stared obtusely as though he were not attending every word. Still, after many sleepless nights worrying about his son, Duncan wasn't about to concede to rationalization.

"What about privacy?" Duncan said.

"What about it?"

"One of your staff's been leaking gossip about my son to an ambulance-chasing attorney who's suing the state, and me."

The warden inhaled as though trying to calm himself. "Mr. Cochrane, many people work here. Hundreds. If one of them took exception to the privileges we've given you, I can't stop him from talking about it to the press."

"I hardly see neglect as a sign of privilege."

The warden reached behind him to lock the door. "If you'd rather, we can arrange for your future visits to occur in visiting, along with the hundreds of other people who come here each week. Otherwise, appreciate that we've been showing you a great deal of professional courtesy. No other visitors, not even spouses, receive contact visits, nor escape our bodily searches before seeing their loved ones."

He pulled the door closed and walked away from his guest, but backward. "Your son is not a guest in our house. He's an inmate, like any other. I can't treat him like a dignitary. And I'd remind you that you are no longer an authority over this facility."

CHAPTER 24

DUNCAN SAW THEM AS HE APPROACHED from the cross street: a phalanx of journalists, twice the number as before, clotting the entire block in front of the Marina towers. At sight of him, they ran as a pack and converged, blocking his way. He recognized a few faces among them: a pretty young correspondent from ABC, a dour radio man in a fedora, and that pest from the *Sun-Times*, looking even messier. They jostled for position, pushing him as they shouted questions just inches from his face—"tell us about your involvement," "why take up this case?" He tried to bore through, but the throng proved too dense to penetrate. Instead, he stood quiet and still, practicing forbearance while he waited for them to run out of questions.

At a lull, he stepped forward. The mass moved with him, but it started a process of inching that led him to the door, where a security guard kept out the invaders.

Of course, he'd experienced similar treatment many times before, particularly after Lindsay died. For weeks, the press had camped outside his home, followed him throughout the day, mobbed his every appearance in public. When the campaign resumed, he'd played off their hunger, feeding them his grief and rage, which carried him into office. As governor, he'd grown accustomed to their company, learned the names of those assigned to the capitol, joked with them off camera, even developed professional respect for a few. Except then he had security around to shield him. The media parasites got only as close as he'd allowed and rarely close enough to draw blood. Now, they swarmed.

Their numbers could signal only one thing: someone had outed him.

***

Inside his room, the air felt hot and stale. He threw open the sliding door to let in the breeze and listened to the squeals and rumbles of the city far below. Forty floors up, not even the journalists could reach him.

The message machine blinked insistently with thirty-four calls. He played the first few—mostly from reporters, plus one from his attorney, asking what "in blue blazes" he was doing—and erased the rest without vetting them.

He checked the clock, saw it was close to five, and turned on the television to monitor the news. All four local broadcasts carried rumors of his advocacy. They spliced together footage of the prison, the police department, and Catherine, braying about the injustice of their case. Could *she* have betrayed him? She never used his name or implied that he was involved. Still, someone had.

Who else knew? His lawyers, but they were the ones warning him off the case. Kai, yet he still trusted his longest confidant. Whitney, but she wanted an exclusive. That woman from the *Sun-Times* attended the throng downstairs, only her sources connected him to Aden, not Harry. Perhaps J. Stone Hudson was at work already.

Of all his associates past and present, the one with the strongest motive had to be Ron. Even though he'd left Duncan's employ years before, he still got called in for questioning by the DA once Aden's guilt leaked out. Plus, he'd put himself at risk just discussing the boy again with his father: a sitting judge helping out the family of a convicted felon. Only, media leaks were never Ron's style. When he wanted to sway his boss, the lawyer found more direct means of communication. Like blackmail notes.

A knock startled him. He ignored it—on the assumption that some news hound had penetrated the security downstairs—until he heard his wife's voice. "What in the world are you thinking?"

A fair question, under the circumstances.

***

For umpteen minutes, Josie excoriated Duncan for his recklessness and thoughtlessness, for exposing them both to scrutiny and ridicule. Reporters had been calling her all day, demanding to know what she knew, surveilling her apartment. Why was her husband involved in the case?

"As you can see," Duncan said, "I'm getting the same treatment."

"What am I supposed to tell them?"

"Nothing."

Not good enough. For another umpteen minutes, she lectured him about his carelessness. Why put forth so much effort for of a man he'd never met while his own son languished in jail?

"Because I believe I can save him."

"And not our son?"

"Our son is guilty."

To avoid her stare, he walked into the kitchen and took out a glass.

"You're willing to sacrifice your career for this man's sake but not for our child's?"

"I've already sacrificed myself for Aden. It's why we're not in politics any longer."

She exhaled with frustration and glared, hands on hips. In public, she restrained her emotions like flyaway hairs, but in private she made no attempt to smooth her features. "I don't think I can wait any longer," she said.

"For what?"

"For you to pull out of this funk." She followed him into the narrow galley. "Two years, I've been expecting the old you to reemerge, the man I married, who built his own business, who beat the Chicago Machine."

He filled his glass with scotch on the rocks. He would have offered her some, but he feared it might provoke her further.

"Maybe I need to stop waiting and start running myself," she said.

"For office?"

"Why not? It's a new era. We've got a female mayor, a female astronaut. Now we've even got a female candidate for vice president. We've broken the male hegemony on power."

To placate her, Duncan nodded. "Why not?" he said. "With Jesse Jackson running for president and a black man seated as Chicago's mayor, *any*thing is possible."

"Except for you. With you, nothing feels possible anymore."

He brushed past her, sat on the couch and sipped his scotch, which already tasted watered-down.

"Only, I can't run," she said. "Not with you creating new scandals every week. I need to separate myself from your self-destruction."

He took another dram to calm himself. "Separate how?"

"Legally."

He studied her face for regret but saw only resolve. "You mean divorce."

"I do. I hardly recognize you anymore, and I can't accept the man you've become."

"Really? I prefer him."

"What do you prefer about *this*?" she said, gesturing to his empty apartment.

"I prefer having time to myself. When I held office—hell, even when I ran a business—I felt velocitized. I worked nonstop, without even a true vacation. I put all my energy into producing *us*, our power and our wealth, maximizing output. Now that I'm out of it, I don't miss the hubbub, the frenzy. Better to live a slower, simpler life than be ground down by the friction of industry."

He turned his back to his wife and moved to the windows so he could look outside. Below people on the sidewalk bustled in every direction, bouncing off one another like random particles. Definitely not something he missed.

"So be it," she said, "but promise me one thing."

"What's that?"

"That you'll divorce yourself from this case."

"Funny, our lawyers said the same thing."

"Then listen. It's why we pay them: for advice."

Silence fell between them as he searched for something more to say. All he could think of was, "I do."

"Do what?"

"Promise."

***

Once she left, he fixed himself another scotch neat and drank it slowly, savoring each sip. After so many years, the breakup felt anticlimactic. Weren't people meant to agonize over such decisions? Every divorce he'd witnessed took months of negotiations—with lawyers and accountants, pastors and therapists—to rearrange familiar lives. Perhaps he and Josie had already concluded that phase. They could conduct their split like so much of their other business, dispassionately.

Would it have come to this if Lindsay were still alive, if Aden were free, if Glynis still trusted them? Maybe not. Six years had passed, yet they'd never reconciled themselves to those events. Lately they dared not even speak of them, but with that tension ever present, they'd become distant, even alienated.

The only solution was dissolution.

Minutes later, another knock interrupted him. In contrast to Josie, Catherine looked ebullient, her long hair streaming behind her, her blues eyes wide. Before he could speak, she hugged him and stepped inside. Duncan wondered if she could sense her predecessor—the scent of her body wash or the indent of her footsteps—but if she did, Catherine acted unaware.

She'd never expected such a response. People were calling by the dozen, offering money and time, eager to volunteer, and all creditable to Duncan.

"Not me," Duncan said. "This is none of my doing."

"Before you joined us, we were in the doldrums. We had no energy, no momentum. Now, we've got more wind behind us than I can control. I don't know how you manage so much attention."

"As best I can."

"I really need your help with this."

"I need to step back now, retreat off stage."

"You can't! Not with our deadline so close."

He offered her a drink, but she preferred to enjoy their triumph soberly.

"When I first joined you, I said my involvement had to remain a secret between us. Now that the secret is out, I can't be the face of your project," Duncan said.

"What about the voice? You know way better than me what to say to the media. What do I tell them?"

"What we discussed."

"We only have three weeks before Harry's time runs out. If we don't get his appeal filed...."

"I can't."

"People already know you're involved. What can it hurt to acknowledge the obvious?"

He returned to the kitchen and refreshed his scotch, the most he'd indulged in months. He wanted the vague blurriness of it, but his mind remained focused. "Was that your doing?" he said.

"What, divulging your role to the media? Certainly not. I promised to keep your secret, and I have."

"Then how did it leak out? Who else knew?"

From across the room, she studied him as though sensing his mood for the first time. "One of the prison guards? At least one must have recognized you when we visited Harry. Probably he checked the log after you left, saw your signature, and made the connection."

"Which is exactly why I can't be involved anymore. I'm too well known, too... compromised. The best you can do now is capitalize on the publicity and deflect the attention to your cause. Highlighting me will only... distract from it."

They stayed silent for an uncomfortable time while he savored the peaty richness of the whiskey.

"What about just one," she said.

"One what?"

"Interview. I've been invited to *A.M. Chicago* tomorrow. Someone named Oprah wants to host us both. She specifically asked for you."

He took another swig and let it lie on his tongue. "No."

"It's strictly local. Chicago only. It'll be your chance to clear things up. It's live, so there'll be no edits later on, no one altering your words."

"I can't."

She crossed the room to stand next to him and lay a hand on his forearm, then left it there to hold his attention.

"She seems very sympathetic. We spoke just this afternoon. She... she's black and poor... grew up poor... and she believes in the failures of the justice system."

He sighed and stared out the window at the lights again. Perhaps one appearance would satisfy the media predators, diminish their bloodlust. No point in killing the same animal twice.

"We'll see."

***

As he lay down for the night, Duncan expected no rest. If pattern held, he'd be tormented by his own consciousness, rehashing the troubles of the day in anticipation of more the next.

CHAPTER 25

BY DAYBREAK, THE WHISKEY HARD WORN off, leaving only stunted clarity. Better to control his own public exposure than to let others reveal him naked. He badly needed a shower, but it offered little relief. After breakfast and a glance at the headlines—"Cochrane Comes Out of Hiding," read the *Tribune*; "Gov. Builds Own Prison," falsified the *Sun-Times*—he pondered the day ahead. Even with the cool air of morning wafting off the balcony, he dreaded spending it confined inside the isolation cell of his apartment. He called downstairs and confirmed that the gang of journalists remained encamped out front. Even if he fled, they'd probably follow him, as they often did while he held office.

Instead, he descended to the restaurant, borrowed an apron, and exited through the kitchen to the river promenade. Despite a negligible wind and the oncoming heat, the water offered relief, its tang mixing fish and sand. He followed a passage below street level for a block and ascended by the Clark Street Bridge, then headed north. He'd brought his usual disguise—Cubs hat, sunglasses, t-shirt—but still walked with his head bowed, ignoring the people around him. That early in the morning, most contemplated their own affairs, making their way to work or school without concern for those around.

However, when he paused at an intersection, a man inquired "Governor Cochrane?" Duncan ignored the summons, but the man continued staring until he raised his eyes and nodded once, hoping the acknowledgment would satisfy his tail. The youngster, who could not have exceeded twenty years, rose barely to Duncan's shoulder and wore a sweatsuit more fitted to a gym than a public street.

"I knew dat was you," he said, in typical Chicago brogue.

Leashed to the guy stood a mastiff, likely outweighing them both, with a head the shape of an anvil and a tendril of drool clinging to one side of its jowls. As soon as it caught Duncan's eye, the dog moved in close to sniff one of his pant legs.

"Gracie, no," said the man.

Duncan stood stiffly, waiting for the light to change while the dog edged toward his crotch. When he reached to block the beast, he came away with a tacky handful of spit.

"I heard about you on da news last night," said the young man. "Good for you, getting out dere again. We've missed having you around. So what's dis case you've got going?"

Duncan smiled and looked for a place to wipe the slobber, settling for his pant leg.

"Gracie, sit!" said the man. The dog complied on Duncan's feet and continued to stare up at him longingly.

"Nothing major," said Duncan. "A prisoner who got more than he deserved."

"Dat right?" said the man. "The news said he's waiting on da electric chair."

"For now."

"If anybody can save him, it's you," said the young man.

The light changed, so Duncan extricated his foot, drawing a mournful look from the dog, and crossed the street, only to be followed by his two sentries.

"Hey, about all dat stuff dey wrote about you? Don't worry about it. Nobody believes Murdoch's mud slingers."

"That's a relief," Duncan said. "Excuse me." He hooked into a corner market as his escort continued up the block, yet they paused beside a fire hydrant for a protracted sniff. To ensure that he would not catch them, Duncan lingered over a magazine rack, then purchased a pack of gum. Once they had advanced out of sight, he crossed to the opposite side of the block. Though less than a mile, the journey felt like many thousand steps.

***

Inside the Newberry library, Duncan headed to the back room and found the discreet librarian seated in her usual place. In keeping with the season, she wore a light blouse that revealed the outline of her bra and a skirt that rose above her knee. A bun still restrained her hair, and her face revealed no makeup. When he took off his sunglasses, she smiled benignly and asked how she could help. From her expression, he guessed that she recalled their prior encounter, but she offered no acknowledgment.

"More research," he said. "This time, a phrase."

He scratched onto a slip of paper the words etched onto his son's body as best he could recall them: ration autumn liberamor. As she studied, she squinched her youthful face until it wrinkled. "My Latin's a bit out of date."

She stood and led him to a narrow aisle of leather-bound books, extracted a Latin/English dictionary with a frayed cover and wrinkled pages, and looked up the second word, which translated to "however."

She frowned and took the pencil from him. "Do you mean this?" she said and corrected the spelling to ratione autem liberamur.

"I suppose," he said. "What is it?"

"The gist of it is that reason will free us."

"You're sure?" he said.

"Four years of Catholic school taught me nothing if not translation." She smiled, and for the first time he could see how pretty she'd be with a minimum of embellishment. Her delicate nose and soft hair reminded him of the girls he dated in high school. Squeezed into the stacks, he felt a moment of guilty intimacy until he noted that he exceeded her in height by a head and in age by two decades. He leaned back and reexamined the sheet for clues. "Reason will free us," he said to himself.

A fitting choice, he supposed, for a man oppressed by incarceration. Still, unless the prison's minister had been tutoring Aden, Duncan couldn't imagine where the boy could have heard such a saying. His military school hadn't even offered the dead language.

"Do you know the reference?" he said.

"It's not one I recognize," she said. "Then again, the nuns only taught us bible quotes. Could be Caesar or Cicero, one of those historic orators."

Again the young woman screwed up her face and turned to her wall of tomes. With minimum effort, she found a Latin phrase book and flipped through the index, then set aside the volume and selected another, and a third when that failed. With each effort, her expression became a bit more troubled and her youth a bit less attractive. After a fourth and fifth try ended in frustration, she said, "Where did you see it?"

"Ironically," he said, "in graffiti."

She shook her head and lowered it as though searching some invisible card catalogue. "Not the sort of thing I'd expect from a vandal," she said. "Still, if you give me a day, I'll keep looking."

***

Across the street from the library, the leaves of Washington Square Park rippled in the breeze, reflecting the sunlight of early morning. The scene would have been tranquil except for a shrill voice competing for attention. A skinny old man in a moth-eaten sweater and oversized pants stood atop a platform, shouting at a cluster of a half-dozen other ragged men and women with shopping carts and backpacks. "The evil empire is us," he called. "With the arrival of Gorbachev and glasnost, our nemesis now more closely resembles our own capitalist excesses. No alternative remains to the winner-take-all competition on Wall Street."

Popularly known as Bughouse Park, the formal square had for years hosted leftist debates. Though the tradition had lately fallen out of fashion, a few practitioners remained.

Duncan paused atop the library steps to don his hat and sunglasses, then scout his options for getting home. A walk back risked more exposure, but a cab could not drop him in front of Marina City without inciting a feeding frenzy. He had settled on a return via the riverside when the voice across the way amplified. "There stands our former CEO of state, Duncan Cochrane, a beacon of the unholy alliance between corrupt business and corrupt politics."

The speaker pointed with an unsteady hand, inciting his few followers to stare balefully at the image of their oppression. Quickly, Duncan descended and turned toward Clark Street to evade the heckler, yet his voice pursued, rising in volume even as the distance between them grew. "See how they run at the sound of an honest voice...."

A bus approached the corner opposite, so Duncan ran across just as it squealed to a stop. He boarded without checking the number and moved to the back, where a young black woman sat between grocery bags. As the bus lurched forward, drowning out the speaker's voice with the engine's grind, Duncan asked his neighbor where they were heading.

Without looking at him, she said, "This the twenty-two. Goes downtown to the Loop."

He sat back, still unclear on the route, but relieved to have escaped scrutiny. The few people ahead of them all faced forward. At worst, he could ride this line as far as the river and then find his way home.

"Was you on TV last night?" said the woman.

Duncan turned to see her studying him with more interest than judgment. Still he shook his head and stared forward.

"You the one helping that poor man in prison," she said.

When he glanced to her again, tears pooled in her eyes. She began to tell him of her own child, a boy of only sixteen, who awaited trial for drug possession. A year before, the young man had turned rebellious, skipping school, staying out late, coming home intoxicated. Still, she'd never expected him to land in a lockup.

"When they found the drugs in his backpack, they arrested him," she said. "How's he going to learn right from wrong if they won't teach him?"

As a parent, Duncan understood. The agony of watching a wayward child nearly equaled that of losing one, so he began to share a bit of his own story, leaving out the details about Aden's latest missteps. While he spoke, a smile merged with her tears.

"You got to tell people," she said. "You got to tell them how it is."

The bus was approaching the Chicago River and his stop, but he lingered another block to take her hand, whose rough texture suggested a lifetime of labor, and assure her that things would improve. The state, which had the power to incarcerate, also held the power to free.

"So you tell them?" she said.

He stood and walked to the rear door, holding her gaze even as he retreated. When the bus pitched to a stop, and the door clicked to offer him escape, he lingered on the stairs, unable to abandon her in a moment of such vulnerability.

"I'll try," he said, and exited.

He backtracked to the bridge at Dearborn Street, crossed the water, and descended to the river level before any of the assembled throng noticed him.

Once he stood inside the safety of his own apartment, Duncan felt the day stretching before him, empty and solitary. He needed rest but doubted he'd find any there. Lately his own apartment had come to feel like an isolation chamber. He moved to the balcony, studying the grid of streets below. With the sun gleaming off the windows downtown, the city felt more threatening than ever before, each block and corner posing some new risk.

Too morose. He shook his head to clear the self-absorption and traced the river to its inlet at the lakefront, and from there across the infinite blue. This view always gave him perspective on the irrelevance of his own problems. His watch told him only a few hours had passed, with several left before noon. Still time remaining.

He stepped inside, ignored the blinking light on his answering machine, and called Catherine. Probably she'd already left home, was sitting in the studio being dabbed with makeup or warming up in the green room. Except on the third ring she answered, as cheery and optimistic as when they'd hung up the night before.

"What time should I meet you?" Duncan said.

CHAPTER 26

OPRAH STUDIED DUNCAN WITH SUCH INTENSITY that he deflected to the television camera, which offered a more impersonal eye. During his years of press conferences and interviews, he'd never met someone who could penetrate his defenses so effortlessly. Her gaze implored him to confess his sins and be absolved.

"How did I get involved," he repeated, stalling for time. Such a simple and obvious question. Then why was he struggling to explain?

"Several weeks ago, Ms. Fontanelle contacted me about this case." He glanced to the advocate, who sat beside him onstage in an elegant black dress. She smiled genuinely to urge him forward. "At first I resisted, as I didn't believe it was my place to second guess the justice system."

Not exactly. Not exactly what he intended to say, but it had escaped already, and he didn't wish to appear uncertain by recanting his words.

"But you decided to intervene," Oprah said. "Why? Why now and in this case?"

Duncan paused to compose himself. The audience in the small studio awaited his words with the singular focus of a jury. They were a varied lot, a mixture of men and woman, black and white, young and old, yet they listened as one body, awaiting his confession, more attentive than any crowd he'd faced in government or politics.

"I did some research and concluded that the system... the justice system had erred in this case. I do not believe he—Mr. Flores, that is—was convicted on... adequate evidence."

He sounded like a stammering schoolboy, unable to express his attraction to a girl trying out her first training bra. How unfitting. Caught between these two women, who probed him with such ardor—not the usual journalistic impatience but a personal appeal—he wished only to escape without embarrassing himself.

"Was that the only reason you intervened?" Oprah said.

He studied the hostess, who wore large sparkly earrings and a stiff helmet of hair. What was it about her that he found so difficult to resist? Her unrelenting glare. She never took her eyes off her guests, even as they related the most embarrassing details.

"As governor, I promised to keep people safe, to put away violent criminals. And I meant it. But I never intended to lock up innocent men. I see now that in some instances—in *this* case—that was the result."

Oprah advanced toward him, stopping just shy of the stage, literally a few feet away. "So your own son's incarceration didn't play a role?"

Despite the modest setting and the limited audience, the studio lights burned his face and blinded him whenever he looked up. His skin prickled as he sweated into his good suit, which bound in the chest and thighs. Instead of thinking about that, he focused on the hostess, this matron of empathy, whose youth and vigor made her all that much harder to resist. She leaned into him, coaxing self-revelation in a way no one ever had—not the police, nor his wife, nor even the ministers and therapists who'd tried to counsel him after Lindsay died.

"My son's case is... is separate from this. Unrelated."

"Governor, with due respect, I find it hard to believe that you, as a parent, have not been in some way changed by the experience of seeing your own child taken from you."

Murmurs of assent rose up from the audience, a few of whom nodded with understanding.

Duncan recalled Aden as he'd last seen him, sitting in the prison chapel, his head lowered in prayer or thought, his father knew not which. The boy had acted so utterly alone. Emotion burbled within Duncan like vomit, trying to escape until he suppressed it with a swallow.

"Certainly that experience has... affected me, but it's not why I joined in this project. My reasons are purely... impersonal. I want to see justice done, not injustice."

Then it came: a single tear welling in his right eye. Whether due to the dry burn of the lights or the gentle breeze from the fan at the far end of the stage, he couldn't say, but he knew that if he didn't do something quickly it would cascade down his cheek for everyone to see. He raised a fist, cleared his throat, then wiped his entire face as though it itched, hoping no one would notice.

Oprah retreated into her audience, extending the microphone to them as hands stretched upward. An older man, with dark, sagging skin below his mournful eyes, stood to speak first. "You may not want to say it, but I can tell by how you sitting there that you feeling the loss of your child." Other listeners urged him on with "mmhmm." Mirroring Duncan, the man wiped away a tear before he continued. "I lost two grandbabies to the jails, and I never forget how it feel, seeing them locked up for the first time. Whether they innocent, like you say about this man Flores, or they guilty as Cain, it don't matter. They still yours and you want to protect them."

Applause rippled through the crowd even as the man remained standing. Did he expect Duncan to answer this non-question, or merely to emote with him? He glanced to Catherine, who stared back with sorrow, as though it were *him* they should pity.

"I appreciate your concern," Duncan said. "But I really don't want this to become about me."

A young woman in a power suit and severe haircut stood without prompting and motioned for the microphone, then began speaking before Oprah could traverse to her.

"Come on now," she said, hands on hips. "How you expect us to believe you not thinking of your own kin when you up here talking about innocence and suffering. There's nothing wrong with you trying to protect your own child. Hell, you quit being governor so you wouldn't have to talk about it. Now you still trying to keep it to yourself, but we all know. We willing to forgive you—God willing to forgive you—if you just ask."

Again, Duncan could think of no fitting response, no contrition he could offer to everyone, much less an audience of anonymous TV viewers. He shifted in his seat and glanced toward a clock on the far wall, hoping that this segment was drawing to a close, only to find nearly ten minutes remaining. To stall, he nodded to himself and looked down at his feet, then recalled the director's advice to keep his head up and watch the hostess. She'd circled again through the audience to a Hispanic man with a stocky build and an angry expression.

"Hypocrite!" he shouted. "You sit up there, talking about how sorry you are, for yourself, your killer kid, while you demanding special treatment for them."

Duncan leaned forward to evade the glare of the lights and so he could see the man more clearly. "If you're referring to some story on the news—"

"I'm talking about that favor of a sentence he got. Murdered his own sister and got off with five years, while my boy got twice that for taking back what was his."

"These matters are not decided by me," Duncan said. "A judge—"

"A judge you hired," said the man, pointing at him. "A judge you paid off."

"That's simply untrue," Duncan said. "I have no more authority over judges than—"

Before he could finish, something hit Duncan's shoulder, spraying him with a liquid both tacky and viscous. It speckled his face and dripped into his eyes, blurring his vision and disorienting his other senses. He tried to rub away the excess, but all he could see was his own red skin. The audience gasped and screamed. People shouted and cursed, at him and each other. Strong hands gripped him under the arms and lifted him from his chair, then carried him off stage.

What had just happened?

Hands continued to lead and prod Duncan until he sat in a dark room with several people hovering over him. One patted his face with something damp while another stripped off his suit coat. He smelled antiseptic and some rosy perfume but couldn't tell if it emanated from his own skin or the hands that touched him. Voices became jumbled and fragmented. A woman said, "A bomb," while a man asked, "Is it blood?"

After what felt like minutes of this tending, the bodies retreated so he could orient himself. He sat in a small dressing room, surrounded by Oprah's staffers, though the hostess was notably absent. Catherine Fontanelle moved in close to study him, touching his cheek and chest. After a tense moment, she said, "It was only a prank."

"What happened?" Duncan said.

"Someone threw a balloon filled with red paint," she said. "Your suit is ruined."

"It's just a suit," he said.

Still she looked stricken, so Duncan swiveled in the chair to see himself in a makeup mirror. His shirt and jacket still bore red streaks, and speckles dappled his hair. His skin flushed almost as red, probably due to all the scrubbing, or humiliation.

Behind him, he saw the reflection of his co-conspirator, who looked crestfallen.

"Can we have some privacy?" Duncan said to the staffers surrounding them. When they hesitated, he said, "I'm fine. I just need a moment."

Slowly they retreated, murmuring to one another and looking back at him with both amusement and embarrassment. Once they'd gone, he turned to face his companion and said, "*This* is why I didn't want to get involved."

She shook her head and looked away. "You expected people to react this way?"

He began to unbutton his shirt, then realized the inappropriateness of stripping in front of her. "I provoke extreme reactions."

"This wasn't supposed to be about you. I wanted people to think about Harry, about all that he's suffered, not their own... private grievances."

"People can't separate the message from the messenger."

"Only one person—"

"It only takes one."

She sighed and shook her head. "You're awfully cynical about it all."

"I'm accustomed to being a target," he said.

She sat on a couch opposite him and inspected her own clothes, which bore shrapnel from the paint bomb. She tried dabbing at them with a towel, but it only smeared the damage. "You think the show planned this?" she said.

"What, the attack?" He listened for sounds in the hallway, but heard only the distant scrape of feet on the linoleum. "I doubt it. Probably someone with a grudge who snuck in the balloon under his jacket." He forgot decorum and stripped to his t-shirt, which had also soaked in the paint and stained his fingers again. "People are still angry with me."

"Can't they see how much you've suffered already?"

"Evidently not," Duncan said, then realized his mistake. "I mean, my sufferings are minor compared to many other people's."

She reached toward him until he offered his hand. "That's not true. You are *very* important."

"I can't afford to think that way anymore."

***

The afternoon passed in a blur, with visits from police and producers, who both assured him that the attacker—a disgruntled parent who'd snuck onto the set through a back door with the ammunition tucked into a lunch bag—had been captured. After launching his projectile, he'd run, but he couldn't escape the building before security tackled him. The cops asked Duncan if he wanted to press charges.

"For what?" said the target. "Immaturity?"

Despite his protestations, the producers demanded to pay for his suit, as though he'd be needing it again, and insisted on having him checked out by a doctor, who confirmed his good health. All in all, they treated him with dignity and esteem despite the ignominy he'd just endured. If only he could redress the public's reaction so easily.

That night, he avoided the news—uninterested in watching his own public shaming replayed or dissected—and audited the Cubs game on TV. From the couch, he watched the lights flicker on downtown and wished for sleep to relieve him. A breeze off the lakefront carried away the heat and smog of the day, leaving a refreshing clarity.

Dusk had overtaken the city, and lights winked on in offices and apartments throughout downtown. The glass also reflected the dim glow of the television in his own suite. What a magical effect, to be able to see both inside and out simultaneously. Like most people, he usually saw only his own point of view although lately even this felt opaque to him, his motives unclear, his actions ill prepared. At a time when he most needed clairvoyance, instead he suffered myopia.

His lawyers had spoken truth. Engagement was a mistake. He still ignited the public, carrying a static charge that could spark on anyone who came too close. Dreifort had left a message on his machine, threatening to withdraw if he continued to "flout counsel," but he knew the attorney liked his money too much to quit.

He poured himself a scotch redolent of frustration, the kind only centuries of repression could brew. Many generations of his ancestors had survived as outlaws, resisting the English occupation by hiding out in the Highlands. He needed to adopt a similar strategy, waiting for his accusers to grow disinterested or fatigued and retreat.

The insight soothed him even more than the liquor. He needed to focus on himself, his children, not be concerned with the greater society any longer. Four years of caring for others had landed him in this state.

A knock unsettled him despite the recent frequency of visitors. He ignored it, unwilling to risk the equilibrium he'd achieved, but when it sounded a second time, curiosity overcame him. Through the peephole he saw a familiar face, warm and welcoming, but dangerous. He could snub the summons, but that would only delay the matter, and he wanted things decided.

When he opened the door, Catherine smiled sheepishly. She had changed into a simple, shift dress and removed her jewelry and makeup but still radiated elegance. Even this late, it felt rude not to invite her inside, so he stepped back into his entryway. She paralleled him as though they were dancing, touching his face and turning it gently toward the light.

"Good. No bruising," she said.

"None that's visible," Duncan said.

He retreated from her for a refill on his drink but did not offer her one. Better to make this quick and blunt.

"I'm afraid this will be our last meeting," he said. "I've decided to withdraw from your group."

"Because of what happened today?"

"For many reasons."

Without invitation, she slumped at his dining table, looking defeated. "We're so close to success, to freeing Harry, and it's all attributable to you."

"Hardly," Duncan said. "If anything, I'm a liability."

"How can you say that? You put us on the front page, on the television. The mayor and the governor are answering questions now. None of that would have happened without you."

Duncan shook his head. "Creating a public spectacle isn't progress."

She smiled. "It was a bit of a free-for-all, and I'm sorry for that. I should have anticipated—"

"No, I should have. I have this... effect on people."

She stood and walked toward him but stopped at the edge of his kitchen. "*Some* people appreciate you."

He felt pinned by her inside his own space, but he didn't want to push past. "If my lawyers discover anything interesting, I'll let you know."

She stared unrelentingly, her pale blue eyes taking in the whole of him. "So you won't receive me anymore?"

Her formality confused him. "Receive, meaning...."

"I can't show up at your apartment uninvited?"

He saw her as though for the first time. The wisps of gray in her hair blended with its original blonde, a more natural look than his wife, who insisted on dyes to cover the effects of aging. Her figure, too, looked more appealing, less corseted and constrained than many women her age. She remained feminine without straining for false youth, a rare combination, so unlike the aerobicized political wives he knew.

"Why would you want to see me?" he said.

She smiled slyly. "I enjoy your company, your insights. I feel a... kinship with you that's... rare."

Was this flirtation? Compared to the younger women he knew—those in the media and government, who displayed their sexuality freely in their dress and their speech—Catherine exhibited decorum. People of their generation restrained themselves, controlled their desires, yet three times she'd come to him, and now she stood in his apartment after dark. Hardly the sort of courtship usually practiced in his day when men initiated every intimacy.

"What would we have to discuss?" he said.

She lay one hand on her throat, stroking the underside of her jaw, which held square and firm. "Many things. I know only what I've read about you, your history."

"And I know even less about you."

She extended an open palm to him. "You see? We're at the beginning of our relationship. Wouldn't it be a shame to end it prematurely when it began so promisingly?"

He thought of his last conversation with Josie, which felt so final. Could one be unfaithful to a partner who'd already rejected him?

She led him to the couch and sat so close that he could smell her soap—something creamy and herbal. When their fingers interlaced, her palm felt smooth except for one index finger, which bore a callus where one held a pen. Even as he stroked it, her grip remained slack, not passive but at ease.

She started by explaining her own connection to prisoners. After growing up privileged and sheltered in the western suburbs, Catherine had married right after high school a man who proved to be both controlling and neglectful. He'd stay out late but call to check on her, then leave for the weekends but demand that she await his return. She'd endured him until the liberation of the sixties made divorce permissible among respectable people. Since then, she'd remained single, raising her son on her own and supporting them as a real estate agent. Like him, she'd assumed her upbringing gave her immunity from criminality until her child descended into addiction at a time when drugs connoted coolness. His stay in jail had spurred her advocacy for reform. Although the boy had stayed clean and free for nearly a decade now, her passion remained.

Duncan's family history needed no explanation. Still he felt compelled to share something, so he clarified his own recent separation and unemployment, alluding to his children's struggles and his devotion to his wayward son without offering details.

Throughout, Catherine listened silently, nodding encouragement but letting him think uninterrupted. Voicing the facts gave them coherence and logic that often eluded him in his ruminations. By the time he'd finished, relief suffused him. To unburden himself to someone who understood and responded without judgment released the pressure that had built inside him ever since they'd met.

By the time he leaned forward to kiss her, any awkwardness or inhibition had drained with it.

THEY TELL ME YOU ARE CUNNING

CHAPTER 27

IT FELT GOOD, AWAKENING NEXT TO a woman again. The warmth of her, the crook of her hip where his arm fit, the lilac smell of her hair against his face. More than the release of sex, he'd missed the intimacy of another, the adhesion of skin on skin. It brought him his first good night's sleep in a week.

Yet at the same time it felt awkward and unfamiliar. Many months had passed since he'd touched another person so, and even more years since he'd slept next to anyone but his wife. Nonetheless, watching her dress and kissing her goodbye on the doorstep, he wondered what this meant: a one-time tryst or the beginning of a new pattern. He said nothing about his concerns and watched her depart, but whether with regret or longing, he couldn't decide.

As he gathered the newspapers and skimmed the headlines, their bombast felt distant—"Attack on Gov. Crime" screamed the *Sun-Times;* "Cochrane Splattered" intoned the *Tribune*—reports from some outpost disconnected from him. Then he noted a column from Mark Rica, his most insightful critic, and committed to a full reading:

> *Yesterday, we witnessed another example of double think from our state's Big Brother, Duncan Cochrane, whose tenure in the governor's mansion most closely resembled mind control.*
>
> *This time, we're to believe, an unperson splattered the former leader in fake blood, an allusion to his victorious war on crime, or his murdered daughter, or perhaps his own martyrdom at the hands of his enemies, we're not sure which.*
>
> *The vandal has yet to explain the symbolism of his protest, owing to his incarceration by the thought police.*
>
> *Regardless, his act should remind us all of the halcyon days during Cochrane's reign, when his Ministry of Truth taught us all newspeak. Like many politicians, he admired the maximal state of Orwell's 1984, setting his Macintosh to track any and all criminal suspects.*

Of course, he added a codicil to the criminal code, excusing himself and his children from such constraints.

The governor would have us believe that since he left office two years ago, he's developed a soft spot for those caught in the dragnet of his sweeps through Chicago's underground. That during his time in power, he overlooked the propensity of local police to induce confessions through whatever means necessary.

Like many dictators, Cochrane has developed a conscience in proportion to his own suffering. During good times, he excused the state's excesses. Now targeted, he would have us believe that he regrets his past impatience with due process.

Which reminds us of his jailed attacker. One wonders if this unman will receive the same empathy from Cochrane that his new benefactor, Harry Flores, has, or whether he'll be another example of the system's harsh treatment of the unconnected.

Maybe if Mr. Cochrane takes up his case, he too can be saved, or maybe this episode was yet another dumbshow to distract us from his true aim: a cult of personality.

Duncan set aside the paper and smiled. To outside eyes his motives might appear selfish, but given the suffering he'd endured lately, his activism felt more masochistic than self-serving. Regardless of the public response to the prank, he'd done more to feed his critics than silence them, and more to endanger himself than protect his child.

Most urgently, he wanted to check on Aden, but given his alienation from the true warden of the facility, he didn't wish to return only two days after his last visit. Better to let hurt feelings settle, especially if the man read about his latest public appearance. How then? He knew a number of other employees at the Illinois Department of Corrections but none with an insider's knowledge of Stateville. Then, an idea came to him.

He dialed the prison's main number and asked to be connected to the doctor who'd treated Aden. He didn't know the man's name, but it was easy to describe him: short, stocky, bald, with a handlebar mustache. While he held, the prison's phone message listed its rules and regulations—no weapons, no drugs, no food, no crop tops, as though these posed equivalent danger—until the doctor's husky voice cut it off.

Rather than play coy, which had spurred many of his recent problems, Duncan introduced himself and explained his dilemma.

"I can't speak to you while I'm working," the doctor said, "but my shift ends at eight."

With an hour to go, Duncan could just make Stateville in time.

"I was thinking of someplace in the city," said the doc. "I know a nice diner in Boystown."

***

Chicago is often called a city of neighborhoods, each distinct in ethnicity and history. It held so many that even Duncan had not visited them all during his campaigns for office, and Boystown proved to be a novelty to him. It squeezed in between Wrigley Field and the lakefront along the North Side. One thing stood out: everywhere on the streets he saw men. Men chatting, men walking, men holding hands, looking as natural as at an all-boys school. Hardly a single woman appeared anywhere.

He found the diner along a busy commercial strip of Halsted Street and sat at a table by the rear, facing the back. Consistent with the neighborhood, all the patrons proved to be male, but none noticed him, more engrossed in one another than in a fallen celebrity. Still, whenever new visitors arrived, he used a mirror behind the counter to check their identities.

The place looked and smelled like a typical greasy spoon, with fried food hissing on the griddle and oil lingering in the air, plus a black-and-white checkerboard scheme reminiscent of the fifties. However, the menu offered many surprises: veggie burgers, vegan milk shakes, a Reuben made with seitan instead of corned beef. To a man who'd made his fortune in sausages, living in a city known for meat packing, it felt as foreign as a primitive village. By the time his host arrived, Duncan had settled on the Caesar salad as the most familiar option, even though it too included fake meat, and a cup of tea, which he assumed would include real tea leaves.

Out of his white coat, the doctor looked far different than Duncan recalled, with a tank top that showed off his swollen chest and arms. Even with his shaved head and handlebar mustache, he somehow fit in with the locals, who exhibited every style but convention.

"Not what you expected?" said the doctor.

"Not what I'm accustomed to."

"Don't worry. People here are discreet."

After ordering and exchanging small talk—the doctor chose the spot because he lived nearby with his partner; he commuted four days a week because he couldn't stand to live outside the city—Duncan asked the obvious: why work in a prison?

"The similarity of our communities." He sipped a fruity soda and glanced around the restaurant before continuing. "We're all outcasts, ostracized and stigmatized by the mainstream. And AIDS." He waited a heartbeat to gauge Duncan's reaction, but on seeing none, continued. "I don't know how much you've heard or read about it. Stories tend to be hidden on the back pages. It's a plague affecting my people and prisoners in equal numbers. Mostly gay men and IV drug users get it, which is why no one talks about it, but it's a hundred percent fatal, and it's spreading like TB. I'm one of a handful of people studying its causes and stages."

Duncan must have looked nervous, because the doctor smiled and said, "Don't worry. It takes more than casual contact to spread it." Still, he leaned back in his chair as though offended by the implication that he could be a carrier. "But that's not why you called me." He waited for his guest to confirm the obvious.

"No," Duncan said. "What I couldn't say on the phone is I need your... your insights on my son."

The doctor nodded and explained the limits imposed by confidentiality, even for inmates.

"I'm not asking for his medical history," Duncan said. "More about... I don't understand the culture where you work. How to... to help him."

Again, the doctor nodded and sipped his drink in contemplation.

"The most important thing is what you're doing already: keep in touch. Many men don't receive any visitors, and they lose perspective on the free world. They get so institutionalized, they forget social norms. So maintaining a link to the outside helps as much as anything."

Duncan lowered his head and spoke to the tabletop as though that would ensure privacy. "Not enough, I'm afraid. My son has been... distant that last few times we spoke. Detached. Like he's given up."

"You mean his recent injuries. As I said, I can't divulge much about his care except to tell you that his life was never at risk. He looked bad, but I always knew he'd heal."

"That's reassuring."

Duncan paused as their meals arrived. His Caesar salad proved to be a close approximation of the original, as rich and creamy as any he'd tried, though the texture of the false flesh threw him, so he picked around it. The doctor ate less fastidiously, taking a large bite from his portabella and licking the sauce from his fingers. After a few nibbles, Duncan lay down his fork, seeking other satisfactions.

"There's something else," he said. "Last time I visited, he had a new tattoo, something in Latin. I don't suppose you studied any in medical school."

"Only the scientific terms."

"It said something like 'reason will set you free.'"

The doctor laid aside his sandwich and wiped his fingers. "Ratione autem liberamur?"

"Yes, precisely. What does it mean?"

"Your translation's correct. It's the context you're missing."

"So it's not about getting out of jail?"

"Not in the Monopoly sense. Many years ago, there was a famous inmate housed at Stateville, Nathan Leopold. You may have heard of him and his partner, Richard Loeb. Philosophy students from U of C. They murdered a child for the thrill of it, and to prove they were too smart to get caught. Turns out, they weren't as smart as they thought, and they ended up incarcerated for life. The media dubbed it the crime of the century.

"Loeb died young at the hands of another inmate, but Leopold spent thirty-something years inside. He worked in the library and the infirmary, tutored other prisoners. I heard he learned two dozen languages, including Latin."

The doctor paused and took another bite of his sandwich, leaving Duncan in suspense.

"That phrase you saw was his motto. He inscribed it onto many of the library's history books, and it became a mantra with the other inmates. No surprise that we still have those volumes. Things change slowly on the inside. Only I didn't know people still read them. Prisoners these days mostly go for westerns or true crime, something more practical. Good to hear your son is choosing books that are educational."

"So it's not gang-related?"

"Not unless he's started some new gang of classics scholars."

"Then that *is* reassuring."

The doctor offered Duncan a few of his home fries, which tasted little different from the French tradition, if perhaps less greasy. For all its unconventionality, this food did ape the original.

"I would take that brand as an encouraging sign," the doctor said. "I'm no psychiatrist, but to me it indicates that he hasn't given up hope. No one who's planning to die would suffer through a tattoo in prison."

Duncan smiled at his joke and tried some more of the fake meat on his salad. If he could ignore the spongy texture, he might mistake the flavor for real chicken.

"Besides learning dead languages, is there anything else he could be doing inside to improve himself, any programs or education?"

"Not so long as he's in solitary. The prison's philosophy is to preserve the body, not the mind."

"What about if he left protective custody?"

The doctor shook his head. "I wouldn't recommend it. Given his celebrity status, he'd be a target."

"Do you know of any other prisons that have more to offer?"

"There's Sheridan, downstate. They have a number of treatment programs for body and soul. I've heard good things about their counseling program. That would be tricky, though. They don't have an isolation wing there, so he'd have to mix with the other inmates."

"So it's possible."

"For you? I'm not sure what is or isn't possible. For a typical inmate, though, what triggers a move is either an overdose or an attack. Without an overt threat to life or health, there's no urgency."

CHAPTER 28

BY THE TIME HE EXITED THE cafe, the sun hovered directly overhead, with little breeze to cut the humidity, giving Duncan a prickling sensation as he walked to his BMW.

He planned to return home even though nothing awaited him there, yet as he sat in his stifling car, which reminded him of the slow roasting awaiting him in his apartment, he realized how close he would pass to the murder site. He could ring the bell, speak to the super again, but he couldn't think what else to ask him. The man said he'd moved in after the killings.

However, someone preceded him in the job.

From a pay phone, Duncan called the city's building department. A clerk revealed the building's owner: Hans Brugner. Another call to a friend at the DMV revealed that the landlord lived not far away. By the time he reached his destination, sweat was trickling inside his Oxford shirt and khaki pants. He paused in the shaded porch of a Victorian, which exhibited the fussy grace of a painted lady, with three colors accenting the ornamental trim work. The driveway sat empty, and the stair treads held a sheen of pollen. Probably empty. He knocked and listened as a dog bayed inside, then tried again when the owner did not answer.

Just as he'd resigned himself to another trip in his sweat box, the door opened. A man Duncan's age stared at him through thick glasses that hazed over his eyes while a Weimaraner danced beside him from foot to foot. The landlord squinted, showed the shock of recognition, and invited him into a living room that featured period furniture—a high-backed couch, a Victrola, a sterling chafing dish—more befitting a grandmother than a bachelor.

The inside offered little relief from out, with only an antique fan circulating the heat. While the dog sniffed his guest's feet, the host padded nervously between his own, assuring Duncan that he'd always voted for him and professing astonishment at his sudden retirement from public life. Was he truly unaware of the reasons? Duncan glanced about the place but saw no intrusion of modernities such as televisions or radios. The ambiance suggested someone who rarely left home, a virtual shut-in.

"My purpose is more personal than political," he said. "I wanted to know about an apartment building you own."

The other man began a defense of his negligence, assuring his inquisitor that he'd never intended to become a landlord, that he'd inherited the building several years back when his parents died, that owing to his poor vision he rarely visited, instead leaving everything to his superintendent, but that the man had proven exceedingly dependable. His defense blended irresponsibility with assurance and incorporated every method to explain his own absence.

"What about the prior manager?" Duncan said. "Do you have his name and number?"

After several guarantees that he did, the man spent five minutes rifling desk drawers and filing cabinets. When at last he produced a torn-off envelope flap with only a first name, George, and a street address, Duncan didn't bother to thank him.

***

The former super lived inland from the lake in a neighborhood populated by auto repair shops and liquor stores. Aside from the typical brick chic of Chicago housing, nothing looked familiar. In his campaigns, Duncan had focused on wealthier, white neighborhoods, ones with people who shared his concern for crime creeping its way toward the high rises.

On the street, a radio played something with foreign beats and instruments, while the scent of exotic foods—with roasted chickens and chilies—drifted on stagnant air. Row houses extended as far as he could see, without a single patch of grass to absorb the heat and few trees to shield the sun, which radiated off the sidewalks.

The man's new place offered none of the charm of his former digs—a tenement with peeling paint and rickety stairs. At the landing, Duncan found no names on the panel of doorbells. He tried several before a female voice crackled over the speaker and directed him to 304, where another woman asked if he could come back. Once he'd explained the urgency, she requested the number of his government ID, as though such a thing existed, then kept him waiting for minutes before buzzing him inside.

He climbed a dark, creaky stairwell to the landing, where a woman met him. She had dark eyes, skin, and hair and was bouncing an infant strapped to her chest.

"At first, I didn't believe you were the governor," she said in a lilting Spanish accent. "But you looked right." She led him inside her flat, which offered solid if inexpensive furniture. "My husband's asleep," she explained. "Give me a minute. He's hard to wake up."

Duncan waited on a corduroy couch and inspected the place for other clues about the owners. Besides family photos hung illustrations of Jesus and the pope framed in gold, and an embroidery of the Serenity Prayer. Typical sights for a home in Chicago, where the Catholic Church ranked second to the political machine in importance.

To his surprise, a man with the red hair and freckled skin of the Irish emerged from the bedroom wearing nothing but boxers. Though his limbs dangled slim and sleek, his stomach bulged over his shorts, suggesting minimal activity. He stopped and stared at who awaited him, then finger-combed his tangled curls nervously. "I thought my wife was bullshitting me," he said.

"Sorry to wake you," Duncan said.

"Forget it." The man sat on the corner of a scuffed coffee table, unselfconscious about his near nudity.

"I have a few questions about the murder at your former residence."

The man shook his head—whether to revive himself or dispel the memory, Duncan couldn't say—and looked between his feet. He watched this witness for shame or guilt at his testimony, which had condemned another to death, but saw only fatigue.

"You were home at the time?" Duncan said.

Eyes still lowered, the man nodded.

"One of the tenants told me that she heard someone running down the back stairs right after. Did you hear anything?"

George threw open his hands pleadingly and said, "No. Like I told the cops, I was asleep. I wish I hadn't of been. If I could of caught that guy...." He smacked one fist against the other to illustrate.

"So the noise didn't wake you?"

"Not till after. I found the bodies, all beat up and bloody...."

His pained expression suggested some lingering memory, perhaps acknowledging his failure as the building's supervisor.

"But you knew the victims?"

He nodded. "Nice people. Never caused a problem."

"So you can't think of a reason someone would want to kill them?"

A baby's tentative cry from inside the bedroom interrupted, and George waited for it to subside before answering. "The cops called it a burglary gone wrong. The guy panicked."

"Did you know the man they arrested, Harry Flores?"

George leaned back, eliciting a groan from the table, and looked toward the prayer wall. "Just from seeing him around."

"Do you believe he's guilty?"

The super threw up his hands, stood, and walked toward his bedroom. For a moment Duncan expected him to leave, but he stopped in the doorway and palmed his bare stomach as though it pained him. "I guess." He paused and inhaled loudly. "You gotta understand. It's still hard to talk about it."

He turned to face Duncan and scanned his apartment with disgust. "We left 'cause of that. Moved into this dump. My wife wouldn't stay in a place where somebody died. Plus, everybody was blaming me for what happened. Said if there was a light by the alley or better locks on the back door...." He shook his head. "Truth is, I'd been bugging the owner for months to beef things up, but he didn't want to spend any money on the place. Told me to fix stuff as it broke and that's it." He shook his head again as though to clear the memory. "Worst thing ever happened to me."

It surprised Duncan how personally he took it all, as though he himself had suffered for it. "I don't know if you've been following the news," Duncan said, "but I'm skeptical that Mr. Flores is guilty of the crime. The police forced a confession out of him, but there's little other evidence implicating him. That's why I asked your opinion. Did you hear or see any of what the police were doing?"

"Too much. I had to let them in and out of the apartment, starting the night I found the bodies. I saw those people...." Again he shook his head at the memories.

"Did the police spend much time there, enough to have solved the case so quickly?"

Once more the baby's cry interrupted, this time more sustained. George glanced into the bedroom, nodded once when his wife said "dáselo a él", then turned back to his visitor. He walked to a battered desk, opened a bottom drawer, and from its back pulled out a velvet bag containing something the size of his palm. He weighed it in his hand, then unwrapped a box and extended it to Duncan like an offering: a battered transistor radio with a bent antenna.

"After the cops left, I got stuck cleaning out the apartment 'cause the landlord was too cheap to pay anybody else to do it, which was...." He shook his head violently. "I boxed up everything, put it in storage, gave the key to the people's relatives. Mostly it was just clothes and furniture, but I found this. It felt wrong to me—not the kinda thing the Mulvaneys would of owned, seeing as he sold expensive stereos. I figured it must of belonged to the killer."

The child's wail intensified, making it impossible to speak for a time, until her mother started singing a ditty in Spanish. The music soothed the child, who quieted, but George closed the door to the bedroom and returned to sit opposite his visitor.

"I showed it to the police, but I doubt they used it. By then they'd arrested somebody, and I'd moved out."

Duncan recalled seeing a photo of a radio in the court files, perhaps the same one. "Why did you keep it, then?"

George stared at it, shrugged, and shook his head. "I dunno. As a reminder of why I left, I guess."

When the baby's crying resumed, with a crescendo loud enough to wake the neighbors, the woman called to her husband from the closed bedroom. He retreated to the door, exchanged some confidence with her, then turned to his visitor.

"I gotta go. Kid needs milk, and we're out."

Duncan stood, thanked him, and asked if he could keep the radio.

"*I* don't want it," said the handyman. "I don't want *any*thing to do with this case."

CHAPTER 29

AFTER SO MUCH TIME IN PUBLIC, Duncan wanted only to return home, but he feared the passage to it. He'd escaped his apartment early—before the media had convoyed outside it—yet by late afternoon he anticipated that a throng awaited him. He parked a block away and walked through a haze of humidity to the corner closest to the entrance.

Peeking around a building, he saw the expected mass of reporters, but their attention focused on some new prey: a dozen people carrying signs and chanting. From down the street, he could not see or hear them clearly, but one word rose above the fray—justice. Then he noted a familiar PUSH logo on one woman's shirt and IDed them: the Rev. Jesse Jackson's followers. They'd heckled him frequently during his administration—usually for his focus on crime and punishment—but had lost interest after he left office. With their leader preoccupied by running for president, they'd focused their attention more nationally. Duncan's TV appearance must have convinced them that he offered more free publicity than a commentary on unemployment rates.

Only, he couldn't decipher their message. Did they support his advocacy, oppose his son's preferential treatment, just dislike him personally? Perhaps even they couldn't decide. Nonetheless, it distracted the news crews from the back entrance.

Duncan circled the building to find more protestors massed in the courtyard by the river. Resolved, he lowered his head and strode forcefully toward the rear doors even as people ran toward him, blocking his way, until he could do little more than shuffle. They shouted and jostled so loud and close he couldn't glean anything but their anger. He craned his neck to see above them but found no escape from the mass encircling him. Instead, he stood still and silent, waiting for their energy to dissipate, until three burly white men bored through from the exterior, all but shoving people aside until they reached the governor. They gripped him firmly by both arms and reversed course, escorting him through the mob and delivering him to the lobby. Only once they stood inside did they release their grip on his biceps, which left a dull ache like a bruise.

Although they wore the sport coats and slacks of business casual, Duncan pegged them as undercover cops by their short haircuts and thick muscles. They gave him the typical ten-yard stare of authoritarians, but stood in a military at ease as though before a superior officer.

"Thanks," he said. "I can make it home from here."

Two glanced to the largest of the three, who equaled Duncan in height and age but exceeded him in weight by at least twenty solid pounds. "Our orders were to see you to your apartment," he said.

Intuitively, Duncan disliked his tone, which commanded more than informed, but it felt ungracious to reject their offer.

In the elevator, with the four of them crowded together, Duncan could smell the smoke and fried food that permeated their clothes, plus something else, like overripe fruit, as though they'd walked through a muddy field to reach him.

"Seems like you've upset a lot of people," said one cop standing behind him.

Rather than turn to address him, Duncan faced the elevator doors and noted thirty floors remained on their trip. "The truth will do that," he said.

"More like digging up old lies," said a second cop behind him.

The grind of the motor echoed through the elevator shaft, and the car seemed to sway under the added burden of five large men inside it.

"If that's the case, then the police have nothing to fear," Duncan said. "I'm only interested in what really happened."

The officer positioned next to him turned. "When you ran for office, you promised law and order. You promised to back us up when the lawyers and liberals tried to stop us doing our jobs."

"Which I did."

Again Duncan checked their upward progress to find a dozen floors remaining. He thought of pressing the button for a lower floor, but the biggest of the detectives stood in the way of the panel.

"Seems like you've gone soft hearted now that your kid is a convict," he said.

Rather than let the insult pass, Duncan turned to him. Up close, he noted a boxer's firm jaw and flared nose, which looked as though it had broken. "It has given me a new perspective on how we treat suspects."

They glared at each other until the car jolted to a stop and the doors opened on Duncan's floor. He waited a moment to show he would not be intimidated, then stepped from the tight box into the hallway. To his relief, the detectives did not follow him, content with silent stares.

"Look all you want," said their leader. "You'll find nothing but good cops and bad crooks."

The bell sounded to warn that the doors would be closing, but the detective stuck a thick arm in the way to block them.

"We have something for you," he said.

With his free hand, he reached into his sport coat as though for a weapon. Instinct told Duncan to duck or run, but he stood paralyzed until the man extracted not a gun nor a club but an envelope.

The cop extended his hand and left it thus until Duncan accepted the letter, then released his grip on the lift doors. As the buzzer sounded again, he smirked and said, "Your man Harry? He gave himself up, easy. And soon, you will, too."

Not until after the elevator had descend non-stop to the bottom floor did Duncan examine his gift: a summons to appear before the grand jury.

***

Upstairs, his apartment felt like a greenhouse baked all day in the sun, which streaked the floor and sparkled in the air. He hunted for his old rolodex, which contained all the numbers for state officials he'd once ruled, exhumed it from the dusty back of a kitchen cabinet, and skimmed through until he located the number he wanted.

Jerome Johns had served as a prison warden during his administration but since then had ascended to head the department of corrections. They'd met only once, at a time when Duncan suspected everyone of treachery, and the interview had not gone well. Johns acted resentful and combative at being paged to answer to his employer, even refusing a job offer at twice the pay. Duncan could only hope *his* memory of the incident had faded.

He dialed, got the jailer's secretary, talked his way past her, and within minutes was speaking to the man who held the keys to his son's cell. First, he thanked Johns for taking his call, then flattered him by noting how busy he must be. Before he'd concluded, he felt a familiar pain in his finger where he'd constricted it with the phone cord. Johns said nothing, exhibiting the typical tactic of all cops, letting people talk themselves into trouble. Still, Duncan recalled his gruff voice and dense body, both conveying the power of his office. In person, Duncan might have at least read his face, divined his mood. Only he lived hours south, in Springfield, where any appearance by the former governor would be noted and analyzed.

Thus, he began a lengthy explanation of Aden's recent misadventures, leaving out the tattoo but emphasizing his hospitalization, winding his way toward his true purpose, until Johns cut him off. "If you're calling for a favor, know that I don't interfere in the day-to-day operations of facilities."

Duncan assured the man that he expected no special treatment, only an impartial review of whether Aden were best served in his current environment or—

"Mr. Cochrane, I don't run a reform school. I'm not worried about whether my residents are achieving their full potential, or whether they're happy and healthy and feel at home. I only care that they're secure, from each other and from the public. You should know that I heard about what happened with your son, and the staff are telling me his injuries were self-inflicted. If you're so concerned about his welfare, I'd suggest you persuade him not to batter himself."

Duncan assured the man that he had, and would, advise his boy how to make the best use of his time, but that in some cases, surely, men who were ill-suited to their environments might benefit from a change. Not necessarily a downgrade in security level, only a transfer. One of the other jail staff had mentioned a facility—

"I'm not moving him because of his famous father."

Duncan paused, unsure how to respond to such a blatant rejection, and recalled his biggest concern when he held public office. "Then do it to protect yourself and your men," he said. "Because if anything happens to my boy while he's under your care, believe that I will use all my remaining power and celebrity to punish you."

Before he could detail the threat, Johns hung up.

CHAPTER 30

DUNCAN DIDN'T WANT TO GO OUT again during daylight, but the hothouse that was his apartment sapped his energy. He sought some direction. What could he accomplish from home? He noted the transistor radio, switched it on to hear something in Spanish that he couldn't understand, spun through all the dials, only to hear news of himself, and turned it off. He weighed it in his hands, felt the cracks and dimples in the plastic denoting heavy use, even removed the battery cover, but found nothing distinctive about it. Had the police even bothered to fingerprint it?

Then he recalled another unresolved lead and picked up the phone. Peruzzi answered on the second ring.

"Any news?" Duncan said.

The detective lowered his voice as soon as he'd heard Duncan's. "I might have something for you. Can I come by your place?"

"I wouldn't advise it unless you want to appear on TV tomorrow."

Silence on the other end of the line suggested not. "You ever hear of a bar on the Near North Side called the Brehon?"

"No."

"Good. Meet me there in an hour."

***

After taking the river route out of his building, Duncan walked several blocks north on Wells Street, a shaded corridor of tall buildings that proved less popular with pedestrians. Near the El station, he found the place, a corner storefront with Celtic signage and a Kelly green façade. Inside, little distinguished it from hundreds of other gin joints in the city: a tin ceiling, pool table, and oak bar that ran its length. Owing perhaps to it age, it emanated wood rot, with floors disintegrating into sawdust. Only after seating himself at the rear and studying a news clipping framed on the wall did he recognize its history.

Several years prior, under the name The Mirage Tavern, it had hosted a sting by the *Sun-Times*, back when the paper cared about journalism. Two reporters, along with the Better Government Association, used it to expose corruption in City Hall. The do-gooders had caught dozens of Chicago building inspectors and tax collectors soliciting bribes in exchange for ignoring obvious code violations. The story had disgraced the city's machine politics on many front pages and cost many civil servants their sinecures.

Now it looked more polished, with clean tabletops and a smell of baked potatoes. The only evidence of such a legacy was the framed clippings, including photos of its exposed wires and leaky pipes.

Why Peruzzi chose it as a meeting spot was the first of Duncan's questions once his host arrived.

"Nobody comes here," said the sergeant. "Since the scandal, it's as toxic as Three Mile Island to anybody in government, like the place is haunted by crooks past."

Peruzzi wore his typical uniform of fitted trousers and tweed sport coat, although he'd balled up the knitted tie that usually accompanied it. While his dress constituted CPD's version of undercover, to Duncan it always stood out, perhaps due to the wearers' discomfort with formality.

They made small talk with the waitress—a middle-aged woman who dressed like a teenager in a denim skirt and blouse open to the sternum. On the menu, Duncan saw typical pub food, including several dishes that reminded him of his ancestors: Shepherd's Pie and Guinness Stew. He ordered an Irish whiskey and a Scotch egg while the cop chose a corned beef and an ale, then they waited for the woman to bring their drinks before speaking.

"I don't want anybody ear hustling us," the cop said. Fortunately, only a half-dozen other patrons occupied the space, most at the bar. "Before I say anything, I need your word that you won't repeat any of this. My career's over if anyone hears I snitched."

"Agreed."

"I'm only finking 'cause I hate sloppy police work. We ought to be smarter than the crooks, not dirtier."

The cop sipped his beer and glanced around them casually as though looking for familiar faces before continuing.

"There's definitely something hinky about that case. First off, no evidence points to your man. Usually there's some motive or pattern that leads you to a guy. He had a fight with the victim prior or he's got a habit of sticking up people on a particular block, but your guy's only bad habits are drinking and passing out."

"He told me that's he's a different person under the influence."

Peruzzi lifted his glass. "Isn't everybody."

"I think he meant more nasty, more aggressive."

"He's had a few dustups, but that's typical for a guy living on the streets. Mostly just fights between drunks." He paused for another sip. "Don'tgetmewrong," Peruzzi said, in a rush to the point, "guy fills up a rap sheet, but he's more of a public nuisance than a public menace."

Duncan tried his whisky, which lacked the complexity of a single malt but did ease the dryness in his throat. "From what I heard, the building's super first identified him."

"Based on nothing. Without a trail leading from A to B, we can't just take people's word. A tip like that might get your attention, but it's not enough to collar a guy. You never know why somebody's pointing the finger at somebody else. Could be some old grudge or rivalry. You always got to have some evidence before you detain a suspect."

A woman with spiky hair passed close by their table on her way to the bathroom, and Peruzzi waiting until the door clicked shut. "Most guys in the department, I could just ask them about a case, and if they remembered it, they'd tell me what happened." He took a larger draught and wiped away the foam on the back of his hand. "Not these guys."

"How do you mean?"

"They keep to themselves."

"How's that possible?"

"The districts all have their own way of doing things, and downtown leaves 'em be so long as they're not messing up the stats. Since the North Side's got a high pinch rate, they do what they want. Whenever somebody'd ask how they do it, they'd say it's 'cause of where they serve—people along the lakefront are more prone to cooperate with the cops. Then you look at their files and the dots don't connect."

"Didn't anyone ever question their methods?"

"So long as they're collaring crooks, none of the brass cares how they do it."

Their food arrived, so Duncan took a break to sample his. Not since childhood had he consumed an egg that he been encased in sausage, then breaded and fried. It conformed to his memory, as savory and rich as a full breakfast skillet.

After a few bites of his sandwich, Peruzzi set it aside. "The detective who handled your case is known for being tough on suspects. Guy lives in Belmont Harbor on a boat named *The Vigilante*."

"I believe I met him earlier today. Looks like a heavyweight boxer, with a broken nose?"

"That's him. How you'd two meet up?"

"He came to my apartment, told me I was wasting my time with this investigation."

Peruzzi took a chip from his plate and chewed it contemplatively. "Shows he's nervous. Must be something to this, or he'd ignore it."

"So how do we prove that he forced a false confession?"

"That's the thing. These guys prefer a Haymarket method."

"A what?"

"A cursory investigation. Their paperwork's thin, they don't take notes. They go for the easy target, figure even if they got the wrong guy, it's one less problem to solve later."

Duncan watched a man wobble to the jukebox, peruse the options, and put in a quarter. Ironically, a woman started singing over a disco beat about the glamorous life.

"Did you see anything in the files about a transistor radio?"

"Nothing incriminating. They found one that didn't belong, but the only prints on it were the victim's and the super's, and the super handed it to them."

They listened to the dance rhythms from the machine while thinking silently.

"Too bad we can't get 'em in here," Peruzzi said. He pointed to the back wall above them. "That's where they put the cameras that caught all those city shakedown artists."

"Don't your detectives tape their interrogations?"

"Not always. Depends on what they expect to get. They typically only record the end result, when a guy's ready to confess."

"Harry claimed they recorded his, but no tape was used at the trail."

"Probably suppressed or destroyed it."

"Could you look again?"

"Sure, but there's likely nothing there."

"We've got to try."

***

By the time Duncan left the bar, the sun had descended below the horizon, yet the streetlamps remained dark, leaving a gray no man's land.

CHAPTER 31

A MAN WALKS DOWN A LONG corridor escorted by two guards who measure a head taller than him and twice as wide. The prisoner limps between them unevenly, dragging one leg, his hands cuffed behind his back. Overheard, a bare bulb swings, creating a pendulum arc of light on the gray walls, yet the passage stretches into darkness, too far to see. Their footsteps echo off the cement tunnel, reverberating like the tick of a clock.

They walk away from Duncan so that he cannot see their faces, yet somehow he knows he is watching Harry. At last they reach the end of the hallway, and the man turns in profile. Instead of the condemned inmate, Duncan sees the face of his own young son, his beard long and scraggly, his cheeks pocked by acne.

A metal door slides open with a clang, revealing an open courtyard painted by moonlight. In the middle waits a scaffold, the rope swinging in a gentle breeze. The boy lets a sly smile crease his face, then begins a slow march to the gallows. As he disappears, his father shouts and lunges toward him until he jolts himself awake.

***

After such a dream, Duncan could not risk sleep again. Instead he lay in bed listening to the wind howling through the bars of his balcony and feeling his building sway with the gusts, a reminder of his helplessness against such forces. Still, at the first sliver of daylight, he rose and prepped for a trip back to prison.

He drove through fifty miles of grain, the wheat and corn and soybeans so high they created a tunnel of green and gold. The monotony focused him on Harry and his options. Go public with his discoveries and risk a backlash. Turn them over to Catherine and hope that she could shame the state's bureaucracy into action. Work behind the scenes and pray that his role would stay hidden. Forget it all and resign himself to failure. None appealed.

As the prison came into view, rising from the fields like a medieval castle, with thin windows and stony turrets, he refocused on his son. Aden's best option remained a transfer, but without help from the prison authorities Duncan could not make that happen. The doctor said suicide attempts received priority, yet Aden's self-harm had made no impression. How far did he need to go? Not that he would ever suggest such a thing to Aden, but a false showing might fool people, especially with help from the doc. It wouldn't be the boy's first histrionic display.

No. Even a feint at self-slaughter would traumatize him and the family.

This behemoth that he'd created, this architecture of punishment and banishment, had outgrown even his expectations. Like many state systems, it had become self-directing. Once perhaps as governor, he wielded the authority to correct its excesses. Now, as a private citizen, he felt powerless.

Rarely did he miss his old position so much.

***

Duncan parked and walked to the prison's staff entrance, as usual. The latchkey inside the control booth stared at him through thick glass, held up a finger for patience, and phoned someone. Minutes passed, during which a half-dozen employees—guards and janitors, secretaries and nurses—passed through the rasping gates. None so much as looked at him, much less greeted him. His latest TV appearance had sent the wrong message—that he opposed the system he created.

When at last the control technician addressed him through a crackly microphone, Duncan felt ostracized.

"You need to check in with the front lobby," the tech said.

The visitors' entrance lay at the top of a long ramp, in a vast control booth of glass and steel. There again he confronted a technician who was visible but unreachable and who ordered him through an intercom to wait. This time, the woman disappeared through a back door, leaving Duncan alone in the lobby.

Posters warned about the risks of drinking and driving, the benefits of prenatal care, even the importance of voting and vaccination—a unitary system of social modification—yet the ambiance suggested the waiting room at a doctor's office, with Muzak playing benign versions of counterculture classics, and a sterile cleanliness to lull people into compliance. Disinfectant masked the rot and decay of the body inside.

A clock encased in wire mesh marked the passage of time: five minutes, ten. After a quarter-hour, Duncan rang the buzzer for service, but no one responded, as though the place had shut down for lunch. At last the technician returned, but she offered no apology or explanation for the delay. Instead, she addressed him through a speaker in the ceiling.

"Sir, you'll have to return during regular visiting hours." Her voice reverberated off the glass and tile like a commandment from God.

He demanded to speak to her supervisor, a guard, the warden, anyone who could overrule his exclusion, but she said all were preoccupied. "I'll wait," he told her.

He sat for what felt like hours, watching the few visitors who came to deposit money into the accounts of loved ones. They'd withdraw worn singles and fives from their wallets and feed them through a slot in the glass booth, trusting that—like any bank—they'd reach the right account. A custodian swept through the lobby with a buffer, polishing the floor to a high gloss. One man emerged from the security door, squinted against the sunlight as though unaccustomed to it, then sprinted down the ramp at sight of his ride. Free at last.

The impersonality of it all struck him. To receive orders from people so indifferent, untouchable. What had once appeared as secure and prudent to him now felt inhumane.

When Duncan grew stiff from the molded plastic chairs, he paced the hard tile floors, watching to see if the tech watched him. She didn't. He marked the clock but stopped after he caught himself checking every five minutes.

Idly, he speculated how he himself would survive inside such a place. Until recently, incarceration felt like a remote prospect, something that happened to other people. In the past week, though, with all the grandstanding by the attorney general and the civil rights attorneys, he questioned that. Would a judge lock him up for protecting his own kin, and if so, where? Some minimum-security prison—a club fed, as Ron called them—where he'd pass the time with macramé and candle dipping, or would they make an example of him, send him to room with those he'd persecuted?

He tried to shake off such morbid thinking, but surrounded by the prison culture, he couldn't escape it.

At last a uniform emerged from the double doors and approached Duncan. He walked with the swagger of a wrestler and bore a typical flattop, although all in gray. Bars on his shoulders distinguished him as a lieutenant, although Duncan had never spoken to him before.

"Why can I not see my son?" Duncan said. He knew better than to confront police with an accusation, but after so much waiting, his emotions got the better of him.

"That inmate is housed in solitary confinement," said the cop neutrally.

"My son is in protective custody."

"According to our records, he is on restricted privileges and is ineligible for visits."

"Is this revenge, punishment for me defending the unjustly accused?"

The man sidestepped into a military at ease, more a blocker than a public servant. "The rules apply equally to all visitors."

"I know that discipline is what you all do best, but there's no need. In case you missed it, I've been disciplined enough."

"Sir, the same rules apply to all visitors."

Duncan studied the man for some signs of recognition at his identity but saw only a cop's steely glare. He considered declaring his pedigree, but surely the guard recognized the person who once signed his checks. A part of him feared that his credentials no longer impressed.

"I need to know how he is," Duncan said.

"Fine. We have never lost a man here."

"Do you *know*? Have you checked on him? Because the last time I saw him, he wasn't fine. He was hospitalized."

"All our inmates receive the care they require."

"Let me speak to the warden."

"He's away from the facility."

"When will he return?"

"Next week."

Duncan backtracked to the door, then paused. "I will not forget this."

***

On the long drive home, he weighed his options, which proved few: submit or fight. If he chose the latter, what powers remained that could overthrow a system designed to coerce compliance?

CHAPTER 32

FOLLOWING HIS RECENT HABIT, DUNCAN PARKED a block from his building and paralleled the river to the back entrance of the restaurant, where people ignored his arrival. As he stood in the lobby waiting for the elevator, an unfamiliar voice summoned him by name: a man in a hardhat and tool belt, walking toward him menacingly. Although several inches shorter than Duncan, he possessed the dense arms of someone who earned a living with his body. The stranger stopped inches away from his target, his breathing heavy and agitated. That close, he smelled of leather and sweat, with wood dust mottling his hands.

"Why are you defending my parents' killer?" he said.

It took a moment, but Duncan recognized the man from artist sketches of the trial: Josh Mulvaney, eldest son of the victims.

He glanced outside, where the doorman stood guard against the media. TV cameras peered through the broad windows to capture this confrontation. How much could they see, and would any of what he said be picked up by their microphones? Above them loomed more cameras for security, angled to the lobby's entrance, but again he knew not how much they'd capture. He wanted to speak to this fellow survivor, to assure him. But not in public, not on tape. Given the man's agitation, Duncan couldn't invite him upstairs. Even sharing an elevator felt dangerous. He scanned the lobby for a private space but realized the delay was only aggravating his visitor.

"Let's take a walk," Duncan said.

They descended to the sunken passage by the river where canopied barges ferried tourists through the Erector Set downtown, narrated by crackly voices that described it in historic terms. "...a monument to the city's industrial era...." Duncan scanned for a shady spot but saw only sunlight. In some respects, the locale presented more dangers than the elevator, with few people to intervene if the talk degenerated, but just escaping the narrow lobby felt safer. Since Duncan thought better while in motion, he headed east toward the lake, which saved him from looking into the man's aggrieved face. Duncan planned to explain his reasons for intervening, in the most empathetic manner possible, but before he could say anything, Josh spoke in a rush.

"Three years ago my parents got beat to death in their own place so I sat through two years of trials and appeals for their killer counting the days till the case ended then this week I had to hear about it all over again." He paused to catch his breath, which came in short huffs. "I just want it to be over I want the guy dead so I can forget about him but every time you breathe his name I gotta hear about it from prosecutors and the press and the wait starts all over." He paused again to wipe his face, whether from sweat or tears, Duncan couldn't tell. "And now you're talking about a new trial."

Duncan assured him that he intended nothing of the sort, though of course he hoped for precisely that. He explained the importance of holding the right men accountable, the futility of false prosecution, the shame of police brutality. He tried all the arguments he'd rehearsed for his public appearances but never delivered.

"You're giving this guy more justice than my parents."

Duncan stopped beside the stone pillars of the DuSable Street Bridge—where the path ended, and they'd be forced up to street level—and faced his accuser. "Don't forget, I've lost family to violence too," he said.

At that, Josh blanched and turned away. "Sorry. That was disrespectful."

Behind the son's anger, Duncan saw the grief that drove so much of what they'd both done and said. "I know I sound like a politician," Duncan said, "but it truly matters to me that justice is done."

The man stared toward the river as though contemplating a suicidal jump. "When you ran for governor, you promised to lock up the crooks. I voted for you 'cause of that. Why build all these prisons if you're going to let the killers go?"

"I'd agree if I were convinced that this man killed your parents. I'm not."

He detailed all the causes of his doubt: the coerced confession, the lack of evidence, the absence of motive. "I assume that you want the true killer to be prosecuted."

Josh nodded slowly. "But what good's letting him go if you don't catch the guy who did it? Once he gets out, everybody's going to forget about my mom and dad."

"I won't."

They reversed course but at a slower pace. With Josh's permission, Duncan reprised what he knew about the crime: that someone entered through the back stairs and got caught when the Mulvaneys returned home.

"That's one thing that never made sense," said Josh. "Dad always locked his place. His store got broken into half a dozen times, so he bought himself a special deadbolt for home and had the super change the locks when they moved in. As a kid, I once left the door open. He grounded me for a week. No way Dad left his door unlocked."

Duncan recalled photos of the crime scene, which showed the back door angled open, leaves drifting inside the hallway. The one thing he hadn't seen were photos of damage to the frame or lock. Wouldn't detectives want to document how a burglar entered the place? It reminded him of the break-in at his own home, where a busted window by the doorknob left glass fragments *out*side.

"Did your father give anyone else a key?" Duncan said.

Josh shook his head. "Just me. He didn't trust anyone other than family. Caught too many people trying to steal things at work."

After Lindsay's murder, police spent months interrogating everyone who knew her—ex-boyfriends, employers, classmates—only to overlook the most obvious suspect. True, Duncan blocked them from interviewing Aden, but not intentionally.

In the Mulvaneys' case, the police so rushed to find a suspect they considered only one. Whom might they have ignored?

Duncan waited for another couple to pass out of earshot before he replied. "Did your father own a small, portable radio?"

Josh half smiled at the memory. "Yeah. He took it to ballgames so he could listen to Harry Caray. Why?"

As quickly as he could, Duncan excused himself with a promise to explain later.

***

Once he'd returned to his apartment, Duncan called Peruzzi. He'd barely IDed himself before the detective sergeant cut him off.

"You ain't gonna believe what I found in our archives," he said. "Tape of the interrogation. You'll definitely want to hear it."

"I do," Duncan said. "But first I need you to check on something else for me: a handyman named George Hajek. Whatever you can find."

They agreed to meet later that day at Peruzzi's home, where no one would notice. Even so, the detective asked Duncan to park in the alley and enter through the rear.

CHAPTER 33

AFTER THEY HUNG UP, DUNCAN ENJOYED a moment of optimism. Although the sun still bored through his windows, slow-roasting the interior, a breeze carried the tincture of evening. The tapes might speak the truth and free Harry. Once more he felt the power to move people and policy.

The telephone disrupted his revelry. When he answered, a recorded voice asked if he would accept a collect call from an inmate in an Illinois correctional institution. He did, waited, then heard rapid breathing as though someone had run to the line.

"Dad? I heard you tried to see me and got turned back."

"Who told you that?"

"A C.O."

"Why would the guards tell you that they wouldn't let me in?"

"Head games. They get off on taunting us."

"He's not taunting *you*."

Through the phone, shouts echoed as though down a long corridor.

"Hold on...."

After a minute of vague commotion, Duncan asked, "Where are you?"

"The infirmary. I told them I needed to see the doc so I could call you."

For once, Duncan appreciated his son's duplicity.

"What'd you want?" Aden said.

"Just to see how you are, how you're feeling."

"The same." His tone sounded more ominous than reassuring.

"I'll be back soon, at the next visiting," Duncan said.

"I doubt it."

"I wouldn't deceive you about that."

"The C.O. said I'd got my last contact."

"Last until when?"

"Ever."

"The guard said that?"

"On the q.t."

"They can't deny you visits."

"It's prison, Dad. They can do whatever they want."

Duncan walked to the window for some fresh air. "Don't believe what they tell you. I still wield some authority."

"Not in solitary. There, it's just me and myself."

"I *promise* I'll have you out of there soon."

"I'll die before they let me out."

More shouts in the background echoed through the phone line, followed by a deep male voice, "Inmate, drop the phone."

"Gotta go, Dad. Call you when I catch—"

The line disconnected before Duncan could respond, even as Aden's last words still resonated. "I'll die before they let me out." What exactly did he mean? The boy never spoke directly, never revealed his true thoughts or emotions, instead forcing others to interpolate. Was it just his typical cynicism, a touch of hyperbole, or something else, some renewed impulse toward suicide?

Duncan couldn't risk misunderstanding, not with his child's survival at stake. Instead, he had to act politically. Except, what resources remained: his lawyers, Peruzzi, Whitney, the doctor? None could grant Duncan access. The people who could he'd alienated.

As governor, whenever bureaucracy or indifference stalled his initiatives, he'd used the bully pulpit of the office to rally his supporters. Back then, he'd counted on voters to exert the necessary pressure. His few encounters with regular citizens—at the library and on the bus, with tenants and landlords—suggested he might still possess that skill. Only how could he reach such people without the machinery of office or the staff of a campaign to spread his message?

From the back of his closet he extracted his best gray suit and his black wingtips, which could be quickly buffed to a sheen. His white shirts remained boxed and creased, in need of ironing, but he might steam out the wrinkles in the shower. Then he reconsidered. This was not a professional matter but a personal one. Better to appear less an authority than a parent. He replaced his office attire and examined his outfit—khakis and a polo shirt—which looked stylish if casual. For appearances, he gargled, shaved, and gelled his hair. Then he descended to the lobby.

Outside, more than a dozen reporters caravanned, including two news crews with satellite feeds and a radio tech with a boom mic, plus several rumpled scriveners from the daily papers. Duncan inhaled his courage and stepped through the door to pandemonium: before he could speak, flash bulbs blinded and layers of voices deafened:

"Governor, a word...."

"...your latest appearance...."

"...will you continue...."

Duncan held up a hand until the cacophony subsided and his vision returned.

"Good evening," he said and paused to take in the surroundings. Rush hour traffic had largely passed, replaced by the still of night and the smell of charcoal. "I'm sorry I haven't been more... available to you all. After leaving office, I decided it best if I kept my activities to myself."

He paused to seek the right phrasing. A part of him wished that he'd scripted this moment. In office, he'd mostly read words that others composed, yet in personal matters he'd always trusted his instincts.

"Lately, some of my private affairs have come to light, and I want to explain my actions.

"When my daughter, Lindsay, died, I blamed strangers, which is why I focused on public safety while I was governor. I wanted to protect all the other endangered children. By the time I realized what caused her death, I'd already set in place all the apparatus of retributive justice.

"I'm sure I don't need to point out the irony of what happened next: that my own son is now subject to this system. Only, the experience has convinced me that I erred.

"Several of you have labelled me a hypocrite for prosecuting other people's children while shielding my own. When I resigned, I told you it would be unethical for me not to protect my own child, even after he erred. Any of you with children of your own will understand that parenthood is a lifelong commitment."

The click of camera shutters reminded him not to appear too grim, so he tried for a determined smile.

"Still, I allowed anger and grief and bitterness to drive me. My intentions were honorable, but my actions weren't always so. I sought personal vengeance through public policy. Looking back, I understand that instinct, but we as a society can't allow our government to act as a vehicle for reprisal. Prisons need to do more than punish. They should also improve.

"Which is why I stand here now. I find that my son—who has already confessed his sins and begun to atone for them—that his welfare is at risk. He sits in a prison like the ones that I built, without comfort or companionship. Because of my prominence, he is kept alone, isolated even from me, without the means to reform himself.

"Surely that's not the intent of our correctional system. Even the name implies its true end: to correct bad behavior."

He paused as a group of black teenagers shambled past on the sidewalk opposite, staring with curiosity even as they jostled one anther and laughed. Their mirth reminded him to drop the political pretenses and speak plainly.

"I'm here today to ask that my son be released from solitary confinement and allowed access to his family. I expect no special favors, only the justice due to all offenders."

He paused, awaiting further inspiration, but when the media chorus began shouting questions about his son's crimes and Harry's guilt, Duncan turned and walked back into his apartment building.

***

The wait to see the translation of his message proved agonizing, like watching a cake rise, only he couldn't remove it from the oven if the top overflowed its mold. He clicked between the three networks awaiting the first footage but found only regular programming. By the time he left for Peruzzi's home, he felt bound up with anxiety. Some relief came to him when he reached the lobby and saw the front of the building vacant, the media vultures satisfied by their most recent meal. Still, he took the back way out.

CHAPTER 34

PERUZZI LIVED JUST WEST OF THE city limits in suburban Berwyn, a large swath of brick bungalows for people escaping crime and blight. As instructed, Duncan parked in the alley and knocked at the back door where a petite woman holding a rolling pin like a weapon eyed him with suspicion before calling to her husband. Duncan felt awkward standing in the kitchen next to her, an uninvited dinner guest lured by the smell of baking bread and tomato sauce. She continued to size him up until Peruzzi appeared in cutoff jeans and a white t-shirt that fit tight across his chest. The cop led his guest into the basement, a dark concrete cell with low ceilings, exposed pipes, and a dank mustiness despite the summer heat. It subdivided into three areas: the center held a sectional sofa and stereo, one corner a small gym with weight bench and speed bag, and the far wall shelves of empty beer cans, mostly exotic and foreign brews. Peruzzi sat in a well-worn recliner next to the sound system but leaned forward so that the chair squeaked on its hinges.

"I haven't listened to the whole tape yet," Peruzzi said, "but the bits I heard were pretty revealing."

Duncan sat perpendicular to him in the sagging couch. "How did you find it?"

"A while back, the brass bought this machine to duplicate all our recordings in case one gets compromised. We put the original with the case file and another in a warehouse downtown. Huge basement under where I work. The detectives on your man's case hid the first one, but they must of forgot about the copy."

He inserted a cassette into the player, and a recording crackled through the bulky speakers. The high fidelity felt like overkill for a simple conversation, but it reproduced every sound, from the scrape of a chair to the clearing of a throat. A male speaker introduced three people, including Harry, whose only words were "yes sir." Despite the tape's grain, Duncan recognized his voice.

The other two had the gruff, blunt delivery he'd expect from police officers. One bore the throaty rattle of a smoker, the other a deep basso.

He imagined a middle-aged Mick from Bridgeport paired with a large black man from the South Side, stereotypes to be sure, but more likely than not.

They started with simple, biographical questions: where do you live, what do you do? No surprises there.

"They're getting a baseline," Peruzzi said, "testing how cooperative the guy is."

Duncan pictured the interrogation rooms he'd seen: bare cells without decor or windows, blocking out all other lights and sounds. Even as a visitor he'd felt their intensity, offering no distraction, no escape. How long before despair set in?

Then the questions narrowed to the night of the murder. Harry couldn't recall much, only that he'd passed out in his closet under the El station. More than anything he sounded confused, unclear why he'd be cross-examined about his drinking habits.

When the gravelly cop shifted his focus to the killing, Harry's answers compressed to monosyllables: no, yes, I don't know. His voice mixed fear with frustration as the purpose of the interview became evident. He repeated his explanation three, four, five times: he'd passed out under the train tracks.

"Then why'd a witness say they saw you leaving the guy's apartment?" said the smoking detective.

Duncan motioned for Peruzzi to pause the tape. "No one saw him. I've read the file, and no witnesses identified him. One heard a person running down the back steps, but she didn't see his face."

The detective shrugged and started bouncing on his heels in typical, hyperactive fashion. "They're testing the guy, see if he'll break."

"By lying to him?"

"It's a common tactic. An innocent man will keep protesting his innocence, but a guilty one's going to change his story. Totally legal."

"That hardly seems fair. Why are people condemned for their own lies when the police are absolved for theirs?"

"It works. You wouldn't believe the cockamamie stories you hear once you prick a guy's alibi."

Peruzzi leaned forward and let his fingers hover over the play button. "Keep listening. There's more interesting stuff coming."

As the cop predicted, Harry did not trip at the ploy, reasserting that he'd been too drunk that night to walk. "When I'm in the bag, my leg locks up," he said.

Duncan recalled his limp as he'd entered the visitors' area in prison. He'd assumed that the shackles hindered him, but plainly some other injury caused his shuffle. Then he pictured Harry slumped against a wall, drinking from a brown paper bag, the prototypical wino. Neither vision flattered him.

A loud crackle, accentuated by the big speakers, brought him back to the interrogation room.

"Hear that?" Peruzzi said. "They stopped the tape."

"Why?"

"Yougotme," he said, blending his words into one. "Usually, the only reason you'd stop recording is if somebody needed to piss. Here, they stopped it right in the middle. Something happened they didn't want heard."

When the tape resumed, Harry breathed heavily as though he'd just finished a hard run. The cops repeated their questions about the night of the killing: where were you, what were you doing. To every one Harry repeated the same answers.

"Are all interrogations so... bludgeoning?" Duncan said.

"Depends on how talkative a guy is. With the ones who like to tell stories, you let them trip themselves with lies, but when a guy's quiet or sticks to one story, like your man, you try to force him into talking. Either way, you got to wear him down."

After another few minutes, the recorder popped and clicked again, reproduced as loud as a gunshot on the sound system.

"Another break," Peruzzi said. "Can't be for the bathroom unless somebody's got a bad coffee habit."

"Why then?" Duncan said.

"That's the thing. With audio, I can only guess, but since your man reported they were bagging him...." He shrugged his agreement.

Again Duncan had to imagine the scene: Harry handcuffed to a chair, with a typewriter bag over his head, approaching asphyxiation.

Once they restarted, Harry's voice laced with fear. He pleaded for them to stop without specifying what. He reasserted that he didn't know "what happened to those people," unable to name them. Then another break, followed by crying. Throughout, the detectives repeated the same questions a dozen times, implying that they would not quit until they received the answer they wanted.

"How much more is there?" Duncan said.

Peruzzi shook his head. "I never got to the end, but there's only the one tape, so couldn't be more than a couple hours."

"Harry said he'd been questioned for thirteen."

Peruzzi shrugged. "It's easy to lose track of time in those rooms. Minutes feel like hours. By the end, everybody's exhausted."

How much time had passed during those silent breaks? Hours maybe during which Harry expected to die. Finally, Duncan understood why a man might implicate himself, anything to escape such abuse.

He flashed to his own encounters with the police, in confined offices and conference rooms, with lights flickering and fluorescent. They too asked him again and again to recreate the night his daughter died, only their queries spanned many weeks, not an endless night. Even so, he grew fatigued and angry with their persistence, then lashed out at their stagnation. As a prominent man, a wealthy man, he could afford to. Harry couldn't.

Peruzzi hit play, and the cops switched tactics, offering to bring the interview to an end if Harry would just tell them what really happened. Something scraped on the table as they proffered a drink—probably just a soda, but Duncan imagined them taunting an addict with alcohol. By this time, their target could hardly speak, uttering only single words between gasps and sobs. "No.... Don't," but they ignored his pleas. It pained Duncan to hear a man treated so cruelly, even at such remove. He wanted to turn off the recording, but he needed to hear the end where Harry signed his confession.

The cops began suggesting scenarios, the one with the deep basso narrating it like James Earl Jones. "You walked to the apartment. You found the back door unlocked. You planned to take some jewelry. You got caught and panicked."

"How would the robber know the door was unlocked?" Duncan said. "Their place was on the top story, in the rear. He'd have to try every other door first."

Peruzzi shook his head, stared at the tape, and bounced on his heels, a boxer ready for the next round.

The narrator continued, speculating that Harry bludgeoned the couple with some weapon he'd brought and dumped, then fled on foot, carrying whatever he could. Throughout, their suspect said nothing, his silence neither consent nor denial.

"Another mistake," Duncan said. "He can't run, not on his bad leg."

"At this point, they're not looking for the truth," said Peruzzi. "They want the confession."

"Why didn't this come up at Harry's trial?"

"For real? They probably hid it from the defense. Tapes like this only help if the guy confesses, and since your man signed his...." He shrugged.

They restarted the cassette, only instead of more dialogue they heard fumbling in the background punctuated by something hitting the table next to the recorder.

"You recognize this?" said the raspy detective.

Even through the big speakers, Harry's reply was too muffled to interpret.

"We found it at the crime scene, tuned to Spanish. Is it yours?"

Duncan stood and paused the tape mid-sentence, drawing a questioning look from the detective. "They're talking about the radio," he said.

Peruzzi nodded. "They're bluffing. They've got no way to connect it to the killing."

"The super claimed he found it while he was cleaning out the apartment."

"Figures they'd leave something like that for him to find. Any rookie would of bagged it as evidence." He shook his head with disgust.

Again they restarted the recording, picking up with more questions about the radio. After several minutes of futility, the detective with the husky voice claimed he'd "found your greasy prints all over it."

Silence followed with nothing but the sound of the tape crackling like a lit fuse. Then Harry spoke. "You're lying." He repeated the same words four times more, each one louder and with more anger, as though inflating himself through practice.

Then, pandemonium.

Shouts and curses and things being thrown or broken, Duncan couldn't tell which. Voices and sounds jumbled into an unintelligible mishmash of anger and reprisal. Duncan imagined Harry thrashing against his tormentors, handcuffed but not restrained, kicking and biting anyone who came near him, a furious whirlwind. Perhaps the detectives had been feeding him alcohol in hopes it would diminish his resistance. Instead it unleashed his id.

The commotion continued for several minutes, with other voices joining the fray, doors opening and slamming, something banging on the table. Then silence as someone cut off the tape.

"That's why they never used it," Peruzzi said. "Your man didn't break, he broke out. If they'd played that at his trial...." He shook his head with condemnation.

Again Duncan recalled his own experiences with the police, who'd taken up residence at his home for days after his daughter's murder. They'd photographed and fingerprinted every surface twice, confiscated every blunt object, from a meat tenderizer to an umbrella.

Despite their doggedness, he'd concealed Aden's guilt. Initially he wanted to protect his son from the trauma of reliving his sister's death. Later, as he grew suspicious of the boy, he kept his concerns private, investigating on his own until he found the evidence he needed: ironically, another tape. By then, the police had turned to less likely suspects, implicating a career criminal much as they did to Harry.

Could he glean anything from the experience? Don't overlook the obvious.

"The woman I spoke to said she heard footsteps on the rear stairs but didn't see anyone in the alley. The police assumed that he ran that way, but what if instead he ran into the building."

Peruzzi shrugged, "Could be, but why?"

Duncan inclined forward in his seat just across from the cop. "What did you learn about the super, George?"

Peruzzi threw up his hands with resignation. "Not a lot. Guy's basically clean. He got popped once for possession, but otherwise the worst I found was a couple unpaid parking tickets."

"No other arrests?"

"Not for him. There were a bunch of other crimes in that building, little stuff getting stolen—cash and watches. A couple bikes disappeared out of the basement. Seems like somebody was targeting the place, only they never took anything big. The uniforms dismissed most of it as people forgetting where they put stuff, but after the murders we pulled all the cases together, and you could see the pattern."

"Did anyone question George about it?"

"Not as a suspect. I saw his name in a couple of the theft reports, but mostly he talked about how the landlord wouldn't pay for any new security."

"He told me the same thing, just before he blamed Harry."

"Shows he's consistent, which usually means he's telling the truth."

"You said the detectives found the super's prints on the radio. What if he left them not during the clean up but during the crime?"

Peruzzi stood and walked toward a gun safe. "Let's see what he says when the cops show up unannounced."

***

They banged on the apartment door a dozen times at least without getting an answer. Under the frame lights shone, and conversation murmured just below their understanding, a couple debating something. At that hour, most family men should be home, so Peruzzi tried the knob and found it unlocked.

He paused with the door cracked. "You hear an argument?" he said to Duncan.

"Sorry?"

"'Cause if there's a domestic disturbance, I gotta investigate."

They agreed that the clamor justified an uninvited entry.

Inside, the home looked slovenly—not dirty, but as though no one had picked up in several days. Stray clothes lay across the sofa and a pan of curdled milk sat on the stovetop, emanating its sour funk. The radio played some talk show in Spanish, the source of the banter. Not at all the way it appeared when Duncan visited just thirty-six hours prior.

They called to anyone present but heard no reply. Where were the man's wife and child, who should have been in bed at such a late hour?

From the side room they heard someone groan and found the super passed out on a double bed, alone, again wearing only boxers. His skin looked even more flushed than Duncan recalled, so much so that even his freckles suffused, and his red hair swirled like uncut grass. From his moaning Duncan couldn't tell if the man was merely asleep or ill. Peruzzi checked his pulse on one wrist, then tracked it using his watch.

"Guy's half dead," he said.

He shook the man, gently at first, then more forcefully, but George only grunted in reply. Next the detective scanned the room. Several drawers on the dresser hung open, but few clothes remained, and the baby's crib sat empty of blankets or pillows, despite the stench of dirty diapers. From a bedside table he picked up a small pipe and sniffed the bowl.

"Heroin," he said. "Explains why he's so dopey."

"Should we call for paramedics?"

Peruzzi located a safety pin next to the crib, then inserted it into the man's open palm. Quickly, the junkie twitched.

"Hasn't ODed," Peruzzi said. "Help me sit him up."

With one on each side, they manipulated the limp man so that his legs hung off the bed, then hefted him to a slumped posture. Though his limbs felt thin and bony, his body felt dense.

"Start moving his arms, get the circulation going," Peruzzi said.

For several minutes, they manhandled him like a marionette, flexing him every which way until he resisted their pressure. Then they pulled him to his feet and carried him between them, forcing him to walk until his legs accepted some of the pressure. Up close, his breath smelled of vinegar, while his skin felt warm and damp. They continued thus for many minutes, reviving him one body part at a time—forcing open his eyes, shouting in his ears, putting stale milk beneath his nostrils—until at last he told them to stop.

Then they questioned him: what had he taken? (nothing); where were his family? (gone); when would they return? (never). Whether out of intoxication or fear, he evaded every question. Only with each dismissal his speech became more coherent, so they persisted.

At last the three sat before the dining table, with George smoking a cigarette and staring anywhere but at his visitors.

"How long you been hooked on the needle?" Peruzzi said.

George muttered unintelligibly.

"A long time, huh?"

Duncan looked to the wall, where the serenity prayer hung askew. "Have you tried to quit?"

George snorted and nodded.

"Nobody gets off the horse," Peruzzi said. "They slow it."

"Says the cops," George said.

Duncan smiled at the insult. His defenses mimicked those of Aden while he was using—answering every accusation with one of his own. Another sign of addiction, but also attention.

"What happened to your family?" Duncan tried.

"You," George said.

"Me?"

"Scared them off."

"How?"

"Asking about the case."

"Why would that bother your wife?"

George shook his head.

"You using back then, too?" Peruzzi said.

"No."

"When'dyoustart?" he said.

The room was growing hazy with smoke, giving Duncan the urge to bum one, but the last thing he needed was to stoke his own addiction. Instead, he stepped to the window to let in the evening breeze until Peruzzi shook his head.

The detective returned his stare to his target, unmoving. "We're staying till you explain some things."

"About what?" George said.

"You told the cops you were sleeping during the murders at your last place. That true?"

George stared at the table and nodded despite a mask of indifference.

"What if we ask your wife? She still back you up on that?"

The handyman studied the Formica tabletop as though unable to guess her reply.

"You high at the time?"

Almost imperceptibly, he nodded.

"So you were using even back then."

They waited a good thirty seconds before George said, "Not like now."

"You were what, a recreational user?"

George nodded with more enthusiasm.

"You never heard Mrs. Reagan?" Peruzzi said. "Just say 'no'."

The super shook his head.

"You can't say no?" Peruzzi said. "I heard you say it a couple times already tonight."

"It's not no," said the super, laconically. "It's no and no and no...."

"What does that mean?" said Duncan.

George sighed and looked past them toward the serenity prayer. "I had it under control."

"A smack addiction?" said Peruzzi. "I doubt it."

"Methadone," George said.

"So you were taking the cure and working your little job," Peruzzi said. "Then things stated disappearing in your building."

George lit another cigarette off his first while ignoring the implied question.

"You know anything about that?" Peruzzi said.

Weakly, George shook his head

"Know what I think?" Peruzzi said. "I think you were stealing to feed your family. You got a wife and a new baby. No way you could support them on a handyman's pay. They give you anything besides free rent there?"

Slowly, the super shook his head.

"You had to make some extra money somehow, and you couldn't of kept a job, not with a skag habit, so you lifted things. Who's gonna report a few bikes missing from the basement?"

George watched the ash from his cigarette fall on the table.

The cop leaned in closer to him. "You keyed yourself into other people's apartments and took things they wouldn't miss: cheap trinkets and jewelry. Only they noticed. I'm checking the pawnshops now. How many tags am I gonna find in your handwriting?"

When the super failed again to respond, Duncan held up a hand to the cop asking forbearance and tried himself. "Why'd you identify Harry to the police?"

George took a long drag and stared at the table. "He always hung around the neighborhood."

"He lived there," Peruzzi said. "Sameasyou."

George huffed but said nothing, drawing heavily on his butt as his eyes drooped.

"AsI'mlookinatit," Peruzzi slurred, "you're no better than him."

The super stubbed out his butt and grabbed a third cigarette, but his hand shook, making it difficult for him to strike a light.

"Really, there's not much difference between the two of you," Peruzzi continued. "You're both addicts, stealing to support your habits."

"I had a job and a family," George said weakly. "I'm not living under a train."

"You're still a hype," Peruzzi said.

"I got clean," George said.

"When?"

A tear pooled in George's eye, "It's not my fault. I wouldn't've relapsed."

"If what? If you hadn't killed those people?"

The super shook his head more forcefully. "If they hadn't made me clean up."

"Clean up what, your habit?"

"The apartment."

"Clean up your own mess, you mean."

The handyman sucked his latest cigarette toward the filter but said nothing. With the window closed, smoke pooled in the air, clouding everything. Duncan looked in vain for a fan but saw none. What kind of people could survive a summer in Chicago without even a fan?

"Tell me about the radio," Peruzzi said.

"Which one?"

The cop pointed to the kitchen counter. "When we entered here, you had it tuned to some Spanish station."

George nodded.

"You speak Spanish?"

"A little."

"Why listen to the radio if you can't understand it?"

"For my boy."

"Your own kid doesn't know English?"

"His mom wants him to learn both."

Peruzzi pointed toward his companion. "You told *him* that you found one like it in the Mulvaneys'."

George reached for another cigarette, but the pack sat empty.

"KnowwhatIthink," Peruzzi said. "I think you left it there."

Silence.

"Were you listening to it in their place?"

"When I was cleaning."

"Before then. The night of the crime. Were you listening to your Mexican radio then?"

Silence.

"How much time you spend in the place before you called the cops?"

He shrugged.

"You *take* anything?"

George shook his head.

"You *sure*?"

A nod.

"So if I search this place, I'm not gonna find anything belonging to the Mulvaneys?"

Silence.

"That a yes?"

After a long pause, George stood and walked to the same drawer where he'd stored the radio. From the back, he pulled a woman's silver stickpin that had tarnished to gray. He palmed it and stood forlornly by the doorway to the bedroom and the drugs.

"I didn't think anybody else would want it."

"You mean you stole it," Peruzzi said.

"After they died."

"You better sit down again."

With a languorous walk, George resumed his place between them. The detective began narrating for him.

"You were breaking into people's homes.

"You didn't get paid enough and figured you'd supplement your income.

"Support your habit.

"Hock stuff."

To each suggestion, George shook his head.

"That night, you heard the Mulvaneys leave and decided to burgle their place. You were listening to your Spanish station so you didn't hear when they came home. You panicked, killed them, and took whatever you could carry."

George placed his head in his hands but shook it more vigorously.

"You waited a while, then called the cops. Except you forget to turn off the radio. After they noticed, you used it to implicate somebody else."

George cupped his face, unresponsive.

"You blamed Harry to save yourself."

Slowly, his head descended to the desktop, where it lay inanimate.

"Isn't that how you did it?" Peruzzi whispered.

After a long pause, George sobbed to the table. "I don't wanna go."

"Go where?" Peruzzi said.

"Prison."

"Why would you go to prison?" Duncan said.

The handyman uncurled himself to look Duncan in the eye. "Because that's where you send people like me."

In his angry stare, Duncan saw recognition of his own crusade against criminals. Again, he felt ashamed. The cruelty of this pantomime, given the tape they'd just heard, became hard to deny. Only, with the roles reversed and Duncan acting as interrogator, the ritual felt necessary. After so many years of evasion, they needed to get the truth from George that night.

"Let's stand for a minute," Duncan said and nodded to Peruzzi.

When the super did not follow their lead, they lifted him and paced a few laps around the small living room. As the smoke mixed with the stifling heat and the fetid odor of decay, it felt as though they were wading through the ashes of a fire. Once it became difficult to breathe, they seated themselves again. The super kept his head up, but he looked pained at the effort.

"I know how you feel," Duncan said. "I carried a great secret too, for many years. I thought it would get easier to bear. Instead, it grew heavier. It felt as though I was shouldering many times my weight, with no way to unload it."

He paused to watch for a reaction, yet the handyman's head was dipping to hide his face.

"I'm sure you've read about it. My son killed his sister, right next to where I slept. It took years for me to be able to say those words out loud. For months I denied it, to myself and my family, until I couldn't ignore the truth any longer. Then I denied it to everyone else: to my friends and supporters, the people who trusted me. Is that what you did? Lie to your employer and your wife about what happened?"

George shook his head weakly, looking as though he were about to cry.

"To my eyes, it's clear that you're hiding more than just your addiction. You remind me of my son. He denied his alcoholism for many years before getting treatment. And his guilt. I've often thought that if he'd sought sobriety earlier, he might not have to live with the shame of having killed his sibling."

At that a tear grew too heavy and followed the rut of George's cheek downward.

"The thing is, the longer you hide something like that, the harder it becomes to conceal. The truth will out, and when it does, the cost will be multiplied by the time it took to reveal it."

He paused, and hearing no reply, tried again. "The only freedom comes from confession."

For what felt like minutes, George stared at the tabletop before finally nodding his head once.

"So you did it?" Peruzzi said. "You killed those two people."

George did not deny the charge, but neither could he bring himself to acknowledge it.

***

Within a half hour, two patrolmen had loaded him into a squad car and driven him downtown, leaving Peruzzi alone again with Duncan. As the detective poked around the apartment, peering in drawers and under furniture, he said almost to himself, "We shouldn't of cut off the interrogation."

"We know the truth," Duncan said.

"From a nod. That's not going to impress anybody in court."

"Even with two witnesses?"

"Two biased ones who the defense will say are protecting themselves."

"He as much as admitted everything."

"But without saying it."

Duncan shook his head. "He isn't ready to admit it to himself yet."

"You had him ready to tumble. Another push and he'd have confessed to anything."

"That's not our purpose."

The detective paused in his search. "We might not get another shot at this guy. If he talks to a lawyer, he might never speak to us again."

Duncan stood before the serenity prayer and studied it. "...taking, as He did, this sinful world as it is, not as I would have it...."

"If he recants," Duncan said, "we need to find other means of convicting him."

Peruzzi lifted a pile of unwashed clothing and dropped it in disgust. "Assuming we can find some."

"You said that you could confirm it with pawn receipts."

"You know how many pawn shops there are in this city? Assuming he even used one? I could spend weeks looking for where he hawked it and never find anything."

"Then through some other testimony. From his wife, maybe?"

Peruzzi withdrew a piece of jewelry from a drawer, examined it, and threw it back inside disconsolately. "That's a long shot."

Duncan stood and moved to the door, satisfied.

"Regardless, a confession should never be enough," Duncan said. "We need more to convict a man of murder."

CHAPTER 35

WHEN HE RETURNED HOME, THREE MORNING papers already lay outside Duncan's apartment. He threw them on the dining table and collapsed on his sofa, exhausted from a night of interrogations.

He needed sleep, but he wanted something positive to fall asleep to, so he reached for the sports section to check on the Cubs score. Instead, on the front page of the *Defender*, he saw a photo of himself talking to reporters under the headline "Guilty Plea." The story detailed his impromptu press conference in the most unflattering terms. It summarized all his admissions but failed to convey his emotions. The only direct quote was, "While my intentions were honorable, my actions were not always so." Its overall tone was less a plea for justice or mercy than a confession.

Also, it hardly mentioned Aden outside of his guilt and incarceration, saying nothing about the conditions in which he lived, nor about his isolation. The tone hinted that his suffering was entirely justified, even deserved, after so many others had disappeared into the vortex of the prison system.

No surprise that the city's Afro-American paper would revel in Duncan's plight. Its editor had denounced him since the time he proposed his three strikes policy, and its reporters had led the inquisition into his son's guilt. Throughout his four years in office, the propaganda sheet had embarrassed and defamed him whenever possible.

He checked the other two dailies, which proved almost as biased, with stories that focused more on his history than his words. Typical. Why expect sympathy—no, accuracy—from the scandalmongers who'd driven him from office?

He lay back into the soft cushions, massaging the tacky ink into his fingers. With enough soap he could remove all visible traces of it, but the evidence would remain imbedded in the grooves of his skin. For days his fingerprints would leave behind its stain. Once tainted, they could never be fully erased.

***

The phone awoke him. He couldn't tell the hour, nor how long he'd slept, only that the sun now bore through his windows, superheating the place. Stiffness and grogginess grafted him to the couch until the machine answered the call. When a female voice said, "This is Governor Vukovic's office calling," Duncan leapt across the room.

"Hold, please, for the governor," said the woman.

In the silence following, Duncan decided that someone was pranking him. Probably a response to all the negative coverage. Except he'd kept his number unlisted and offered it only to close friends, so how had anyone else obtained it? Probably the same way reporters did.

"Governor," said a familiar voice, and at once Duncan realized this was no hoax.

During his last campaign, Duncan had come to despise his successor. In every way, the man acted as a moralizing hypocrite, shaming Duncan with his son's addiction and his daughter's unsolved murder while disguising his own failings. To hide a skinny build, Vukovic wore bespoke suits funded by his wealthy family. Despite possessing the weak chin and hooked nose of a bird, he preened for the cameras like a peacock. He courted Christian evangelicals while drinking offstage, hiding a gay son, and downplaying his two divorces. Only the revelation about Aden's guilt had tipped the election to him.

"Yes," Duncan said with deliberate chill.

"It's been a while."

Duncan let silence convey his distaste.

"I would ask what you've been doing, but the papers have answered that for me."

"Are you calling to gloat?"

"More to sympathize. I'm sure you've read some of my own... coverage."

During his first two years in office, Vukovic had endured several scandals: corruption by his advisers and cronyism with the legislature. None implicated him personally, but all attached themselves to his name. Embarrassments to be sure, but nothing compared to Duncan's woes.

"All kidding aside, I wanted to talk about your son."

Duncan heard himself inhale, anticipating some new punishment from the state.

"I understand he's having a difficult time in custody. Hardly a surprise, given his celebrity." That familiar, snarky tone made Duncan want to hang up. "Still, I wish you'd called on me instead of speaking through the media."

What could Duncan say—I didn't have your number? He pictured Vukovic sitting at the broad mahogany desk he once occupied, the memory so vivid he could almost smell the linseed oil. Even under the circumstances, he couldn't admit that he did not trust the man. "I don't expect any professional courtesies," he said.

"Come now," said the governor. "After four years in office, you should know that little happens in the capital without favors."

"I guess I've been out of town for too long."

"You're not missing much. There have been times...." He signed and chuckled. "Let's just say I've been tempted to offer you the job back."

A pain in his little finger alerted Duncan that he'd wound the phone cord around it so tightly it cut off circulation, like a teenager talking to his first girlfriend. He uncoiled the tourniquet but felt little relief. "I have enough problems of my own."

Vukovic chuckled, but genuinely. "You mean Muskegee? I wouldn't worry about him. The rumor here is that his investigation is running out of fuel."

"That doesn't stop him searching the state for more."

"Your time here should have taught you not to fear the threats you can see as much as the ones you can't."

Duncan exhaled audibly, surprised at the relief he found in talking to one of his few equals. Still, he allowed silence to force the other man into revealing his purpose.

"What exactly is it," said the governor, "that you'd like for your son?"

Duncan pictured Aden as he'd last seen him: seated on a pew in the chapel, alone, his shame engraved into his skin. Even to put it into words pained him. "Help," he said.

"I got that, but in what form?"

In brief, Duncan described what he'd lately learned about the penal system—how few avenues for reform it offered, how isolating and demeaning it felt. He spoke more honestly and bluntly than he had to his wife, his lawyers, even to Catherine, who understood it already. At the end, he mentioned the Sheridan prison, which the doctor said offered more therapeutic treatment.

"I *can* arrange a transfer," Vukovic said, and paused.

Duncan again felt the blood rushing into his numb hand.

"On one condition," Vukovic continued. "That you call *me* next time you need something. I don't want any more scandals in the press."

"Understood," said Duncan.

CHAPTER 36

THE CROWD FILLED THE GRANDSTANDS TO capacity, buzzing with anticipation. Few could recall the last time the Cubs had held first place at all, let alone in mid-July, more than halfway through the season. Could the curse of the billy goat have finally lifted?

During the '45 World Series, one spectator and his pet had been evicted from the stadium, provoking a spell worthy of Grimm's fairy tales. Thus, on Opening Day of the new season, the team had performed an exorcism to rid it of the hex—inviting a descendant of the billy to Wrigley Field, where its ancestor had been unwelcome—yet they had performed that ritual previously without success. Forty years between playoff bids had convinced everyone of its potency.

Duncan also vibrated with excitement, only for different for reasons. This was his most public appearance since he'd left office. Unlike the previous game, where he'd hidden in the chancel of the press box, now he sat on the third-base line among the other congregants.

Fortunately, with the field shimmering under the midday sun, his hat and dark glasses blended. That day, everyone dressed in the team's red and blue. Still, he stared straight ahead as the players warmed up with soft toss and gentle grounders.

"Are you nervous?" Catherine said.

She laid a hand atop his own, forcing him to look at her. With a headscarf and cat eye sunglasses, she reminded him of Liz Taylor or Grace Kelly. Unlike those icy movie stars, or his wife, she liked to touch him, found excuses to do so.

He shook his head.

"It shows," she said, seeing through his denial.

He couldn't think of an appropriate reply in public and so remained silent.

"Not because of me, I hope."

Again he shook his head but more emphatically. For their first true date, Duncan wanted to take her somewhere special to him. He considered a swank restaurant or the symphony, but both felt too formal, too society for his current status. He needed somewhere that showed his history, before ambition and politics had compromised his character, and nothing captured his essence like baseball and hot dogs.

"It's been a while," he said, leaving the "it" intentionally undefined.

"So tell me what we're seeing," she said.

"Well... we're playing our historic rivals, the Cardinals. Rick Sutcliffe is pitching. He's won ten of eleven since they traded a backup outfielder for him. They really needed a number one starter...." He paused at a look from her that betrayed not boredom, but what—indifference? "That's not what you meant."

She smiled and shook her head.

He paused to take in the scene as he composed his words: old men filled out scorecards as the PA announced the batting order. Children sprawled over the dugouts, reaching for autographs. Vendors stalked the aisles, hawking peanuts and beer. All around, strangers conversed about the team's chances to make the playoffs.

"You're seeing the city at its best," Duncan said. "Forty thousand people all supporting the same, righteous cause."

Catherine smiled more genuinely, her blue eyes creasing with satisfaction, and said, "That I understand."

Next, he summarized his own connection to the game: his years in little league, his starring role in high school, his scholarship to Northwestern, his dream of playing professionally, which ended with the reality of the minor leagues— six months a year traveling by bus to Podunk cities in the farm belt. He omitted his engagement to Josie and the need to support his impending family, but she left it unquestioned.

Before he'd finished his autobiography, the national anthem interrupted them. Duncan stood and, following the other men, removed his hat. Before the last note from the organ had faded, he replaced it and fell again into awkward silence.

After a few moments, she said, "I saw Harry this morning. I told him how optimistic we both are about his release."

He held up a hand to stop her. "I wouldn't promise him anything yet."

"But your lawyers are filing a habeas motion."

"Which will take months before even a hearing is set, and the evidence is far from overwhelming."

"We have the tape of his interrogation."

"Which only suggests police abuse."

"And we have George."

"Who didn't confess."

"What about the things the police found in his apartment?"

"My detective friend is tracing them to previous burglaries, but he's found nothing else from the Mulvaneys."

"Besides their radio."

"Which he claims he found after their death."

"But with so much new evidence...."

"We have a chance."

The Cubs took the field for the top of the first, which passed quickly, with Sutcliffe retiring the side in order. At the break between innings, Duncan said, "I saw the Mulvaneys' son recently."

"How's he taking it all?"

"He's... adapting. After so many years believing that Harry killed his parents...."

"I don't suppose you ever fully recover from something like that."

"No, you don't."

As the home team's leadoff man took his warmup swings in the on deck circle, Catherine districted him, asking, "How's Aden?"

Duncan glanced about them for eavesdroppers before answering, "Better. He's in a new... facility, one that suits him."

"They have what he needs?"

"I think so. Only time will tell. He's still...."

"I know." She squeezed his hand parentally. "It's temporary."

"That's what I keep telling him, but the young don't have that perspective. Only experience teaches the long view."

She squeezed his hand more tightly and held on as the Cubs mounted a rally—two singles and a walk—but failed to score. At the next break between innings, they talked about the Innocence Inquiry and other cases it was pursuing—a man convicted of rape who didn't fit the victim's description, another imprisoned fifteen years on the testimony of his alcoholic roommate—but without the same passion. The thought of more men like Harry depressed Duncan in ways not even the game could lift.

He distracted himself with the play-by-play. In the top of the second, the Cards scored with a hit, an error, and crafty base running, drawing a groan from the crowd. After so many years of failure, Chicagoans flinched at the first hint of it.

During the next break, Duncan asked, "What can we do?"

"About the innocent? What we've been doing."

"About them all. How can I undo the damage I've done?"

"By admitting it. Tell people you were in error."

"We Protestants aren't big believers in confession."

"Not confession. Just acknowledge your mistakes."

"More of them? I think people are tired of my mea culpas."

"People don't know how to take honesty from a politician."

"A retired one."

She left that claim unchecked as well.

"You really believe confession is the answer?" he said.

"Not in the Catholic sense. Don't ask for forgiveness. Just tell people what you intended."

"Does it even matter what I intended? I'll sound like every criminal I put away, claiming it's not my fault."

"That's why you ask forgiveness, not for what you saw, but for what you failed to foresee."

In the next half inning, Ryne Sandberg evened the score with a majestic home run that fell outside the stadium onto Waveland Avenue. On the transistor of a man sitting in front of them, Harry Caray described the scrum among the boys waiting there for just such a souvenir.

Duncan felt himself relaxing into the easy rhythms of the game— until a vendor stopped beside their aisle to sell hot dogs to the family seated adjacent. His steamer released a savory whiff of Duncan's past. Surreptitiously, he watched to ensure the man dressed the Smokie Links properly with mustard, relish, onions— everything except ketchup— but Duncan decided to hold out for a bratwurst. Because he sat on the end of the row, Duncan had to pass the food across, followed by the money. The vendor remained too engrossed in his job to notice this intermediary, but Duncan noted a flicker of recognition from his neighbor as he accepted his change.

Once they'd completed the transaction, Duncan exhaled and smiled to himself. The city had forgotten him.

"Hey governor," said a voice to his left.

On instinct, Duncan turned to face the father, who leered at him. His two children also stared with the curiosity and forwardness of early adolescence. Under such scrutiny, Duncan could not ignore them, so he tried for a smile but felt the strain.

"What do ya' think of our chances?" said the father.

Confusion silenced Duncan until the man nodded toward the field.

"For once, I'm optimistic," Duncan said. "I think it's finally our year."

ABOUT THE AUTHOR

STORIES ABOUT CRIMES HAVE ALWAYS RESONATED with me, whether it was *Crime and Punishment* or *The Quiet American.* Maybe it's because I started my career as a police reporter, or because I worked for a time as a teacher in the county jail.

More than a decade ago, when I decided to finally get serious about writing, I started with short stories based on real misdeeds I'd witnessed. I wrote one about my next door neighbor, who'd been murdered by a friend, another about an ambitious bike racer who decides to take out the competition, and a bunch of others based on characters I met in jail.

Over time these got picked up by various magazines online and in print. More than twenty now exist, including a prequel to the Duncan Cochrane series in the political crime anthology *Low Down Dirty Vote.*

For my debut novel, *They Tell Me You Are Wicked,* I drew inspiration from the most infamous event in the history of my hometown: the real life killing of a political candidate's daughter (though I made up all the details).

Book two in the series, *They Tell Me You Are Crooked,* is set two years later, after my hero, Duncan Cochrane, has become governor. He's haunted by the family secret that got him elected and fighting a sniper who's targeting children in Chicago.

In the latest book, *They Tell Me You Are Brutal,* he searches for a saboteur who is poisoning pain medications, all while trying to protect his family from personal and political ruin.

In all my work, I am inspired by efforts to right criminal injustice.

Please connect with me online at:

Website: www.DavidHagerty.net
Facebook: www.Facebook.com/DavidHagertyAuthor/
Twitter: www.Twitter.com/DHagertyAuthor

WHAT'S NEXT?

David is plotting what comes next for Duncan and the other characters who occupy his thoughts. Watch his website for news about future publications:

www.DavidHagerty.net

Or stay tuned to developments and plans by subscribing to our newsletter here:

www.EvolvedPub.com/Newsletter

MORE FROM DAVID HAGERTY

Be sure to grab all of the books in this critically-acclaimed series of crime/political thrillers. You'll find all the "Duncan Cochrane" books at our website, and their purchase links at various retailers, at the link below:

www.EvolvedPub.com/DuncanCochrane

MORE FROM EVOLVED PUBLISHING

We offer great books across multiple genres, featuring high-quality editing (which we believe is second-to-none) and fantastic covers.

As a hybrid small press, your support as loyal readers is so important to us, and we have strived, with tireless dedication and sheer determination, to deliver on the promise of our motto:
QUALITY IS PRIORITY #1!

Please check out all of our great books,
which you can find at this link:

www.EvolvedPub.com/Catalog/

Thank you!

CPSIA information can be obtained
at www.ICGtesting.com
Printed in the USA
BVHW031250010719
552377BV00016B/1615/P